About the author

Born in India, Archie Macdonell started out as an author after being invalided out of the army during World War I. By 1919 he was writing dramatic criticism for the London Mercury. Then in 1933 came his novel *England, Their England*, and one morning he awoke and found himself famous. Other novels followed including *The Autobiography of a Cad* in 1938. He also ventured into history with *Napoleon and his Marshals*. In the early part of World War II he made frequent broadcasts for the BBC. He died in 1941.

The Autobiography of a Cad

Prion Humour Classics

* for copyright reasons these titles are not available in the USA or Canada in the Prion edition.

The Autobiography of a Cad

A G MACDONELL

with an introduction by
SIMON HOGGART

PRION

This edition published in 2001 by
Prion Books Limited,
Imperial Works,
Perren Street,
London NW5 3ED
www.prionbooks.com

First published by Macmillan Publishers Limited 1938.
Copyright in all countries signatory to the Berne Convention.
Introduction copyright © Simon Hoggart 2001

Cataloguing in Publication Data
A catalogue record for this book is available
from the British Library

ISBN 1-85375-414-5

Jacket design by Jon Gray
Printed and bound in Great Britain
by Creative Print & Design, Wales

To Leonora

INTRODUCTION

by SIMON HOGGART

I first encountered A G Macdonell at secondary school when chapters from his most famous novel, *England, Their England*, were read to us as an end of term treat. It's a very funny book, and the episode everyone remembers, about the village cricket match, seemed hilarious to a class of light-headed schoolboys gleefully looking forward to the holidays. Looking back, it seems almost painfully dated. Its whimsical vision of warm beer, old maids cycling to church and the thud of willow against leather (as another bored spectator kicks a tree) was already growing cloudy by the time I was a boy, and is now as distant in the memory as the works of Arthur Mee. I was reminded of it decades later when I read Bill Bryson's *Notes from a Small Island*, another beautifully written book which flattered us by lingering on our loveable eccentricities and ignoring our real faults.

The Autobiography of a Cad, by contrast, is as fresh as tomorrow's front page. It is also, in my view, much funnier than *England, Their England*, though its cynical tone meant that it would never match the huge commercial success Macdonell had had with his great hit. *The Autobiography of a Cad* was published in 1938, (five years after *England, Their England*) and its bleak and bitter view of the landowning aristocracy and British politics – especially the Conservative Party – did not suit the mood in a country which was already gearing itself up for war. In retrospect it's hardly surprising that the only two languages into which it was translated were German and Italian.

The cad in question is one Edward Fox-Ingleby. The autobiography, moving from his earliest years on his father's estate through Eton, Oxford, the Great War and a life in politics, is a manic, bravura attempt to excuse a life lived without scruples. A life in which – through his remorseless and relentless quest for power, sex and money – he has abused family, friends, colleagues and lovers without once troubling his conscience. But what gives the book its truly savage quality is the *coup de grâce* – it has, for its unspeakable narrator at least, a happy ending:

> In May 1926 I had defeated all my enemies. I was a Minister of the Crown. I was rich and young and a bachelor again. I was untarnished by public scandal. I was respected and honoured by all. And I was at peace with myself.

This is followed by a brief appendix, to which we turn anxiously, hoping that fate has finally dropped the two-ton anvil on Fox-Ingleby's head. But we are deprived even of that; the last few pages merely record with smug satisfaction how, in writing his memoir, Fox-Ingleby has managed to diddle his publisher, agent and researcher. Macdonell offers us no glimmer of light.

Anyone who reads any of today's self-regarding political memoirs will recognise the overblown style Macdonell was satirising even then. The following, while not a real quote, having been invented by me, could easily be a genuine excerpt from any of the dozens of ministers who wrote their account of the Thatcher years:

> There are those who now – with the benefit of hindsight, needless to say! – who claim that the community charge, sometimes mischievously misnamed the poll tax, was a mistake. I am not among those. In my view, had we persevered, a course I tried with might and main to urge upon my 'elders and betters'...

In this same style, Fox-Ingleby's words of self-justification roll on. Of course he is not merely justifying his political actions. His appalling certainty remains unchecked by a friend betrayed, a woman abandoned, or wartime shares and armament deals which make him rich at the cost of British lives. He spends most of Great War in soft, well-paid civilian jobs while taking advantage of the absence of men at the front to frolic with their wives and girlfriends (for its day, the book is surprisingly frank about sex). He is horrified to learn that an old adversary is attempting to have him enlisted. He seems puzzled why this nemesis has it in for him, and concludes that it may be because at university, "I had playfully cut him across the face with my riding crop." In the same period he takes time out to express his "distaste for the semitic financiers who profiteered all day in the city and bolted like dogs in the evening." He is outraged when his "Buy British" campaign is undermined by the fact that all his three cars are foreign. As with any true politician, anything his opponent does is execrable, anything he does himself easily excusable.

Obviously the character is a monstrous grotesque. But we can still meet his descendants today. He would, perhaps, have been proud of Jonathan Aitken, who told a wholly unnecessary lie and was destroyed by his conviction that laws and morals did not apply to him – though Fox-Ingleby would have despised the way he let himself be caught. (He might have arranged for George Carman to be found in bed with a dead woman or a live boy.) Certainly he would have identified with Neil Hamilton, who apparently remains unaware to this day of what he did that was wrong. Cash for questions? Nowadays Fox-Ingleby would have taken his credit card machine into the central lobby to operate that little scam, and if caught would have managed to pin the blame on whichever colleague complained. I read the second, that is to say the earlier and more candid, volume of Alan Clark's diaries just after *Cad*, and was struck by the remarkable similarities – though at least Clark didn't pretend he was doing his women a favour, and didn't destroy his wife as revenge for her resentment.

Many of the book's episodes are drawn from Macdonell's own experiences and you soon realise that every one of Fox-Ingleby's opinions is the precise opposite of his creator's. His anti-hero has a particular distaste for Lincoln: a place where Macdonell was twice a Liberal candidate. There is a throwaway line expressing contempt for Winchester, where Macdonell went to school. Unlike the cowardly and lubricious Fox-Ingleby, Macdonell spent two years in the artillery during the Great War before being invalided out. Fox-Ingleby expresses his utter indifference to the post-war sufferings of Europe: "the only detail of those post-war international politics of the world which moved us to any sort of emotion was the League of Nations, and the only emotion to which the League moved us was laughter." The line's force is increased by the fact that Macdonell spent five years working at the League's HQ.

Macdonell died in 1941 at the age of 46. He lived in Oxford at the time. One account claims he died suddenly in his bath, another that he was killed in an air raid. We are fortunate that, three years before, he had left us such a magnificently abusive satire on a way of life and a cast of mind which are not yet quite extinct.

Contrary to what some of my readers will think, no reference is made in this book, nor is any intended, to its author.

CHAPTER I

I, who write this little book, am in my fiftieth year. For I was born in 1889 and I am writing in 1938. But I am only presenting to you the story of the first thirty-eight years of my life. That is to say, it is in 1926 that I come before the curtain at the end of my performance, to receive your applause, your derision, or your execration, whichever you will. For myself, it is equal, as our French friends say. Cheers, laughs, or hisses, are all one to me. It is a long time since I was touched or moved by the opinions of the herd.

But a reason is owed to you for this apparently arbitrary selection of dates. Why do you not bring your story down to 1938? it may well be asked. Why break off just at the moment when the world is a-tiptoe to follow your life and career down to its latest moment?

But there is a reason. I do not suppose that a high sense of artistic rightness is implanted deep in the bosom of everyone. But, on the other hand, no one was ever less ready than myself to claim a monopoly of such a sense. There must be a few others, scattered here and there, if one only knew where to look for them, who also have this fine appreciation of what may be called Symmetry. The modern style is slipshod. No one takes the trouble nowadays to tell a story, to tie up loose ends, to build an arch in which every stone falls truly and certainly into its predestined place so that a thing of symmetrical beauty is left at the end. But those of us who have clung to the classical tradition think otherwise.

I chose the year nineteen hundred and twenty-six as the end of my story, because it represented the climax of a symmetrical story. It was in the month of May of that year that I dropped, gently but with what an exquisite accuracy, the keystone into my arch so that my arch stood graceful and strong against whatever storm might blow. Beginning with no influence, with no title, with the handicap of parents who were obsessed by an inferiority complex, with a hatful of inherited disadvantages such as the unpopularity of my father for his political views and the tradition of commercial vulgarity left behind him by my grandfather, and, above all, with the dead weight of provincialism which life in the Midlands, unmitigated by the possession of a town house, inevitable hung round my youthful neck, nevertheless I fought clear of it all.

Single-handed, by my own unaided efforts, after years of laborious toil and endless planning and thinking ahead, I overcame every obstacle and, in the year 1926, rounded off a tale of far-sighted endeavour with a series of triumphs that placed me upon the top of the world. No third son on the last page of a fairy story was ever manœuvred by the Fairy Queen into such a position of commanding success as I had reached in that year. Only I needed no Fairy Queen, and certainly no manœuvres, whether of hers or of anyone else's. All that was necessary for me was my own talent, supported and encouraged by my own exertion.

That is why I have closed my tale on my thirty-eighth year. The whole romance of "from pit-boy to Cabinet" is contained in those years, so why spoil a work of art, however fascinating it may be, by continuing it after the essential effect has been achieved?

It is usually an act of vanity to assume that the world is sufficiently interested in one's personality to spend twelve-and-six on one's autobiography. Nowadays autobiographers either begin early in their life and describe their reactions to daffodils, and Greek statues of boys, and God, and the Oxford Union, and the rugged kindliness of their dear old father, and so on, or else they wait till they are ninety and babble of crinolines, and the Tranby Croft scandal, and what Cardinal Newman thought of Disestablishment. Both of these types are consumed with vanity. They really think that an elegant dislike of calceolarias, or a recollection of John Brown's repartee to Queen Victoria outside Crathie Church on an autumnal afternoon in 1878, is the sort of thing which the world wants to know. But for myself, I am not concerned with vanity. It is not, and never has been, one of my weaknesses. After all, vanity can never go hand in hand with clarity of vision. The two are incompatible. And by clarity of vision, of course, I mean that clarity which not merely understands and dissects the foolish and comic and pathetic world about us, but which turns inwards and enables a man to understand himself.

Nor am I writing this book to make money. Few people of this materialistic, nay, hedonistic, age of ours have cared less for money than I have. It has meant very little to me, except as a commodity to exchange for the odds and ends which have from time to time constituted my small wants. Besides, I have always had plenty of it.

Nor again is it celebrity that I am seeking. When you have read through to the end—and in all modesty I make no doubt that those of you who have reached as far as this will find it difficult to put the volume down, as sycophantic reviewers so often say, until you have finished it—you will find that before the end of my thirty-eighth year sufficient celebrity had come my way without the necessity of seeking more.

Why then am I telling you my story?

The reason is because it contains a moral which it might be to the advantage of the growing generations to examine. These growing generations have had all too seldom a sheet-anchor on which to depend in times of stress. Their world was knocked askew by the war, and by the fits and starts of the post-war years. They live too often upon sand. They have no standards.

It is only right, therefore, that a man like myself, who has not merely survived the slaughter of Armageddon, but has emerged from that cruel time of death and, worse, disillusion, with his ideals untarnished and his principles uncompromised, should place his conclusions at the service of those, less fortunate, who are groping in the dark.

In a word, the moral of these thirty-eight years of my life is that if you do what you think is right, you are bound to win. I do not mean that you are bound to win the ordinary, often sordid, prizes of the outward life. But I have proved, and I have written this book to show how I have proved, that if a man clings fast to what he believes to be the Right and the Truth, he cannot fail in the end to win the only prize which is worth winning, and that prize is Peace within himself. A consciousness of duty done, come what might, is worth far more than every other reward which Society can bestow. Shakespeare coined a phrase about "the fault, dear Brutus, is not in our stars but in ourselves," and Sir James Barrie gave it currency in a foolish play. The sentiment is all right, so far as it goes. But it should have been added that the merit is also in ourselves and not in our stars.

CHAPTER II

My name is Edward Percival Fox-Ingleby and I was born in 1889. My father was a wealthy landowner in the neighbourhood of Midhampton, Midhamptonshire. We were not an aristocratic family in the sense that we were quartered with the Dukeries or mentioned in Domesday Book, but we were of good solid upper-class stock. Naturally I would have preferred, when I grew sufficiently old to understand these things, to have been the viscount heir to a marquis, or even the younger son of a Nova Scotia baronet, always provided that my income was no smaller. But at no time in my life would I have exchanged my father's competence for an impoverished title and a mortgaged estate. We live in a world of realism in which a coronet, however pleasant, is seldom the equivalent of a large block of War Loan.

For those who are acquainted with the true relative values of these matters, a title is by no means everything. Many a family which has not even a baronetcy at its head is more ancient, more renowned, more essentially noble, than a dozen dukedoms and a score of marquisates. The Inglebys (Fox- was added later) are not actually mentioned in the Roll of Battle Abbey nor is their escutcheon among those which adorn the fringes of the Roll, but there is a very strong presumption that they were present in some strength at the Battle of Hastings, as there is no record of any Inglebys remaining in Normandy after the early spring of 1066. My descent, therefore, can be traced direct from father to son—with a trivial gap between the battle of Tewkesbury in the Wars of the Roses and the accession of Henry the Seventh, during which it is presumed that loyalty to the defeated Yorkists necessitated a temporary change of name, and a few other trivial gaps later on—right back to that fine old Norman family. So you will readily understand that I can hold up my head in any company, although only a plain commoner, with this resounding fanfaronade of ancestry behind me.

Of my great-grandfather on the paternal side—I have never taken much account of maternal relations; they are unimportant in deciding a man's heredity—little, if anything, is known. But the fact that he bequeathed neither money, nor land, nor ancestral Ingleby plate, nor the family portraits, nor even a crested snuffbox, to his son Jedediah Percival, my grandfather, leads me to think that he must have gambled away the Ingleby fortunes in the company of Fox and Pitt and Sheridan and the Prince Regent. I fancy he was one of the inner clique of the Corinthians and the Hell-Fire Club. Probably he was famous as Beau Ingleby. There is no actual proof of this but it is the only possible explanation of Grandfather Jedediah's humble start in life. Thrown out, a pauper infant, into a hard world by the early death of the aristocratic spendthrift, poor little Jedediah was brought up in a middle-class, nonconformist household near Dulwich—a strange milieu for an Ingleby—and by the time he was sixteen years old he had so far assimilated his bourgeois surroundings that he had acquired a passionate admiration for John Bright, a belief in the teachings of Wesley, and a determination never to regard anything less than fifteen per cent as an adequate return upon outlaid capital. The only exception he ever made in the third of these tenets was in the case of other people's capital. For this he always thought four per cent was more than sufficient.

I do not remember Grandfather Jedediah very clearly, but I have heard enough about him to make me revere his memory, and at the same time to feel extremely glad that he is dead. He was a Liberal of the good old school. He hated privilege and tyranny with equal vehemence, and was always ready to denounce, upon the private hearth or upon the public platform, the Tories, Ferdinand of Naples, the Tsar, the Sultan, Disraeli, Napoleon the Third, and all those who used the feudal system of birth and prerogative and salon-intrigue to keep the Claimant out of the Tichborne estates and title. He subscribed to good causes at the rate of a guinea each per annum, and threw all his influence against Lord Shaftesbury's attempts to interfere with the normal and natural relations of capital and labour. I have been told that Grandfather Jedediah was animated against Lord Shaftesbury—Lord Ashley as he then was—by the fact that he, Grandpapa, was at that time financing a number of small chimney-sweeping enterprises in various towns in the north Midlands, and resented his Lordship's meddling campaign to prohibit the use of young lads in the chimneys. But this I know to be a malicious accusation, for my grandfather's religious, Wesley-inspired soul would not have allowed him to do anything so wicked as to exploit children in chimneys unless the system had been economically sound. He was as vigorous as even his Lordship was in the denunciation of all abuses which did not show a reasonable profit at the end of the financial year, and he was particularly philanthropic in his desire to stamp out the monstrous exploitation of humanity which was so often practised by his rivals in trade.

Jedediah Percival Ingleby made a large fortune out of his various business enterprises, and even the sudden expropriation of his numerous slaves upon his West Indian estates (he never visited them, of course, but he held a controlling interest in them through a majority holding in a parent company) did not do more than shake a little the solid structure upon which he had built his fortune. "I am a religious man," he used to say reverently—I was only a child, but I can remember the occasion vividly, the big iron-grey head wagging, and the straight blue eyes gazing at the ancestral Bible which never left the desk in the dining-room "I am a religious man, and the Almighty God will not, I think, misunderstand me when I say that the Ingleby Estates Company is the Rock upon which I have founded my Church."

Jedediah took an active part in Liberal politics in the Midlands and was chairman of the County Liberal Association and a frequent visitor to the Party Councils at Westminster.

It was greatly to his credit that he did not sever his connection with Liberalism after the Acts were passed which prohibited the employment of children under six in factories for more than fourteen hours a day. He must have lost many thousands a year by that piece of bureaucratic interference. From his letters of that mid-century period I gather that he would have thrown in his lot with the Tories, had it not been for Lord Beaconsfield's abrupt and ill-considered extension of the franchise to the ten-pound free-holder and his equally undigested Factory Acts. Such iniquities revolted my grandfather's essentially Liberal soul, and he remained loyal to the old party, surviving even the imposition of the income-tax and the proposal—of all criminal lunacies—to give Home Rule to Ireland.

Grandpapa Jedediah died in 1896, full of years. He cut up for close on a cool quarter of a million. He was a man. His wife was negligible.

There is no virtue in the world, in my opinion, to equal the grandeur of filial piety. If I may call from the vasty deep a vague spirit of the classics which I studied as a youth, I would refer you to pious Aeneas, who carried his old father either out of Troy or into Rome—I forget which. But anyway, the point is that he carried him somewhere or other; the particular city which was the starting-point or destination is immaterial. Aeneas was a good son, and I have always admired him for it. I, too, was a good son and, although my father has been dead for many years, I think that I still am. For, however deep my grievances against my father, and with whatsoever unfairness he treated me, no one ever heard me say or write a word against him and no one ever will.

The trouble about Father was that he inherited Grandfather's Liberal ideas in theory without Grandfather's Liberal ideas in practice. Thus, he sold all the family shares in the Ingleby Estates Company, invested the proceeds in consols, and settled down at the big house at Grantly Puerorum in Midhamptonshire to lead the life of a squire.

Grandfather Jedediah had bought the house—it was the old Manor of the Grantly-de-la-Vignes, who were contemporaries of ours, having left Normandy at the same time as the Inglebys—after one of his finest financial coups. When the Prussians scored their unexpected military successes at Mars-la-Tour and Gravelotte and Vionville in the war of 1870, shrewd old Jedediah saw what was going to happen, down to the last detail. He sent an agent, with a large credit at the Banque de France, to enlist the services, on a commission basis, of all the available rat-catchers in Paris. In the weeks which elapsed between the disaster at Sedan and the Prussian investment of Paris, Jedediah's agent and his rat-catchers had pretty well cornered the metropolitan sewer-rats. They put them into cages in a couple of hotels in the Rue St. Honoré which Jedediah leased for the purpose, and waited for the siege and its inevitable pressure. Weeks before the surrender of Paris on January 26th, 1871—if my historical memory serves me aright—rats were selling at seven and eight francs a head. Mind you, francs in those days were francs, and you cannot be surprised that a frantically starving populace, still retaining some francs and madly anxious to buy a sewer-rat almost at any price, should have materially assisted my grandfather to buy the Manor House of Grantly Puerorum.

It is, indeed, on record that old Jedediah was heard to grumble once or twice that the Siege of Paris had ended too soon. If it had not been for the untimely capitulation signed by Favre (I am not pretending. I looked it up in a history book), Jedediah claimed that he would have disposed of the two hundred and twenty thousand rats which still remained on his books. But even as it was, he did not do very badly out of the transaction. The remaining rats went back to the sewers of Paris and, out of the profits, he bought the Manor House of Grantly Puerorum. But if the siege had gone on long enough, and if it had not been for that iniquitous Favre with his craven hurry to surrender, Grandfather Jedediah always maintained that out of the surplus rats he could have bought Grantly Grange, Grantly Place, and the grazing and turf-cutting rights over Grantly Common as well. Which just shows that you can never trust those French. Indeed, all through my life I have found it difficult to distinguish between French and rats. I suppose it is a hereditary trait with which I have been endowed owing to Grandfather's financial disappointment.

To return:

Father cut loose from all Grandfather's commercial affairs within a few days of coming into his inheritance, and settled down at Grantly.

He was a passionate believer in a quiet life and a fixed income.

It is difficult to see where he got these defeatist ideas from. The Inglebys have been traditionally fighters, ever since the old days in Normandy. Jedediah was a fighter, and I do not suppose anyone could say that I have been conspicuously backward in an affray.

But Father was painfully mild.

He looked painfully mild. His face was red and hearty, his long moustaches were white and middle-class, his blue eyes were almost grotesquely gentle, and his kindness to his inferiors was the laughing-stock of the young bloods of the county. His behaviour as the squire of Grantly Puerorum was, alas! that a son should say it, undignified.

Father was, to put it in a nutshell, a sort of amateur saint. Professional saints have always seemed to me to be pretty awful—all those peculiar Italians and Swiss and Frenchmen and Spaniards, who wore dressing-gowns and made liqueurs and kept large dogs. I have always been proud to belong to a race which did not mess about with professional saints.

But amateurs, whether in theatricals or in literature or in sanctification, are even worse, and Father was an amateur saint. I have no time to do more than sketch the lines which his unpaid canonization took. For example, he developed a painful knack of espousing lost causes and, worse, of subscribing heavily to them. Gone was the old notion of the grandpaternal guinea. The new paternal notion was seldom less than a hundred guineas. Then Father had the repairing habit. That is to say, he re-roofed leaky cottages on the estate, rebuilt tottering barns for the tenant farmers, laid on water and gas for peasants who probably never washed and couldn't read, maintained fences and gates, and paid for hedging and ditching. Not only did he indulge these extravagant whims, but he stubbornly refused to add the interest charges on all this capital expenditure to the rent of the peasants and, on more than a dozen occasions in my own recollection, he actually excused the entire estate of its annual rent on the ground that the harvest had been ruined by the weather or something. I am a little uncertain what it is that ruins harvests, but, whatever it is, it was that.

It is difficult to understand where Father got these ideas. Jedediah never spent a penny on the estate unless he was legally compelled to—and then the man who legally compelled him got it hot and strong in double quick time—or unless he could see a way of getting twopence back. But Father threw solid gold into what he facetiously called "these green and pleasant fields," and never expected to get anything back except what he called "good-will." I am all in favour of good-will myself, but I am not so keen on it when you have to pay for it, and

I simply detest it when you have to pay through the nose for it.

Then there were the two infuriating blunders which Father made about temperance and blood-sports, either of them sufficient in itself to ruin my social career. I have to speak about them, not to disparage my father—that would be unthinkable—but out of ordinary honesty to myself. If I am to give you any idea of the background against which I was brought up, I must not shirk any of the relevant points.

Briefly, on temperance and blood-sports, my father disastrously revised the sane and practical policy of my grandfather. Jedediah Ingleby, like a good Liberal, was a strong temperance man, but he was sensible enough not to be bigoted. He employed none but rigid abstainers upon the estate, and inexorably discharged without a character—and in those admirable days loss of job and character at a week's notice also meant loss of cottage at a week's notice—any employee who was suspected of having entered the local inn. Chairman of the local bench, his sentences for inebriety were exemplary. But he was broad-minded enough to admit a certain elasticity into his principles, and he seldom retired to bed before he had drunk, in addition to his bottle of favourite claret, two bottles— smaller, of course, by a good deal than our modern bottle—of port or Madeira wine.

As for field-sports, Grandfather neither hunted, fished, nor shot. His youth and middle-age had been too fully occupied with the creation of his fortune to allow of such pastimes, and in his later days he preferred, when he wished for diversion, to amuse himself in a manner which required less money and less time, and which, moreover, required no new apprenticeship.

I have often in my life been told by seedy, dingy persons, who seem to be only one step removed from blackmail, that they are my first cousins on the wrong side of the blanket, and it certainly would appear that Grandpapa Jedediah's interpretation of "blood-sports" was inclined to casuistry. He would not shed the blood of an animal by way of sport, but he would not deny himself the sportive play which hot blood made possible, and infinitely desirable, until he was seriously advanced in years. Be that how it may, I admire him for it. He knew his own limitations. A pheasant on the wing was one thing, a village maiden quite another. He could not bring down the former, and he knew it, and he did not try. But he could bring down the latter, and he knew it, and he did try, and he did succeed. In consequence the local gentry liked and respected him. They put up with his accent and his manners for the sake of his wine, and, exhausted as they were, as a local gentry always is, every evening by their tramps after partridge or their gallops after foxes, they did not fall foul of him in the rustic courts of Venus. They were tired after their own hunting and so they were not rivals in his. In consequence the old man was fairly popular with his well-bred neighbours, and they gradually came to regard him as "a rare old character."

Father's attitude was very different and, considering the effect which it had upon my social career, I would not have hesitated to stigmatize it as unforgivably mean, low-class, selfish, and vulgar, if anyone else but my father had been the person concerned. Father, the moment he came into the property, with Grandfather hardly cold in his grave, relaxed all the firm rules about alcoholism on the estate. He sent Christmas presents of firkins of ale to all his dependants and broached enormous barrels at the annual tenantry ball in the village Institute. Yet he himself was a teetotaller, and no drinks were served at the Manor House. The festive parties at the Manor soon faded away. Father's invitations to dinner were only accepted by the nonconformist parsons, the big tradesmen in Midhampton, the Radical politicians, and a handful of people, here and there, who, one can only suppose, came because they liked him. The big neighbouring squires simply would not sit at a board which was graced by lemonades, barley-waters, and even, to my shame, cocoas.

Worse quickly followed. My father declared publicly, on a

Liberal platform at the election of 1901, that encouragement of field-sports was incompatible with the tenets and spirit of Liberalism, and that the whole estate of Grantly Puerorum was to be wired forthwith. And wired it forthwith was. This gratuitous insult to the surrounding country, together with Father's almost comically light sentences on poachers when-ever he found himself in control of the bench, alienated us completely from the cultured society and the elevated milieu in which I had naturally expected to be brought up. My contemporaries of eleven and twelve years of age, triumphant in the victory of the Unionist Party at the polls in 1901, lost no opportunity of jeering at me as "a dirty little Rad" or "Foxy the spoil-sport" or "Ginger-beer Neddie," whenever we chanced to meet in the country lanes or on the way back to school. And, bitterly though I suffered, I could not find it in my heart to blame them. After all, I was a little Rad, and I was the son of Fox-Ingleby, the Spoil-sport, and my name was Edward, and ginger-beer was drunk a good deal in our house, so how could I say that I had a legitimate grievance? But it irked me sadly all the same. Boys of that age are pathetically sensitive, and it would probably be no exaggeration to say that I was perhaps even more sensitive than the ordinary run. But how I envied them, those swaggering young sons of true-blue Tory landowners with their ponies and their trout-rods and their twelve-bore guns and their hereditary grooms and their freemasonry of class and their instinctive domination. I was as good as they. I knew it, and they—I fancy—knew it. But my father, whom I loved and against whom no word shall be spoken in my presence, was a damned anti-blood-sport Radical.

My mother was an ideal wife and mother. She was placid and comfortable and well-meaning. She fussed, of course, and she had an extraordinarily irritating trick of assuming that everyone had got a cold and needed eucalyptus on their handkerchiefs. The faintest clearing of the throat by the butler, the most casual sneeze by the kitchen-maid, the merest snuffle by a nasty adenoidal boots, was enough to send Mother off into a paroxysm of solicitude. During the winter months the whole house reeked of disinfectant like the dress-circle of a West-End theatre when the play is faltering, and the incompetent country doctor made a very comfortable income out of Grantly Manor.

Mother was a champion pauperizer. She used to give so many old clothes, and boots, and blankets, and sacks of coal to the wives of the tenants and workmen on the estate that it was really hardly necessary for them to do any work at all, and her extravagant generosity when any of them had a baby was a positive encouragement to plebeian incontinence. And she used to spend hours sitting in their frowsty little parlours, talking to them about nothing. A little geniality from the master or mistress is a wonderful tonic to a semi-feudal community such as ours was, but Mother overdid it to such an extent that she must have seemed undignified to the dependants. Her excessive familiarity caused me agonies of shame when I was a small boy. Even at an early age I had an instinctive sense of the essential fitness of things, and Mother's free-and-easy failure to play the part of the Grande Dame was distressing to me. But the truth is that Mother was in many ways an irritating person. She had a knack of looking after Father when she ought to have been looking after her only child which never failed to annoy me, and she scarcely made any secret of the fact that she was a wife first and a mother second. This was wrong. Nobody wishes to be spoilt, but there ought to be a middle course between spoiling and positively putting the child's interests after the father's.

But it is not for me to criticize. In her own fussy fashion, she was a wonderful woman and I loved her very dearly.

She was a Fox, and Father added her name to his when he married her. I rather fancy that she was descended from Gaston de Foix, who figures, you will remember, in the Chronicles of Froissart.

CHAPTER III

Cut off as I was by Father's short-sighted folly from the society of those of my contemporaries who were wrongly supposed to be superior to me in length of pedigree, and were certainly inferior in talent, I was forced to spend most of my holidays in the society of the only son of my father's estate-agent. His name was George Bedford and he was almost exactly the same age as myself. The estate-agent himself, William Bedford, was a man for whom I had a keen contempt even in those early days. In old Jedediah's times, William Bedford had been a keen follower of the pack and a fine shot. But he accepted the fatal edict of 1901 with a servile lack of protest which I could never forgive, and put away his pink coats and guns and rods without a word, and threw himself with energy into my father's Utopian experiments for improving the breed of potatoes, and running a model farm, and such-like nonsense. Serf-like humility is not a thing which I care for very much. And I always disliked the endless drain of money which these experiments involved.

I have always thought that a man who has once worn a pink coat ought to be proud to go on wearing a pink coat, and that a man who throws a thousand pounds away in an endeavour to improve the pedigree strain of brussels sprouts would be, if he were not my beloved father, a fool.

But William Bedford put as much servile enthusiasm into the jettisoning of his pink coat as he did into Father's experiments in the in-breeding of cabbages, or whatever it was. He seemed to take a pride in his work as work, without ever enquiring whether one sort of work might not be more worth while than another. He had that dull, rustic type of mind which has no sense of discrimination. Still, take him for all in all, William Bedford was not a bad fellow.

He was a big hearty man with a red face and huge hands, and very popular with the farmers and the farm servants, which was only natural because it was William Bedford who had to carry out Father's reckless schemes of improvements and to announce the rent dispensations in bad years. No wonder he was popular with them. Any man can cultivate the good-will of savages if he takes them a bag of beads or a musical box. The surprising thing about Bedford was that in some mysterious way he managed to retain the esteem of the gentry, which he had acquired in his hunting days, even after he had supervised the construction of the wire fences. The Master, of course, and one or two of the younger and clearer-sighted members of the Hunt could not be anything more than coldly civil to him after the apostasy, but many of the older landowners in the Grantly country, and the sporting Archdeacon, and most of the High Church parsons, used to chaff him about the wire fences and his conversion from sport to farming as if it really was a laughing matter.

William Bedford had one outstanding quality which I have always hoped was an honest quality. He was utterly loyal to Father and Mother. Indeed, he seemed to adore them both. It was difficult for me at that age to make out whether he really loved them or whether he merely loved the hands which fed him, but there can be no doubt that Father and Mother believed in the sincerity of his affection for them and that they genuinely loved him. The three-cornered friendship which existed between them unbroken for nearly thirty years was a peculiar English anomaly. Probably I am hereditarily a throw-back to my Norman ancestors, but I never could feel anything but uneasiness at the idea of sitting down to supper with one's estate-agent. Father and Mother were so essentially English that they did it every Sunday for nearly thirty years. Yet what is an estate-agent but a paid servant, when all is said and done? And who would sit down to supper with his footman, except on the annual occasion of the servants' ball? But my parents thought otherwise, and it was their business, not mine. They loved William Bedford and—let us give him the benefit of the doubt—he probably loved them.

George Bedford, the son, inherited from his father the subservience which made his father follow mine without a murmur from hunting to brussels sprouts and from blood-sports to benevolence. But it was the only quality which he did inherit, for in every other way he was the opposite of William Bedford.

He was born at the old Dower House, just outside the north gate of the Park on the Weltonborough Road, in the same month as I was born at the Hall. He was tall for his age and thin, with sloping shoulders and a pigeon chest and a pale face and spectacles, and he was a precocious reader of books. There was none of his father's yeoman bluntness and rusticity about him. Nor was there much of his father's practical bent. At least William Bedford knew on which side his bread was buttered when he put up the wire fences. He lost his hunting but he kept his salary and his house. But George, from my earliest recollection, wasted time on book-learning that could be of no future material value to a man in the position which he was likely to occupy in after-life. It was all very well for me to study the classics and learn the poets off by heart and master the jargon of the art-galleries. A knowledge of Homer and Southey was obviously an investment for me. For George it was a waste. *The Elements of the Law of Trespass*, or *Halliburton on Pigs*, or *Elm Disease, its Cause and Cure*, would have been far more useful for an estate-agent's son who could hardly hope to rise higher than an estate-agency himself. Many and many a time I used to point this out to young George, and he always listened attentively. But not even my advice could stem his output of misdirected energy.

This disregard of my advice—for although I was in a position to order the little fellow, I never dreamt of giving him my opinions and ideas in any other form than that of brotherly advice—used to annoy me a good deal in those days before I got my temper under perfect control, and I doubt if I would have continued to extend my friendship to George if it had not been for two alleviating circumstances. Firstly, his submissiveness of nature took the intellectual form of admiring me and following my slightest lead and falling in with my lightest wish, and that is a form of flattery which not even the highest characters can easily resist. It is the age-long secret of the dog's popularity with certain types of human beings, and, conversely, the age-long secret of the cat's unpopularity with the same types. George regarded me with the same immeasurable devotion as the cow-eyed spaniel regards his master, and I could not help feeling the same half-amused, half-contemptuous affection for George that the master feels for the cow-eyed spaniel. And the second reason was that, after my father inherited Grantly Puerorum and began his cynical campaign—for I can regard it as nothing else —against my social advancement, there was no one else except George Bedford in anything remotely like my own walk of life with whom I could play. So I made the best of it and, in my holidays, played with George Bedford.

He used to bicycle up to the Hall every morning of the holidays on one of my old bicycles which I had grown out of—it was too small for him, as he was even taller than I was when we were entering our teens, though I was a good deal more symmetrically built, but it sufficed and he was justifiably grateful for the gift—and we used to climb the chestnut trees in the park, bicycle down the long avenues, swim in the lake in fine weather, play croquet, a pastime at which I was already proficient, or carpenter in my handsomely fitted carpentry shop. At one time we experimented with lawn-tennis but I found it a tedious game and we soon gave it up. Oddly enough, George developed a decidedly skilful knack at lawn-tennis during the short time that we played it, and I often wish that I had been sufficiently interested in it to encourage him to make progress. But I preferred the more intellectual game of croquet. During the years that George and I played croquet, I can hardly remember a single occasion on which he beat me.

He did not, of course, go to a preparatory school in the proper sense of the word. In spite of the large salary which my father paid to his father, nearly fifty per cent more than old Jedediah had paid him, George only went to a small local school in Midhampton, a queer place, where the boys went home on Saturdays and did not mind the other boys knowing the Christian names of their sisters, and wore knickerbockers at football to save the expense of soap, hot water, and towels for the washing of muddy knees. I well remember my astonishment—I suppose I was eleven by that time—at eliciting from George the extraordinary statement that no one in his school cheated at French. Of course I was at an age when creative imagination cannot be expected to flower—whatever may have happened to me since—and so perhaps I may be excused for having found it difficult to imagine a school in which one did not cheat at French. Even more difficult was it to imagine a schoolboy to whom it had not occurred to cheat at French. Such a lack of enterprise and common-sense seemed then, as it seems now, quite unbelievable. But that is what George was like then, and in after-life—the epitome of the smug little bourgeois. It was, in fact, symbolical of George's character that it was the subject of French on which he elected to be conspicuously honest. In his walk of life the French language and France meant only four things: unbridled licence in morals, sinister perfection of manners, naked feminine breasts, and a glorification of queer cards like Gambetta and Boulanger.

I am not suggesting for a moment that George, at the age of eleven, paid any attention to morals, manners, Gambetta, or feminine breasts. But the atmosphere in which he was brought up, of an English estate-agent's house in the Midlands—so different from the atmosphere of the Boul' Mich'—was enough to make him suspicious even of the word French. So, in learning the language of those slippery and immoral foreigners, George was characteristically careful to display all the Britisher's dull and self-conscious integrity.

That, I think, sums up the essence of George's early life and the preparatory school to which he was sent. Middle-class honesty was the keynote, and if one had to make a differentiation between the varying degrees of middle-class honesty, one would say that George belonged to the slightly lower middle-class, with which, of course, goes a slightly higher and more self-conscious brand of honesty. George was, in a word, at the age of eleven, a very nice lad, not talented, not even a gentleman, but certainly not a boor.

My own preparatory school was, of course, rather different. We did not run home to our mammies every Saturday—indeed we found it rather a bore to have to go home at the end of the term for the holidays. We did not adhere to a rigid code of "playing the game," in spite of the quaint exhortations of some of the junior, and therefore still idealistic, masters. We soon discovered that " playing the game" inevitably meant a low place in class, a target for fouls at football, and from time to time a sharp spanking from those in authority for failing to reach the high standard set by those who did not play the game either on the football fields or in the class-room. When we discovered this, we ceased to play the game in any of the departments of school-life, and we enjoyed ourselves immensely in consequence.

The high light of my four years at my prep. school was

when I stole a parrot from a passing circus and put it into Matron's bed. The parrot, on being suddenly uncovered by Matron in her grey woollen nightdress, screamed repeatedly "Jezebel, Jezebel, Jezebel". Matron had a fit of hysterics and was only saved from a permanent derangement by the kindly action of Jenkinson Ma., who threw a basin of water (in which Jenkinson Mi. had been washing his famous trio of white Albino mice) over her; and the headmaster, entering abruptly and mistaking the sequence of events, beat Jenkinson Ma. and Jenkinson Mi. very sharply indeed. As I was the only witness of the entire episode from beginning to end, it was largely on my evidence that the Jenkinson brothers suffered. The parrot escaped. So did I. And so, I believe, but I never bothered to enquire, did the triplet mice.

But, in the main, life was dull at that prep. school, and it was with a lively hope of the future that I shed the dust of it, and departed to Eton, at the age of thirteen years and a half.

CHAPTER IV

I greatly enjoyed Eton. I was a wet-bob, of course. Cricket never appealed to me very much and even in those Edwardian days, when the Harrow eleven was dimly perceptible on the field at Lord's—it has not been visible to the naked eye since 1910—I could never muster up any enthusiasm for it, even as a spectator on a fashionable coach. Indeed it always seemed to me that the cricket was the great drawback to the annual school outing at Lord's. Our other annual school treats were not thus compulsorily marred, St. Andrew's Day being in mid-winter, and on the 4th of June the cricket matches being easily avoidable. It is true that every second year we were invaded by the Winchester boys, quiet, gentlemanly lads with their eyes fixed, even at that early age, upon the various branches of the Civil Service. They came to encourage their cricket eleven, but as there was no social importance attached to the game very few of us were in the habit of attending the match. It was, in fact, an ideal opportunity for a quiet day with a book on the river.

The advantages of being a wet-bob were great. So long as one did not become hypnotized by the competitive fetish which is such a tiresome part of an English education, there was no necessity to row in a boat with other lads. Thus the team spirit could be successfully side-stepped. So far as I remember, I never once rowed in a boat with more than a single companion, and then only with one whose friendship

23

I valued for one reason or another. This preservation of individuality, so infinitely precious, can only be achieved at Eton by non-competitive wet-bobs, and it allows complete scope for the two main activities of any rational Etonian, the cultivation of friends likely to be useful in after-life and the avoidance of Collegers.

There was only one serious worry in my school career at Eton, and that was the fear that my father's eccentricities might become public property. Several times sons of our neighbours, who were in the School, threw them up in my teeth in a way that gravely alarmed me at the moment, but on each occasion I succeeded in minimizing the damage by a judicious outlay of my very handsome allowance— for I will say this of Father: whatever his faults, and he had many, poor old fellow, he was always generous to me about money. My assiduous work with the beagles also helped me to tide over several awkward incidents, and of course I was a perfervid Unionist in our Debating Society, seldom missing an opportunity of scourging the wretched Campbell-Bannerman or lashing the miserable Asquith. Those were the days before the 1906 election, when the Unionist cause was being unscrupulously attacked by the Radical propagandists, and it was the duty of every right-thinking man, of whatever age, to rally to the defence of Mr. Joseph Chamberlain.

I remember how astonished I was at my father's apparent indifference to my conversion to Toryism during my first half at Eton. "Everyone must think for himself," he said mildly, and he added: "Somehow I never thought you would stick to Radicalism. That is why I sent you to Eton."

"Are you sorry?" I remember asking.

He shrugged his shoulders and changed the subject. Looking back on it, I cannot help coming to the conclusion that he was not a particularly intelligent man. Presumably he hoped to gain something by sticking to his political opinions.

Where else would be the point of sticking to them? But to my knowledge he never did gain anything, and he certainly lost a great deal.

George Bedford went to one of those lesser public schools which have always seemed to me to possess no merit whatsoever except that they provide some sort of education for people like George. I have no idea what the school was like, because I never encouraged George to talk about it in the holidays. Not that George ever displayed any particular desire to talk about it after a few abortive attempts in the earlier holidays. On the contrary, he preferred listening to my accounts of the wide, Athenian, cultured life of Henry the Sixth's great old foundation. At first I had some scruples about describing scenes and customs and dignified amenities which could not fail, I thought, to arouse wistful regrets and even, perhaps, secret envy. But though George was an eager listener, he never once allowed even a sigh of sadness to escape him.

The truth, of course, was that George then, as always, knew his station in life. He was the son of one of our servants, and it was as the son of one of our servants that he listened to my descriptions and did my holiday task for me every holiday. It is, I think, and at that time also thought that it was, somewhat to my credit that I never discussed politics with George during those old days. I was independent and could afford to think, as Father said, for myself. George was an offshoot of a family that was paid to believe that death-duties and health-insurance and land-taxes were good things. He could not afford to think otherwise so long as Father was alive. I could not help admiring his reticence about his beliefs. I kept silent about them out of tact, but George kept silent because he was determined, I am certain, to be ready to switch across to the right side when the time came. For it was obvious to every Tom, Dick, and Harry on the estate that the moment the Vicar had said his "dust to dust, ashes to ashes" stuff over Father, there would be some pretty drastic changes at Grantly Puerorum. Everyone knew it, and George was no stupider than his neighbour. He had the hereditary gift, at least I gave him the credit for having it, of spotting the difference between the side of a piece of bread which has been buttered and the, so to speak, virgin side. So George, dear good fellow that he always was, held his tongue about controversial matters and listened to my views on current politics without the least attempt to argue.

It was in these unhappy surroundings that the early days of my life were passed. Cut off as I was from the society of the neighbourhood, condemned to choose between solitude mitigated only by George Bedford's company and the sons of Midhamptonshire haberdashers, unable to discuss world affairs in a rational way with my Father, I was probably as unlucky a boy as it is possible to imagine.

But the dice have not always fallen against me, for on my eighteenth birthday I was elected to Pop at Eton, and within an hour received a telegram to say that Father and Mother had been killed in a railway accident while on their way to open a Liberal bazaar and jumble sale at Wolverhampton.

It was naturally a terrible blow to me. To lose both one's adored parents on the same day is a pretty grim shock when one is only eighteen. It cuts away one's sheet-anchor. It sets one adrift upon rough, uncharted seas without a navigator.

But youth is resilient. Youth is buoyant. No one, I am certain, will misunderstand me when I say that my overwhelming grief was made just faintly possible to bear by the knowledge that the world must go on. My loss was irreparable, but my duty was to the future and not to the past. Passionate weeping would not set back the hands of time. Like the leaves of the forest, said Diomedes, so are the generations of men, and there was nothing to be gained by pretending that Father and Mother had not outstayed their utility. There is nothing macabre in the saying that youth will be served; it is simply the Law of Nature. One may revere Old Age without necessarily thinking that it should last for ever. And so, when I received the calamitous telegram on that summery day at Eton, I retired quietly to my room and shed a tear or two, and mused a little upon the past, and upon the dear old days that never, never would return. Then I dried my tears, and squared my shoulders, and went out to face the world, and that afternoon celebrated my election to the Eton Society with a surreptitious champagne party—a party re-markable in Etonian annals for the circumstance that of the nineteen guests, my fellow-members of Pop, eleven were peers or heirs of peers and seven were sons of bankers and the nineteenth was an American millionaire. After the party had come to a hilarious conclusion, I hastily bought a black armband, obtained special leave, and hurried home to see what William Bedford was doing with the estate, and to stop him from doing it.

I think that that was one of the most wonderful days of my life. At last I was my own master. And not only that, I was master of Grantly Puerorum as well. The servants were all drawn up in a row when I arrived at the Manor in the brougham. They were pale and frightened, as if they did not know what was going to happen. Some were weeping— mostly of the housemaid type, I fancy—obviously trying to create the impression that they were mourning the death of my parents. Young though I was, I was not to be bamboozled by flagrant histrionics of that sort. Either they were acting their tears, or they were crying with fear at the prospect of having a real true-blue, landed-gentry master at last. If the former, they were obviously worthless anyway. If the latter, they had at least the merit of being good judges, for they would have been right. I was face to face with the first of the important decisions in my life. I was at a cross-roads. I had to make up my mind, at the age of eighteen, suddenly, whether I was going to accept the tyranny of ancient, pampered, covertly insolent servants, or whether I was going to assert myself and be master in my own house. Remember, I was barely eighteen and, unless I showed a bold and decided front at once, I might easily have slipped under the domination of "old retainers." It did not take me long to decide. As soon as we all returned to the Hall from the cemetery, I instructed the entire staff to attend me in the library—William Bedford was there too, and also the Vicar, the Reverend Ernest Blythe, whose future was now to all intents and purposes in my keeping—where it was my intention to entertain them with a glass apiece of the cheaper sherry which my father had injudiciously bought in 1901.

After a short speech in which I welcomed them into my service and promised that I would do my best to be a good master to them, adding that the details of certain small changes in their conditions of employment which I proposed to make could be discussed on some future occasion, I instructed the two footmen to hand round the sherry.

Everything fell out as I had expected. Banks, the butler, an elderly man who had been with us for nearly twenty years, declined his glass. He was a pillar of the local Rechabites and a Good Templar, and was, in fact, one of those cranky busybodies who miscall Prohibition by the name of Temperance and try to force their views and habits into the lives of other citizens. He used to speak at Prohibition meetings on his evenings off, and often used to distribute leaflets for the Salvation Army in Midhampton. I had always disliked Banks. There was a smugness about his self-righteousness that had annoyed me from the earliest moment that I could distinguish smugness as a nasty quality. Also he was on far too friendly a basis with Father. Whether it was Mother who infected Father with the germ of undignified intimacy with the staff, or *vice versa*, I do not know. But just as she used to spend hours gossiping about second teethings and whooping-cough and such-like drearinesses with the wives, so used Father to talk to Banks as if he was an ordinary human being. Indeed he went even further and used to consult him about local politics and the feeling in the village on matters connected with the parish council. On several occasions, during my third and fourth years at Eton, Father actually asked Banks for his advice after I had already given him my own.

On that afternoon when we all stood in the library after the funeral, I faced my crisis, and, with a full consciousness of what I was doing, I raised my glass and said, "I bid you drink to a happy and harmonious future in our relations." The domestics respectfully murmured "Hear, hear, sir," and nervously sipped at their glasses, with the exception of the two footmen, who swallowed theirs at one gulp, and Banks, who set his glass down untasted.

"You are not drinking, Banks," I said quietly.

"I warmly subscribe to the sentiment," he replied in that unctuous diction which is so common among Liberal politicians, and which I fancy he had learnt from Father.

"But you are not drinking," I repeated.

"No, sir," he answered.

"It is my wish that we all should drink this toast," I said, raising my voice a little.

The upshot was as I had foreseen. The man refused and I discharged him on the spot with a month's wages instead of notice, and, as he had not been in my employment for more than a few minutes, I could not in common honesty towards Society in general give him a character. Few actions are so dishonest and so cowardly as the action of the employer who lets an employee loose upon the world with a "character" to which he could not subscribe on oath in a court of law. As I had expected, the parson raised his voice in protest and I was able to deliver a neat little speech which I had prepared beforehand.

"So long as I am patron of your living, Vicar," I said, "I will not interfere in your pulpit, and I must ask you to return the courtesy and not interfere in my house."

He started to say something but, happily for the dignity of his cloth, thought better of it and retired from the field.

Later in the afternoon the cook, who had been with us for eighteen years, and the senior parlour maid, who had completed twelve years, came to see me with a request from the whole staff that I would reinstate Banks. This request they were foolish enough to support with a suggestion that the whole staff might possibly tender their resignations if it was not granted, so I took the opportunity of discharging them all on the same terms as I had discharged Banks. I then ordered William Bedford to provide a new staff before the next holidays, and returned, cheerful and triumphant, to Eton.

CHAPTER V

My last year at Eton was a happy one, marred only by a long warfare by letter with Father's younger brother, Uncle Arthur. The *casus belli* was a codicil to Father's will in which he had appointed Uncle Arthur as my trustee until I was twenty-one. Father had, however, very luckily forgotten to get his signature to the codicil witnessed, and I was perfectly justified in using this flaw to repudiate Uncle Arthur's claims to authority over me. Arthur, a foolish fellow anyway, greatly interested in what are called for some reason "good works," asked me over and over again not to take a stand on a trivial technicality, as he always described it in his boring letters. In the end I grew tired of answering his appeals and I wrote to him a stiffish letter, pointing out that I was now head of the family, that at last an opportunity had arrived to lift the family out of its bourgeois antecedents, and that I proposed to do so forthwith. I said that by way of a first step in this direction I intended to have nothing more to do with him and his family, and that all future correspondence about the ridiculous codicil would be answered by my lawyers and that their bill of costs would be sent to him for settlement. I re-read this letter before posting it and, thinking that it was perhaps a little harsh, added a postscript in which I offered to defray the cost of the education of my two cousins, Martin and Edgar, his sons, on condition that they were sent to a school for gentlemen. Uncle Arthur was not courteous enough even to answer this postscript, but for a long time he wrangled with my lawyers. It did not matter to me, and it cost him, together with the expenses of the writ that we had to serve on him, a matter of fifty pounds. In fact the only ones who really suffered from the whole farce were Martin and Edgar, who were sent instead to Harrow.

But with this exception my last year at Eton passed quite pleasantly. I had a great deal of money, which is nice anywhere but especially nice at Eton, and I was able to entertain lavishly during the holidays. The difference between being the son of a simple, Radical bourgeois who is alive, and being the inheritor of a simple, Radical bourgeois who is dead, is pretty considerable. From nothing I had become in one moment the young Squire of Grantly Puerorum, rich, popular, and independent.

The first and incomparably the greatest advantage to be gained by attending an educational establishment such as Eton, is the acquisition of friends. Scholarship cannot be forced upon those who are unfitted to receive it, nor can it be denied to those who are naturally endowed with a passionate capacity to acquire it. A love of games, the second gift of the public school to the embryonic Empire-builder, is all very fine for the muddied oafs but there are many men who in early life repudiate the suggestion that they are oafs and have a sensitive distaste for mud. For these a straight bat is as repugnant as a clean slate, because both imply a submission to an artificial discipline.

My particular friends during my last year at Eton were Lord Plaistow, Le Comte de St. Etienne-de-la-Fosse, Lord Bletchley, Eddie Duncatton, whose father was chairman of the Pacific Insurance Company, and Charles Hudson, the heir to the American Zinc fortune. We were all of the same year, and shared a taste for the elegances of life and a distaste for cricket, schoolmasters (whom Eddie once described as men amongst boys and boys amongst men), and the lower classes.

We also were alike in taking an interest in the fair sex, although it was not until we went to Oxford in the following year that we fully realized what an admirable form of entertainment the fair sex can be.

Our life was altogether delightful during that last year. We were all rich, we were all old for our years, we had all escaped that dreadful period in the lives of most young men when their faces are covered with red spots, and half the drawing-rooms of Mayfair were open to us during the holidays and Long Leave. Our influence in the school was always thrown in upon the side of normal common-sense and rational conduct, and we made an especial point of beating severely and frequently all those younger boys who took an excessive interest in anything, whether it was work, games, literature, housemaids, archaeology, or science. We also dealt ruthlessly with all vulgarians, such as the sons of nouveaux riches, or snobs, or the occasional offspring of a country parsonage whose education was being paid for by some Lord or Lady Bountiful. In short, our idea was to create a wholesome tradition of respect for the right kind of authority, coupled with a sense of proportion which should discourage middle-class enthusiasms. We were not popular with the masters, but we had never expected to be. They caused us infinite amusement.

But pleasant though Eton was for men of our qualities and position, we were glad to move on to the University. One gets tired even of beating bourgeois posteriors. Bletchley and Duncatton had been originally designed by their parents for Cambridge, but we decided to stick together, and in October 1908 we all went up to Oxford. In the same term I sent George Bedford up to Oxford to study agriculture as a non-collegiate student.

The careers of myself and my friends at the University moved along a predestined course to an abrupt predestined end. Any reasonably intelligent man who had a knowledge of our high-spirited, restless, eagerly-enquiring, impatient minds, could have foretold the sequence of our joint careers to a hair's-breadth. Academic honours were not for us, nor were the tedious restraints of academic life. The monastic discipline at Eton—for we had, from the very beginning of our time there, scrupulously accepted de-la-Fosse's dictum that a man to whom femininity does not appeal is lower than the beasts of the field—together with the occasional glimpses into a strange and beautiful new world which we had enjoyed during our last two or three holidays, combined to unleash us upon the stage-doors and tobacconists' shops of the University City like a sextette of young wolves. Life was an incessant whirl of excitement. We were continually being pursued by proctors, fined and gated by the college authorities, and harried by indignant fathers. But we did not care two straws for any of them. We were young and handsome and hot-blooded, and the world was at our feet.

There were a few unfortunate incidents, of course. Such things are bound to happen when life is being lived at high pressure. But the quarrel between de-la-Fosse and Plaistow was sad, because it is always sad when old friends fall out. I do not know whether it is that I have an especial genius for friendship, but few things have distressed me more in my life than the defection of a man whom I have loved and trusted. Both de-la-Fosse and Plaistow felt that the other had betrayed him, and it certainly was true that neither of them came very well out of the episode, for both of them lost their tempers in a very common way. Indeed, I got rather a shock over the whole business, because it had never occurred to me that two aristocrats, of the genuine old aristocracy of Europe, could descend so miserably into the gutter. For de-la-Fosse came of a stock which had ruled in Touraine for centuries, and Plaistow's forebears had sold vegetables to Edward the Fourth.

The quarrel arose out of the legendary glamour which surrounds, in the eyes of the women of every civilized country in the world, a French nobleman. St. Etienne-de-la-Fosse, an exquisite product of hundreds of cultured years, found no difficulty whatsoever in seducing a very attractive young girl who, as everybody knew, was being far-sightedly groomed by Bill Plaistow for his second year. She was very lovely and very young, and Bill, being essentially an artist, had heroically resolved not to pluck the fruit before it was ripe. So he was preparing her, gently, smoothly, and on cosmopolitan lines, for the ultimate sacrifice upon the masculine altar. I well remember Bill's rage when he discovered that all his preliminary work had gone for nothing. He used very harsh words about St. Etienne and went about for days swearing vengeance against the treacherous frog who had forestalled him with the fair Melinda. I brought them together in the end, and at a small champagne party in my rooms I persuaded them to shake hands. But they did not mean it. They were sworn enemies for life. For me the whole episode was tragic because it was meaningless, and so it was faintly comic. Two old and trusted friends were quarrelling over the virginity of a sweet but stupid girl in a provincial town. What else could I do but smile, because if the gallant Frenchman had forestalled Bill with Melinda, I myself had forestalled the gallant Frenchman? But naturally I could not tell them that. After all, a gentleman's son does not say these things about a woman's honour. Besides, there was Melinda's baby, and it was obviously more judicious to allow St. Etienne to accept the responsibility, and the paternity order, rather than admit my own delectable priority. And by the time that the youngster was old enough to resemble anything but a carrot, we had all left the University. This was, perhaps, fortunate, for I received a very angry letter from St. Etienne some years later. He had paid a visit to Melinda for the first time since going down from Oxford, to discuss financial arrangements with Melinda's father, and had instantly spotted the resemblance which the child bore to its father. A scientist once told me that the children of particularly masculine men are apt to resemble their fathers more closely than the children of others. This is a drawback for us, but it has the compensation that at least we can take satisfaction from our powers. St. Etienne, in between his rambling sentences of abuse, made repeated demands for the repayment of all the money which he had paid out on the paternity order, but, as I explained in my reply, nothing could be proved and he could whistle for his money. I lost St. Etienne's friendship, it is true. But I had carefully weighed the value of it before I made my decision, and it was with the most careful deliberation that I chose to sacrifice St. Etienne rather than pay the twelve hundred and forty pounds which he had disbursed for the child. No Frenchman, with whatever exquisite charm he may be endowed, is worth all that amount of money. Besides, he had been paying too much, as I pointed out. I also added that if he had had a tenth of my brains he would have passed the brat on to Bill Plaistow. Incidentally, it just shows how wise my decision was to prefer twelve hundred and forty pounds to St. Etienne's friendship—dearly though I loved him—for the war broke out a few weeks after his second threatening letter reached me, together with a strange document from a Notaire Publique in Limoges which appeared to correspond to what we know as a solicitor's letter, and he had to join his regiment of French artillery and was killed almost at once near Compiègne. It was a lucky circumstance for me.

Years later our College at Oxford put up a memorial to him, and I subscribed rather handsomely to the list. This was only right and proper. I was grateful to St. Etienne-de-la-Fosse for having enriched my life with his friendship, and I was also glad that he had been translated to the Valhalla of those who have died for their country on the field of honour before his rascally attorney in Limoges managed to serve a writ on me.

I have related this incident for no other purpose than to point out the ancient moral that women can play hell with the lives of strong and decent men. There we were—three exceptional men. And a little tradesman's daughter, a worthless creature, entered into our lives with no other contribution to the world's gaiety except beautiful ankles and a certain wanton charm, and smashed up two friendships. Dear Melinda. She was soft and silly and she gave me one of the best laughs of my life when I sat as arbiter between St. Etienne and Bill when they furiously claimed priority as deflowerers (or is the word deflorists?). But all the same it is queer that three such men, with an unusual power to control their surroundings and mould their lives, should have been influenced by such a creature.

It occurs to me to wonder where the child is now. It is the first time in my recollection that I have wondered that. It does not matter anyway.

By an extraordinary sequence of good fortune, coupled with the exercise of social influence and personal charm, we survived a whole year at Oxford. But it was clear to the world that the pace could not last. A smash was inevitable. It came in the beginning of our second year, on my twentieth birthday.

By this time I had passed through—if indeed, I had even been in—the callow stages of weediness in appearance and floppiness in mind which normally afflict the eighteenth, nineteenth, and twentieth years of a young man's life, and I was sturdy, healthy, and—to make no bones about it—good-looking. The only handicap which I possessed was my comparative lack of inches, for I was barely five-foot-ten. This may be considered by most people to be a very fair height, but it always irked me in the presence of the six-footers who abound in the ballrooms and drawing-rooms of our aristocratic circles. It was, I know, absurd for anyone of my other advantages to feel this malaise, but, however hard I have tried to get rid of it, and with whatever extra touch of self-confidence I have garnished my demeanour, the malaise has remained all through my life. It was all the more absurd as I grew older and as each succeeding year proved with the best of all practical proofs that women are not swayed in their attachments by mere brawn. A silver tongue and seventy inches can give an hour's start to a booby with seventy-five, and still win in a canter. But even this knowledge, consoling though it was, never quite dissipated my resentment that such an otherwise admirable piece of work should have been marred for a ha'porth of millimetres.

It is not that one is afraid of physical violence from the bigger man. In our walk of life the use of fists is taboo, and even at Oxford where an occasional outsider had forced himself into colleges that ought in common decency to have been reserved for his betters, the danger of becoming involved in a brawl was slight. During my time I only remember to have taken part in one. This was when a party of us were surprised by the occupant of a set of rooms in the act of wrecking them. We had thought that he would not return until later. He was a big, coarse brute of a youth named Stukeley, whose father, we had ascertained, actually kept a public-house near Newmarket, and although there were six of us he did not hesitate to attack us single-handed when his slow mind had grasped the connection between our presence in his rooms and the scene of havoc. It was an unpleasant affair, and such was Stukeley's strength and dexterity that it might have gone hardly with us if I had not used strategy and, grasping one of his ankles from the post of vantage under the table which I had secured at the outbreak of hostilities, brought him down with a crash. We learnt one lesson from this episode and never again wrecked anyone's rooms unless we could muster a wrecking party of at least eight. But this was the only occasion on which I was in danger of physical violence from a bigger man than myself. For the episode of Cyril Hereward, whose pale, pasty face annoyed me so much one winter's afternoon when I came upon it suddenly round a corner in college that I gave it a good slash with my riding-crop—I had been out hunting—was different. There were those who blamed me for the action, as Hereward stood six-foot-four in his horrid grey woollen socks, and they considered that I had been foolhardy. But I knew that there was no danger, as the fellow was a poet and a disciple of Tolstoy. The only blame that might attach to me over the affair was that I had acted impulsively without waiting to consider the pros and cons of such an action in the judicial way in which I have almost invariably acted through life. But the answer to that argument is that Hereward's face was a standing temptation to anyone who happened to have a riding-crop in his hand, and that my sudden impulse was as right as a judicial choice would have been.

I mention this apparently trivial affair because of the consequences which followed from it and which afforded one of many examples of my talent in circumventing ill-fortune. A petty incident which, with anyone else but me, would have been completely forgotten in a couple of minutes, returned to dog me years later, and it was only by great exertions on my part that it did not engulf me in catastrophe.

On my twentieth birthday, then, I was a well-set-up, fairly tall, broad-shouldered young man with white teeth, black hair, neat black moustache, greenish brown eyes, and well-shaped hands and feet, and it was with some reasonable satisfaction that I sat at the end of the dinner-table in my rooms and listened to the speeches of my guests in praise of their host. For I was giving a small party to celebrate the occasion. I see from the autographed menu which lies before me as I write that nine of us sat down that evening. There were my five Etonian friends, of course, and three others, namely: Gerald Chippenham, whose father was high in the Conservative world and who had run up some pretty stiff debts in Oxford, a pair of facts which might seem disconnected but are not; Hugo Walsh-Aynscot, brother of a very beautiful sister; and Kennerly van Suidam, the only Rhodes Scholar of the year who had the entrée into the most exclusive society in the world, the Newport yachting crowd in America.

As I leant back in my chair and twirled my brandy-glass, and listened to Walsh-Aynscot's eulogy, I remember that I fell to wondering which of all these delightful men was the one I loved the best. To which was I the most deeply devoted? It was a difficult choice. My Etonian friends were of longer standing than the three others, but then their little faults and foibles were correspondingly familiar and were becoming increasingly irritating. Bill Plaistow, for instance, was beginning to bet fairly heavily and, as his efforts to beat the book were seldom crowned with success, he was developing the habit of coming to me for loans. Not only that, but he cut up very nasty indeed when, on the fourth request, I told him that I would go through fire for a pal—everybody knew that—but that I wasn't going to lend him any more.

"Then I'm not your pal?" he asked angrily. I assured him that most certainly he was still my pal, but not to the tune of a cool monkey.

"To the tune of a hundred, then?" he demanded, and I was forced to tell him that one does not assess one's friendships in terms of money. Natural delicacy for his feelings prevented me from adding that his present course of behaviour, heading straight downhill as it was, made it exceedingly unlikely that he would develop in the future into the useful friend which I had hoped for, and on the expectation of which I had wasted so much time and money. Is not Hugo Walsh-Aynscot an even dearer fellow than dear Bill? I mused as his glowing speech went on and on. Ruth Walsh-Aynscot is a very, very beautiful girl, with whom I would like to be more intimate. Yes, Hugo is a dear fellow, and when I visit Winterley End, his father's place, in the vac, it will be strange, I thought, if a girl with such full, red lips resists, or wants to resist, a silver tongue. Needless to add that these musings were not in any way interrupted by thoughts of the marriage ceremony. There would be plenty of time for that sort of thing later on, and not necessarily with any of the first few Ruths, so to speak, who might happen to fall by the wayside. Now van Suidam is speaking,—how it all comes back to me across the mists of years—...dear old Ken...such a good chap...and there has always been a queer fascination about Newport....I am not sure that Kennerly isn't the best of them all...though his accent is deplorable and his manners are sadly old-fashioned, and his dinner-jacket is quite terrible ....Chippenham—how strangely the memory works. It is more than a quarter of a century since Jerry Chippenham made his speech, yet I can recall my thoughts as if it was yesterday. Debts and an influential father—that was the theme. Get Jerry out of his hole, on the strictest condition that old Chippenham should not be told, and then let the news filter round to old Chippenham by a circuitous route, and then what about a safe seat in the safe old Tory districts? And there sits dear old Hudson...heir to American Zinc...splendid fellow...and Bletchley...bound to end up as a Governor-General...Eddie Duncatton...de-la-Fosse... useful fellows both...I loved them all, and they, I think, were pretty fond of me.

The last speech was made, the last toast drunk, the last magnum of Armagnac circulated, and then we trooped off gaily to wreck the rooms of the Senior Tutor, who was visiting a sick friend in London. We made a very complete and capital job of it. Seldom indeed can the venerable college have seen a more workmanlike piece of execution. We smashed everything that was smashable—that goes without saying—but we also added some neat new touches, such as pouring vermilion paint over the first editions, tearing the fly-leaves out of the autographed presentation copies of books, and signing fictitious names in indelible pencil across the water-colours and etchings which hung upon the walls. I am always proud to think that it fell to me to make the crowning suggestion—it was, after all, my birthday, and I was the centre of the party—and after a vigorous search through drawers and desks, we found the manuscript of the verse translation of Lucretius on which the Senior Tutor had been engaged for the last seventeen years. We gave it every chance and it was not until Walsh-Aynscot had declaimed the whole of the first hundred lines in his admirable baritone—his sister had a vibrating contralto that was not dissimilar—that we unanimously voted it to be complete bilge and burnt it, leaf by leaf, in the quad., dancing round it and singing as much as we could remember of the hundred and twenty-second Psalm, which, as it was precious little, we eked out with some of St. Etienne's barrack songs, learnt by him from conscripts in Epinal and taught to us on winter evenings.

It was not until we had consumed about four-fifths of the bulky manuscript in the flames that I perceived the imminent approach of authority. In the distance several dark figures were creeping towards us, taking every advantage of the shadowy buttresses of Chapel and the angles of the walls of the quadrangle and the numerous ill-lit doorways to mask their approach. It was obvious to me at a glance that their object was not so much to extinguish our bonfire as to identify us. A mad rush towards us across the open quad. would have given us warning and enabled us to scatter beyond hope of identification, and this stealthy approach was much more dangerous.

It was doubly characteristic of me that I should have been

the only one of us who saw the advancing shadows and that I should have kept my head in the crisis. To have warned my companions and persuaded them to fly might have taken time. They were in that stubborn, unreasoning mood which adolescent intoxication so often induces, and while arguing with them for their own good I might easily have caused my own harm. Without a moment's hesitation, therefore, I withdrew unobtrusively from the glare of the bonfire and retreated into the darkness. Once out of sight, it was the work of a few seconds to reach a well-known angle in the College wall where it was possible to effect an exit, or entry, and within five minutes I was knocking up George Bedford in his small but adequate lodgings in the town. The poor fellow was still toiling at his studies, dressed in a brown woollen dressing-gown and drinking cocoa, and he was delighted to see me. In a few words I explained that I wanted his word of honour, on the following day, that I had spent the last two hours in his rooms. At first he was inclined to demur, but when I reiterated my instructions and threw in a casual enquiry about whether his father enjoyed his position as my estate-agent, and gently asked him whether he himself was enjoying life at Oxford sufficiently to make him wish to remain up any longer, George quickly saw reason and engaged himself to furnish me with the required alibi. I then returned to College by the main entrance and duly had my name taken by the porter for coming in after the prescribed hours. The penalty would be, I knew, a "gating" and a fine. But whatever it was I felt that it would not be a greater penalty than that for wrecking the Senior Tutor's rooms and burning the manuscript of his verse translation of Lucretius.

Nor was it.

Next morning my eight guests were sentenced to expulsion from the University and a fine of fifty pounds apiece, while I was fined ten shillings and gated for a week.

There was an interesting sequel to the episode which

throws, I think, a good deal of light on the difference between my individualistic character on the one hand and the sort of stereotyped mass-character of my friends on the other.

While they were being tried, convicted, and sentenced by the College authorities, I hastened into the town and purchased three magnums of Bollinger 1900, which I brought back to my rooms and put on ice. It was pretty obvious that expulsion would inevitably be the sentence and I wished to entertain them for the last time before we parted.

Half an hour later, as I had confidently expected, my eight friends came marching up the stairs and entered my rooms. In a trice the first cork had popped and nine glasses were being filled.

But there was no gay shout of approval as the liquor foamed and sparkled into my lovely Venetian goblets. There was a dead, almost menacing silence. I looked up from my Ganymede labours and scanned the faces of my friends. I have always been an exceptionally shrewd reader of faces, and it did not take more than the briefest glance to detect in those eight darkened scowls something more than the natural vexation of men who have been sent down from their University. There was a very palpable air of hostility in their demeanour, and I made all possible speed to dispel it. Unluckily, although I had accurately diagnosed the temperature of the meeting, I did not at the first attempt diagnose the cause of the temperature, and I began: "Don't look at me like that. I didn't give information against you. I never said a word."

From the babel of sound which can only emerge from the mouths of one angry Frenchman, two angry hundred-per-cent Americans, and five averagely stupid angry Englishmen, all trying to explain the same thing simultaneously and at the top of their voices, I got the impression that if I had given in-formation against them they would have assassinated me there and then. Even in that hectic moment, when all one's wits were necessary, there was time for the thought to flash through my mind that these men had a very queer notion of the meaning of the word friendship. They were saying things to me and using expressions to describe me which were quite incompatible with the spirit of David and Jonathan. But I shrugged my mental shoulders, so to speak. It is not to be expected that all of us should treat friendship with such an especial—possibly such an exaggerated—sanctity as some of us do. Perhaps we are wrong to do so, but there it is. We do, and we must be humoured.

Long before the babel of abuse and indignation had died down a clearer view of the position had unfolded itself and, for the second time within a handful of seconds, I had obtained a lamentable sidelight upon my friends' ideas of friendship.

For the thing which was vexing them was not the ignoble thought that I might have turned King's evidence against them—as if such a thing had been remotely possible for a man of my character; and in any case, as they might have seen, and as I had seen hours before when pondering over the matter in my mind, to have turned King's evidence would have automatically ruined my alibi and landed poor little George Bedford in the cart for perjury. No. The thing which was enraging them was the fact that they were being sent down whereas I had escaped all penalty except a "gating" and a smallish fine.

This seemed to me at the time, and still seems to me after the long lapse of years, a singularly ungenerous attitude. Surely if they had been true friends, of the sort that I have all my life held before my eyes as the ideal of friendship, they would have rejoiced in my fortunate escape.

"We have sinned," they would have said, "and we must pay the penalty for it. Justice is justice, and we accept our fate. But dear old Edward," they would have gone on, "has escaped, and good luck to him." They would have rejoiced in my success and would have thrown themselves with enthusiasm upon the Bollinger in their eagerness to drink to my good health and to my subsequent academic career.

But alas! for human nature. These were good chaps, but not quite so good as I had hoped. I had put them on a pinnacle from which they abruptly descended at the first opportunity, leaving me standing there alone. I looked from face to face in that flushed and angry semicircle. A very big decision had to be made, and made very very quickly. It was another crisis in my life. How clearly it all comes back to me —the chiming of the clock over the porter's lodge, the merry chirping of the starlings under the Dean's eaves, the cries of the undergraduates in the quadrangle, and the tinkle of the *Merry Widow* waltz upon a distant piano, and the puffings and snortings of the expelled octette.

I looked from face to face. Were they worth it? That was the whole essence of the decision I had to make. On the one side there was my academic career—I was certain to get my first in History—and on the other there was Chippenham's father, that prominent Conservative, there was Plaistow's position in the New Forest, there was van Suidam and the Vanderbilt yachting crowd, there was American Zinc, and there was de-la-Fosse's château in Burgundy. I looked from face to face, and it is characteristic of me that I dismissed Walsh-Aynscot entirely from the balance of forces. Ruth was a lovely girl, but lovely girls are plentiful in this world and, in a matter of such importance, need not be reckoned for one moment. But Charlie Hudson would one day control American Zinc, and St. Etienne's lineage marched with the Montmorencys and the Rohans, and Eddie Duncatton would be a very rich man when his father died, and Bletchley was related to half the nobility of England. Against all that, what did a ridiculous first in History matter? Besides, they were my friends. They might have been ready to let me down, but that was no justification for my letting them down. Those of us who have higher standards must keep to them, come what may. So, just as the tumult was about to break out again in real earnest, I raised my hand, silenced the incipient tempest, and informed them that I had already confessed to the authorities and had insisted on suffering the same penalties as the others.

After the cheering had died down and a tremendous toast had been drunk in Bollinger to the "Prince of Good Sportsmen," my friends repaired to their respective rooms to make ready for their departure and I slipped off to make my confession to the Dean.

That evening we all went to London, dined at the Piccadilly Hotel, visited *Our Miss Gibbs* at the Gaiety, and sent round enormous baskets of orchids to Gertie Millar, Denise Orme, Maisie Gay, Kitty Mason, and Olive May, removed a policeman's helmet in Shaftesbury Avenue, and ended up traditionally in the cells at Vine Street.

It was, in fact, such an exciting day that it did not occur to me for a long time that I had landed poor little George Bedford in for perjury after all. He was fined ten pounds, I discovered afterwards. I thought for a moment of paying him the money, but decided not to. He was sufficiently dependent on me as it was, without the addition of cash benefactions, and I dislike anything that resembles servility.

CHAPTER VI

I have never regretted my decision to leave Oxford University. A degree would have been a pleasant asset from the worldly point of view, but, after all, no amount of academic honours can alter the fineness of the brain which wins, or fails to win, them. A first in History stamps a man in after-life. But if that man takes his first and hides it in the Board of Education or in the Chancery of the Legation in Belgrade, he might just as well have never toiled for it. If, on the other hand, he was capable of winning it, and did not, owing to circumstances out of his control, or even in his control, actually win it, he is still capable of carving a way for himself in the world. What I am trying to say is that a degree is only the outward and visible sign of brain. I took no degree, but my brain has been none the worse for that.

And, against the loss of my first in History, I can always put the reason for the loss. I take no especial credit for sticking, even against my own interests, to my friends. It was a thing which any English gentleman would have done, and I would have held him a dastard who did otherwise. For me the choice between career and comradeship simply was not on the map. My friends came first all the time.

Those years before the war were, of all years since the days of the Regency Bucks, the halcyon time for rich young bachelors. In the early part of the reign of Queen Victoria— that unutterable woman—the world stood upon lavender-

48

scented stilts. In the middle part of the reign of that still unutterable woman, the world was a mass of chimneys and German ideas and such men as my Grandfather Jedediah. And towards the end it was all the frothy idealism of Gladstone, and Disraeli's theoretical ideas about women, and the Boer War with its Krugers, Cronjes, De Wets, and comic City Imperial Volunteers, and increased income-tax from a shilling and a penny to a shilling and twopence, and the ludicrous idea that the ludicrous Kitchener was a great man.

But the Accession of King Edward changed all that, and young men came into their own if they possessed an adequate income. My income being on an admirable scale I quickly settled down to lead the life of the *jeunesse dorée*. That is to say, I kept Grantly open for occasional visits, but in the main I concentrated upon the neighbourhood of Piccadilly. I had chambers in Albany, an account at half a dozen Bond Street jewellers, a rapidly improving taste in orchids, a handsome Napier motor-car, and the acquaintance of half the stage-doorkeepers in the West End. For naturally I and my friends gravitated to the theatre. It was the normal promotion, as it were, from our giggly shop-girls at Oxford, with their cheap scent and their unreasonable and avaricious parents. We could not yet aspire to the higher ranks of the theatrical profession—there were too many men of the world, headed by a most august figure, in the field to give us youngsters a chance—but our money, our youthful good looks and high spirits, our titles or our titled friends, our unlimited leisure, all combined to make the second and third rows of the chorus easy game for us. Those were the almost Corinthian days of Maida Vale, and each of us kept a flat or small house in that discreet suburb, furnished with thick carpets and divans and bright cushions and dim lights, libraried with *La Vie Parisienne* and the translated works of Paul de Kock and Pierre Loüys, and with the walls hung with reproductions of pictures by rising young artists such as Raphael Kirchner,

Léonnec, Barribal, and Lewis Baumer. These little havens of luxury were in marked contrast to our austere chambers in Albany, Jermyn Street, Albemarle Street, and the rest, where we entertained each other to bachelor parties or, occasionally, gave tea to relations who had refused to take obvious hints that they were not wanted. In that spacious era we were able to keep our two establishments entirely separate. No pipes, guns, fishing-rods, or male friends were ever seen in the one; no camisoles or carelessly discarded black silk stockings hung over chair-backs in the other.

It was a point of honour with us never to refer in conversation to our secondary establishments, nor to recognize each other if we met by chance either going to or coming from Maida Vale. Indeed there was only one circumstance in which the existence of each other's mistresses-for-the-moment was admitted at all, and that was another point in our inflexible code of honour. Each of us kept all the rest informed of the names and addresses of such medical men as we happened to hear of in the course of the daily round who could be relied upon to put their surgical skill at the disposal of any girl who could pay the requisite fee. I need hardly add that we invariably provided the fee ourselves on these tiresome occasions. It was a third point in our code never to let a girl down in such times.

It comes back to my mind that I brought off a notable coup in this connection, and one that brought me infinite credit among my circle of associates. Let it be recalled that in those pre-war days the art of gentle dalliance without tedious consequences had not been carefully studied by the female sex as it is now. In consequence, the girls of the upper-classes, the Ruth Walsh-Aynscots, so to speak, were dominated by fear. The desire to enjoy the fleeting hours of playfulness was no less strong then than it is now, or ever has been, in the feminine breast, but it was stifled by the terror of "disgrace." And, as the economic factor, the driving fear of starvation, did not enter into the matter with these daughters of Towers, Granges, Courts, and Places, and of Mayfair and Belgravia, terror overmatched desire. It was far otherwise with the second and third rows of the chorus. The difference between life on a miserable wage in Soho or Seven Dials and life on an allowance in Maida Vale was so enormous that they found it worth while to take a chance. We did our best to minimize the odds against them in taking this chance, for we were honourable gentlemen, but mistakes were bound to occur and we were young and comparatively inexperienced, and, when all was said and done, they were only chorus-girls.

To return, however, to my coup.

I had joined a number of clubs, among them White's, Brooks's, the St. James's, the Portland, the Bath, and the Beefsteak, and often used to fill the interval between dinner and the hour of attendance at the stage-door with a game of auction bridge, poker, or baccarat, at one or other. Now it so chanced that there was a certain young surgeon, by name Willoughby West, who used to play a good deal of poker with us. He was a dark-haired, rather sallow young man, with deep brown eyes and thin hands, always dressed a little better than one thought a medical man ought to be dressed, and always giving the impression that he disposed of considerable private means. I was all the more surprised, therefore, when he took me aside at a club one evening, and asked me bluntly if I would lend him a thousand pounds. His cards had been running badly, he said, and he was in a hole. There was a good deal of paper out against him in the club, and he would be called upon to redeem it sooner or later. I explained to him as gently as I could that such a thing was quite out of the question, and, having promised to say nothing about the incident to a soul, I returned thoughtfully to the card-room. It was not until several hours later that the correct course of action presented itself to my mind, and I repaired to the office of the club secretary, one Major Coot-Turner. I first of all instructed him, in the peremptory tone which is the only way of addressing paid club-servants, that there was a piece of work before him which required the utmost tact. The Major, an elderly man who had commuted so much of his pension that he was practically dependent on his salary from the club, hurriedly assured me that he would do his utmost to please me, and I unfolded my plan. "It has come to my knowledge," I said, "by a roundabout route with which you are not concerned, that Mr. Willoughby West will shortly be unable to meet his card-room liabilities in this club. He is a personal friend of mine and, rather than see him hammered and inevitably ruined professionally, I am prepared to buy up all his IOU's which may be held by our fellow-members. I know it is quixotic," I went on, lifting my hand to scotch an interruption, "but he is my friend. You, Coot-Turner, will go round the members, tactfully of course, and do the actual buying for me, offering in each case sixty per cent of the face value of the note."

"Forty per cent discount!" gasped the Major.

"People will call me a fool," I replied, "but I wouldn't dream of asking a penny more. Willoughby West is my friend, and I am going to get him out of this mess." The upshot of it was that for a matter of six hundred pounds I bought a first-class surgeon. So long as I held West's paper—and he signed a promissory note to pay me interest at a rate which made it unlikely that he would ever redeem it—I could insist that his services should be at the disposal of myself and my friends whenever necessary. It is hardly to be wondered at that this coup caused satisfaction. A number of charming girls were freed from the ever-threatening cloud of dirty Armenians, Egyptians, Hindus, and Roumanians. And I had the additional personal satisfaction of having saved the professional career of Willoughby West, my friend. It cost me money. But it was well worth it, not from my own selfish point of view, but from the point of view of those girls and of West himself.

*

Even all through this round of gaiety in the glittering world I did not forget my responsibilities to those dependent on me. Frequent visits to Grantly kept the staff keyed up to the highest pitch of efficiency, and I made a point of arriving at least once a month without giving any warning beforehand. The first three or four of these sudden descents were great successes, and after some idling gardeners, an under-keeper, and a couple of stable-boys had been by this method detected and discharged, there was a continual buzz of activity upon the demesne. The removal of the barbed wire endeared me to the hunting folk, my generous invitations to shooting parties endeared me to the shooting folk, my public and frank embrace of the Unionist cause and my recantation of the Liberal heresy of my father and grandfather, to the political folk, and my cellar, newly laid down, to the drinking folk. And to crown it all, the young Squire's popularity was greatly enhanced by the stories which began to circulate—I never quite knew how, because I myself hardly mentioned the affair to a soul—of the circumstances in which I had preferred loyalty to my friends at Oxford rather than academic success.

It was at about this time that George Bedford obtained his degree in Agriculture and left the University with, I imagine, the respect of all the worthies whose very existence had been unsuspected in our set. He himself had developed into a very worthy youth, proper and upright, no doubt, but damnably priggish. I set him on, at a nominal salary, as assistant to his father, to learn the trade of estate-agency. It had always been understood between his father and mine that he was to succeed his father at Grantly. For myself, I had never felt absolutely certain about young George's suitability. He had very clear slate-grey eyes and a way of looking very steadily and straight at people when he disapproved of their action in something or other. It was a trick which I disliked a good deal, and what made it all the harder to bear, he was perfectly respectful with it. He just looked at you.

There was a most irritating example of this trick a year or so after I had gone down from Oxford.

It happened like this. On the north side of my estate, and outside it, there lay a rough expanse of heath and bracken and brambles and undergrowth. Scattered about were a few ragged trees, an oak or two, some hawthorns and a lot of seedling pines. The land was of no value to a soul except rabbit-poachers. If it had been, I would have taken steps at once to add it to my estate by enclosure. It is true that it was common land, and that there were certain rights of pasturage and turbary and so on, belonging to the commoners. But the manorial rights were mine, and in those Edwardian years there were few of those precious societies which meddle nowadays in defence of the peasantry against their natural defenders, the Lords of the Manors and the Squires. Had the common land been of any value, no commoners' rights would have been of the slightest use against me if I had wished to take action. But even though I was only twenty-one or twenty-two, I had a perfectly clear-cut view of my responsibility towards the villagers, and nothing would have induced me to infringe their poor prerogatives. Their rights were of pathetically little value, but such as they were I was determined to respect them.

Nineteen hundred and eleven was a year of blazing sun, day after day. It was the year in which Warwickshire so surprisingly won the County Cricket Championship, a success which was only made possible by the lightning wickets on which their fast bowlers bowled. Although I still profoundly despised cricket as a waste of time, nevertheless I had begun to feign an interest in the game. All my most influential neighbours—the riding, shooting, and drinking set—patronized their village teams and so I began to patronize mine. But the sun, which was of such assistance to the Warwickshire cricketers, played the very devil with heather and bracken, and in the middle of July the common-land beyond my wall caught fire. The wind was from the north-east and it soon was obvious that the flames, thirty and forty feet high, were sweeping rapidly towards my magnificent beech-wood, which stood just inside my wall. My own men were quickly mobilized to try to arrest the fire, but they were too few to keep it back. I therefore sent George down to the village with an offer of half-a-crown to any man who would come and help to save my lovely beech-trees. The villagers came swarming up—they were a mercenary money-grubbing lot—and set to work. But after about fifty minutes there was a sudden change in the wind, and the fire, driven back on to the area that had already been burnt, quickly died away of its own accord. In the circumstances it would have been absurd to have paid out half-a-crown for fifty minutes' work, especially as the final extinguishing was achieved by Nature and not by the men, so I told George to give the men a shilling apiece and my warmest thanks.

"You promised half-a-crown," he said. I explained my reasons for the change, and it was then that he looked at me in the way I have described, and it was from that moment that I began to have my doubts about his suitability as an estate-agent for me.

"Will you go and explain it to the men yourself?" he asked when I had finished.

"Certainly not," I replied warmly. "What the devil do you suppose I keep you and your father for?"

He looked at me again for a moment or two in just the same way and then he said, quietly and civilly, "Very well," and off he went. Later in the day an even more unpleasant episode occurred. Old William Bedford, trading upon the privileged position of a family friend, actually came up to the house after dinner to make a protest against my action. At first I refused to see him. It was the first week-end at which I had had the pleasure of entertaining little Lottie, a certain little Lottie from *The Dollar Princess* at Daly's, and I was unwilling to be disturbed at that hour of the evening.

He waited, however, with stubborn persistence in the library for nearly an hour, so there was nothing for it but to give him an interview. But, although somewhat tired after the exertions of the day, I was feeling mellow and good-humoured and I listened to his silly mouthings with patience. William Bedford was over sixty by this time and, with his weather-beaten red face and short, thick, white moustache and his short iron-grey hair, he looked the perfect type of an English agriculturist. Which is precisely what he was. It is a type that will go on for many generations. An innate stupidity and lack of enterprise will prevent them from being killed in aeroplanes and motor-cars or from dying of over-work; fresh air and exercise will keep their bodies in trim; and an ancestry of yokels has bequeathed to them a certain low cunning in circumventing the lesser accidents of Nature. Strength, Stupidity, and Cunning, these are the three qualities of the peasant all the world over. William Bedford had them in full.

"Look here, you've not done right, Edward," he opened bluntly, so bluntly that I could not help laughing. It was fortunate for him that Lottie's charms had created such a mellowness. "You promised the half-crown," he went on, "and you're going to pay the half-crown."

Again my only reply was a laugh.

He took me by the lapel of my new velvet dinner-jacket—and it is to my eternal credit that I did not wince, for Heaven knows what dreadful bucolic things that hand had not been touching during the day—and said earnestly, " Listen, lad. The villagers are a good lot. Their fathers respected your grandfather, and loved your father. I don't want to see you get wrong with them for a matter of a few shillings."

"Over-payment is the same thing as charity," I answered. "I'm not going to begin pauperizing them."

"A promise is a promise," he said slowly, but my answer

was ready:

"Not if the circumstances alter."

"I beg you to change your mind," said the old fellow, shifting the ground to an appeal to sentiment. "Think of your good name, think of your honour."

This was going a bit too far. "My honour is safe in my own hands," I replied stiffly.

"Three of that Venables family came up to the fire," he remarked with apparent irrelevance.

" Well ?"

"They're terrors to poach."

I began to get angry. "Look here, Bedford," I exclaimed, "are you suggesting that dirty scum like the Venables are going to blackmail me into paying this exorbitant sum by threats of poaching?"

"It pays anyone who's got a pheasant or a partridge to be as well liked by those Venables as your father was."

"What are the police and the magistrates and my keepers for?" I demanded.

"For getting convictions of people that there's evidence against. There's never been evidence against a Venables yet. It's a proverb in the county."

I thought carefully for a few moments, and then made up my mind that perhaps a little generosity would not do any harm.

"Very well, Bedford," I said gaily. "The fellows don't deserve it, but they shall have it. Get hold of them all to-morrow and give them the extra money."

"I paid them out of my own pocket as soon as I heard about it," replied the old boy. I burst into a great shout of laughter at having caught him out so completely.

"So all this solicitude for my honour and my pheasants was simply to get your own money back, you old rascal," I shouted delightedly.

He began to say something but changed his mind, and his

face grew even redder than usual, blushing, no doubt, with mortification at having been found out.

I wrote him a cheque on the spot, laughing all the time, and dismissed him. And, a perfect sequel to a good joke, the old boy tore the cheque up on his way home, for I found the pieces in the avenue myself next morning. He must have mistaken it in the dark for a piece of waste paper. And what is more, he did not even miss it, because he never asked for another, and it was not for me to refer to the matter again.

But for all his faults, William Bedford was a decent old cock, and on the whole he managed my affairs at Grantly pretty well, especially after I had hammered into his head the changes of principle which were to be introduced into the management of the estate.

These changes were in the direction of the elimination of waste. To a tidy, well-ordered mind, such as my own, the whole idea of waste is abhorrent. To repair a cottage roof before it is actually necessary, or to allow a reduction of rent simply on the score of a poor crop, or to grant extra days of holidays to gardeners so that they may visit a market-town and buy a pig or two, all these are to me examples of waste. They encourage inefficiency, which is the same thing. A few drips through the roof will soon persuade the cottager to look after his own repairs; a poor crop is generally the result of arrant bad farming; and a visit to a market-town is simply nothing else than an excuse to get drunk.

Of course you must remember that I am still talking of the happy pre-war days. The spread of education, the influx into our local life of Socialist agitators who have taken the niggling trouble to find out the legal rights of tenantry and who come and advise the tenantry what its legal rights are, and the increasing independence of the lower classes—all three of which may be generally summed up as Bolshevism—have entirely altered the friendly, informal, genial relationship between landlord and tenant, master and man, upper-class and lower-class, which was such a characteristic of the Edwardian era.

Things were different in the days of which I am speaking. An employer and landlord could eliminate waste without being harassed on the one side by bureaucrats and on the other by labour regulations and Trades Union officials. It was the era of individualism, and individuals with a touch of— shall I say—outstanding talent, had great chances of doing good. Nowadays, we are all regimented, and Whitehall tells us how we are to treat our dependants, men and women who look to us for everything in the world except air and the running water in the rivers. Efficiency and the elimination of waste are impossible nowadays when the land is treated as a subject for the filling up of forms.

But in my early days there was still a chance for an employer to strike out an independent line of his own for the amelioration of the conditions in which his men and women lived and worked.

It was in precisely this spirit of individualism that, for example, I instructed William Bedford to amend my father's wage-sheet, and to amend it drastically. Father—rest his soul—had year by year raised the wages of his outdoor staff to heights far beyond the scale paid by his landowning neighbours, and this could not and did not fail to cause annoyance to his neighbours and unrest among their staffs. The wages at Grantly Manor in Father's time were, in fact, a positive disgrace and, to anyone with a sensitive social conscience, an inexcusable disgrace. I made it one of my inflexible principles that I would never try to compete with my friends in the labour market, that I would never offer wages that would be tantamount to a bribe to the rustic proletariat to leave my friends' service and enlist in mine. Indeed I was so scrupulous in the other direction that William Bedford had the strictest orders to discover the minimum wage that was being paid in the district for each post, gardener, under-gardener, gardener's boy, stable-man, stable-boy, and so on, and on no account to exceed that amount at Grantly Manor. And the same principle applied, for it will be understood that I have never been the man to countenance favouritism in the application of a rule, to William Bedford himself, whose salary in my father's unfortunate times had been at least thirty per cent higher than that of any estate-agent within a twenty-mile radius of Midhampton.

But while I am describing a few of the rules of orderliness and system which I introduced, candour compels me to admit that the financial savings in which these rules resulted were in themselves very welcome.

For, to tell the truth, I had been over-spending very considerably since leaving Oxford. Everyone has to pay for experience. True. But ill luck was causing me to pay at this period rather more than the experiences were worth. For Lottie, of Daly's, was not the first young lady whom I had installed in the discreet little mansion in Maida Vale. There was Daphne Vavasour (her real name I forget, but it was something like Stone or Rudd), whom I remember because she was the first. There was Beryl Somerset (I think she was Martha Baggin really), whom I remember because it was to Beryl that I wrote some foolish letters. Beryl was a sad disappointment to me. My acquaintance with her was, in fact, the very earliest occasion on which I had the faintest twinges of doubt about the divinity of women as a sex. She was sweet and soft and yielding at the beginning of our time together, but as hard as flint when she discovered that her reign was over, and that her throne was required for another queen. The return of those letters cost me no less than five hundred pounds. The third whom I remember from this period was Irene, though her surname escapes me. The reason why she remains in my mind is simply that she was the only one of them who managed to steal the diamonds which I had given to her, temporarily of course, to adorn her handsome little person during her tenure of office. It was my invariable practice to slip up to the Vale a day or two before announcing a change of companion, choosing, of course, a matinée day, and to run through the flat for such trinkets as I had bestowed. Irene, as it turned out afterwards, had come to me almost direct from Bill Plaistow and had lost her jewellery in the same way on the matinée afternoon preceding the final rupture with Bill. Once bitten, she bought a small but impregnable safe, and I suffered from Bill Plaistow's un-fortunate precedent to the tune of nearly fourteen hundred pounds. Nor would Bill listen for an instant to my suggestion that we should share the loss, a refusal which has always seemed to me to be verging on distinctly sharp practice.

It will be readily understood, therefore, that life with these ladies, although they were all daughters of country clergymen, was by no means cheap, and that any economies which William Bedford could bring off for me at Grantly were very welcome.

It was only to be expected that during these years between 1911 and 1914 such promising young men as Plaistow, Walsh-Aynscot (of whom, by the way, I was seeing a good deal less at this time than before, the fair Ruth having somehow succeeded in repelling my advances and having married an incredible Major of Dragoons; she was a silly girl, anyway), Eddie Duncatton, and myself, should be approached by the Unionist authorities to nurse constituencies against a General Election at some future date. It was Gerald Chippenham's father, in the inner councils, who made the overtures to me, but my scheme for paying off Gerald's debts and thereby acquiring the reversion of something pretty solid in the way of a constituency in the Thames Valley had been frustrated by a most untimely legacy to him from an aunt, and so the old fool, Chippenham père, offered me nothing better than a constituency in Wolverhampton which had been Liberal since the Flood.

"Don't be ridiculous," I said to him at our interview. "If I go into politics I want to go in on the winning side. No young man of sense or spirit—and from what one can see of the Unionist Party, it's a type it badly wants—is going to hang round a place like Wolverhampton till 1917 and then get beaten after all his trouble and expense." The old boy was not pleased. He was the sort of man who has a big white moustache, and a slip inside his waistcoat, and spats, and a clumsy-looking limousine car driven very badly by an elderly man who has spent the first fifty years of his life among horses.

" You must gain experience," he said, clucking at me like a hen.

"I'd sooner gain it in the House than at Wolverhampton," I replied. "Why not give me my own seat—South-east Midhamptonshire?"

"Sir Edward Knighton-Berry has held it for fifteen years," he said stiffly.

" Precisely," I answered. " It's time we had new blood. Knighton-Berry is an old fool. Look what Smith has done to put new life into the Tory Party. Do you think that Knighton-Berry could do what Smith has done? You want a few more Smiths."

"Where are we to get them?" he snapped.

"That's hardly for me to say," I replied modestly.

But he simply would not see my point, and so we parted.

But Edie Plaistow accepted a dismal hole in the East End, and Walsh-Aynscot and Duncatton set out with gallant folly to a pair of nonconformist strongholds in the West of England. As political meetings in between elections are mostly held in the evenings, the frequent absences of this well-known trio were mourned in Maida Vale, and in the Savoy and Carlton, Oddenino's and Romano's, the Piccadilly and the Berkeley, and other haunts of fashion. On the other hand, the field was left more open for those who resisted the lure of the platform and despised the waste of the forlorn hope. During these pre-war years, therefore, I took no active part in politics, beyond giving a general support to Knighton-Berry, our local fool of a member. He was an elderly man of no sort of brains, whose ideas of political strategy were simply laughable. Thus, after duly marching through the lobbies over and over again in the hopeless attempt to defeat Mr. Lloyd George's iniquitous insurance schemes, when the bill became law Knighton-Berry actually declared his readiness to help to work the very self-same schemes in South-east Midhamptonshire. There was consistency for you! There was party loyalty! He also sat on boards of arbitration to administer the Work-men's Compensation Act, another offspring of the "rascally little Welsh attorney," and he openly, and I am sorry to say, unashamedly, advocated the so-called rights of the Trades Unions.

Such a man was a menace to the party and to the fair name of South-east Midhampton, and it was clearly the duty of some public-spirited citizen to "bell the cat" and get Knighton-Berry ousted from his seat in favour of a younger, more progressive man.

Of course, at this time I could not come out into the open against him. To wage a successful campaign—and to a man of my temperament anything in the nature of an unsuccessful campaign is repugnant—against a man so craftily and sycophantly entrenched in the sympathies, and votes, of the labouring classes, as well as being in control of the party machine, was impossible without careful preparation of the ground. Besides, an unfortunate controversy between us had leaked out and become public property, so that any political action I might have taken against him would have certainly been misconstrued, and my public spirit would have been written down as personal spite. The whole affair was, or ought to have been, absurdly trivial, and but for Knighton-Berry's unwarrantable intrusion into the private affairs of a brother-landlord, would never have been heard of.

It all started with a simple desire of mine to diminish the overcrowding of families in the cottages of Grantly village—an overcrowding which was a legacy of the bad old days—and for which Grandfather Jedediah must bear his share of responsibility.

Father had built some stables for his farm-horses on an outlying quarter of the estate, called, locally, Grantly Bottom. He built them, as he always built everything, of the solidest material, regardless of cost. The walls were stout, of the finest Peterborough brick, and the roofs were strongly tiled, and the lofts were well-boarded and well-ventilated. They were, in fact, as everyone who knew Father's character was certain they would be, the finest stables it was possible to imagine. Most unluckily, however, they had been built in the summer of the third of three consecutive dry years, and my father and William Bedford and the architect from Midhampton had all forgotten how damp Grantly Bottom could be in a really wet winter. The clay was heavy, and the mists hung about the small valley in a way that would give rheumatics to the healthiest horse, no matter how fine his stables.

And so it fell out. A wet, dank, dripping winter followed the three dry years, and the veterinary surgeon declared that the horses were getting no good from their handsome quarters. Father, always a recklessly improvident man, at once cleared them out and left the stables to lie derelict.

Ten years later I converted them, at no small expense, into workmen's cottages. That is all. But to listen to Knighton-Berry you would think I had committed some deadly crime, instead of doing a service, as I had done, to our little community by providing some extra cottages. He wrote to me privately; I answered courteously that he would be better occupied in defending the Protestants in Ireland, a job for which we had sent him to St. Stephen's, rather than in playing the nosey Parker—I wrote in a vein of humour—in a neighbour's affairs.

Next he attacked me in the smoking-room of the club in Midhampton on a market-day. I fobbed him off with some banter about what I called, lightly, his humiliating crawl in search of plebeian votes, and I remember adding that the country would not always tolerate dastards. How the members laughed at his discomfiture, especially when he trotted out the time-honoured phrase about "insolent young whipper-snappers." But the old fool was not so easily put down. He had tried the written word and the word spoken in the semi-privacy of a club. Both had failed, so he then denounced me from a public platform in Kettering, to the groans and hisses of a mass-meeting of boot-and-shoe operatives who, for some grotesque reason, fawned upon the senile ass. By this time I had been fairly—or rather, unfairly —driven into the open and something had to be done.

All my life I have been difficult to rouse to action, but when I am roused in a just cause, the action which I have always taken has been firm, even drastic. On the day after the Kettering speech, I ordered my Norwegian sledge to be brought round to the front door—for it was the depths of an exceptionally severe winter, and the mechanics of snow-sweeping had not been carried to the fine art to which they have reached in the last twenty years, when we have had practically no snow at all—and I set out, muffled in my new set of magnificent Nijni Novgorod furs, behind two fresh young horses, to visit my solicitor in Midhampton. There I ordered a writ to be served on Sir Edward for defamation of character, and thence I drove over in my beautiful sledge to Grantly Bottom and superintended personally the labours of my keepers, foresters, and stablemen, who had been ordered to perform the actual details of eviction upon the tenants of the cottages.

I had every reason to feel sore and angry at the conduct of these tenants. I had spent a considerable sum of money upon these cottages from no other motive than a desire to better the housing-conditions on my estate. And then, after all that, the tenants went to Knighton-Berry and complained. (I have no actual proof that they complained but obviously they must have, for otherwise he would never have heard of the cottages at all.) I could not possibly continue to house men and women who made treacherous complaints behind my back, so out they had to go. When the last—or almost the last, for I was becoming impatient and the horses were getting seriously chilled in the falling snow—stick of wretched furniture had been flung out of the cottages, petrol was thrown over the ex-stables and all was consumed in flames. No one was going to say of me that I neglected my dependants and forced them to live in unhealthy cottages. The actual writ against Knighton-Berry was subsequently withdrawn. There was no point in pursuing the matter further. By destroying the cottages voluntarily and thereby losing several hundred pounds of capital value, at the precise moment that Beryl Somerset was threatening me with a breach-of-promise action, I had sufficiently vindicated my honour. Not, indeed, that it ever wanted vindicating. I had, to express myself more accurately, not so much removed a blemish from my escutcheon as demonstrated that no blemish existed upon its white surface. The long-drawn-out bother of a legal action was, therefore, unnecessary. Besides, Knighton-Berry was an old man, at least sixty, and no one wants to harry grey hairs. Besides, such was the old fool's grip on men of affairs in Midhampton that my solicitor not only refused to act for me in the event of my pressing the writ to its logical conclusion, which was the High Court, but swore positively that no other solicitor in Midhampton would act for me either. I told him, tactfully, that it stood out a mile that Knighton-Berry had bribed them all, and he had the nerve to reply that it was Knighton-Berry's popularity that did it. I laughed in the dreary little attorney's face at this comical idea, and said that I would employ a London solicitor.

"If you do," the little fellow replied, "you may win your case. But the whole world will know about the cottages. And you don't want that."

"Why not?" I shouted furiously. "I want the whole world to know about it. The whole thing was charity on my part."

"Well, if you take my advice," said Wigg, for that was his absurd name, "you'll go back to where charity begins and say nothing more about it."

I paid no attention to Wigg, I need hardly say, beyond transferring my affairs to a rival fool called Styles, but the thought of Knighton-Berry's grey hairs haunted me and I finally decided to let the matter drop.

One of the children of one of the families which, for no other reason than simply to fit in with Sir Edward's social theories, were forced to leave the Grantly Bottom cottages on that perishing winter afternoon, died a few days later of pneumonia. I can hardly expect you to believe me when I record the solemn truth that Sir Edward flatly refused to contribute towards the cost of the child's funeral or to share the ten-pound note which I proposed to give, without prejudice of course, to the child's parents. In the end I had to pay both out of my own pocket, and I was bitterly, and justifiably, incensed to learn a few weeks later that Sir Edward, the avaricious, calculating dotard, had taken all the tenants from Grantly Bottom and housed them at very small rents in some of the squalid pig-styes on his own estate at Grantly Episcopi. To me they were human beings. To him they were simply votes.

That was the whole of the petty incident. I did not pursue

the matter beyond one additional small public service. In order to show the people of South-east Midhamptonshire precisely what kind of nincompoop they were represented by, I secretly engaged, at my own expense, three of those detestable Scotchmen who are not merely interested in politics but take a diabolical pleasure in mastering the intricacies of political questions, and who sit up far into the night reading Hansard and White Papers and so forth. These three men I fetched down from Glasgow on a year's contract, to follow Sir Edward from meeting to meeting and ask him questions about his attitude towards the importation of bevel-flanges and the disestablishment of the Church of Wales and the committee stage of the Livestock Bill. Then, having set these hounds of hell upon Sir Edward's traces, I was free to return to London, to the two problems of getting rid of Lottie, whose physical charms were rapidly palling under the rattle of sniffs and snores with which she was liable to make any night hideous, and of ingratiating myself with F. E. Smith, the obvious star to which a Unionist with strong idealistic leanings should hitch his wagon.

The actual business of getting rid of Lottie was ordinary routine. There was no trouble about that. But the expense of it was a bore. It is a truism that everything has to be paid for. We are all aware of that. But the hackneyed nonsense that "the woman always pays" still was popular in those old Georgian days. It is one of the least true of all platitudes, and it could only have been invented by women for the advantage of women in a world that is run almost entirely for the benefit of women. As if a woman could pay. For one thing she never has any money except what we give her or what she flagrantly steals from us, as Irene stole my diamonds. And as if a woman would pay even if she did have the money. Many and many a time in my life have I taken a woman out to dinner and paid the bill with a five-pound note that I could ill afford, knowing all the while that her bag was stuffed with notes that some other man had been wheedled out of or welshed out of.

Let me give you one instance of what I mean. It happened later, during the war in fact, but it is a good illustration and fits into the argument.

It was in 1916, when the war had become really serious and everyone was making sacrifices, or ought to have been. I was doing my bit in the Ministry of Food—you will hear about it later in this small record of a humble life—working long hours and getting precious little thanks except from those who were working with me and knew exactly what I was doing. The girl was a Julie Babyface, or something, and she was doing nothing at all to help her country in its hour of stress. In fact she was one of those worthless parasites who think of nothing but how to amuse herself. She had a part in *Chu Chin Chow*, and lunched and supped incessantly with officers on leave. One day she telephoned to me and asked me to take her out to luncheon. Leave from France had been stopped owing to the Somme offensive, and I suppose even Julie, despite her vast circle of victims, was feeling the wind. We had at one time been intimate and had parted on the most good-natured of terms, so I was glad to be of service to her in the matter of a luncheon. But not on a week-day. Experience can be bought, and in this case had been bought, dearly. So I was wary.

"Julie, my darling," I said into the telephone, "I should be enchanted to take you out to luncheon one day while this ridiculous Somme affair is spoiling every good girl's fun. Let us say the Savoy restaurant, one-thirty, next Sunday."

There was a distinct sound of a rather unpleasant oath from the other end, and then Julie said, oh, so sweetly, "Make it Monday, angel."

Firmly removing my halo, I repeated, "Sunday, then, at one-thirty, sweetheart," and rang off.

But the little devil beat me. As we drove up Haymarket after luncheon on the way back to her flat—for I have always recklessly acted on the principle of "in for a penny, in for a pound"—and as I was regarding with a good deal of satisfaction the drawn blinds and iron shutters of the shops, she suddenly gave a groan, put her famous and beautiful hands to her equally beautiful and almost equally famous breast, and muttered, "I'm feeling faint. Stop at a chemist."

What could a gentleman do? We were exactly opposite Heppell's. I stopped. I offered to go in and purchase sal volatile. Sobbing and gasping, Julie insisted on accompanying me into the shop. Once inside, she recovered miraculously and in less than seven minutes I had been forced to pay out thirty-one pounds and a few odd shillings for scents, soaps, and, worst of all, sponges. If anything kills a romance, it is the compulsory purchase of twelve of Heppell's biggest sponges. And after we had left the shop, Julie suddenly remembered that a dug-out colonel of the Army Service Corps was waiting for her at her flat, and so I was not even rewarded for my devotion and my expenditure. And they used to have the nerve to say that the woman always pays. They do not say it now. Admitted. But now we live in an age which, if not saner, is at least one that is not bamboozled by cant. In those Georgian days that egregious fallacy used to be thrown in our teeth by every single girl of whom one got a little bored. It was the inevitable slogan. One used to wait for its inexorable appearance in the usual torrent of expostulation, slang, and abuse. Sooner or later it would come, with its accompanying shrug of white shoulders and its specious air of being a world-truth. "Well, the woman always pays." Bah!

This brings me back to Lottie. As if she paid! The idea is laughable. I gave her two hundred pounds down, four pounds a week for two years, allowed her to keep all the dresses, hats, shoes, and lingerie which I had given her. She may say that in return she amused me, that she helped me to spend many gay and memorable evenings. But did I not amuse her? Did I not help her to spend many gay and memorable evenings? Of course I did. No, no, it simply will not work.

The dismissal of Lottie was the only occasion that I can recall on which I violated my otherwise inflexible rule: never be off with the old love until you are on with the new. After Lottie there was a gap of almost a year in the ranks of what might be called my permanent mistresses. There were naturally small *affaires du cœur* here and there, but there was no regular occupant of the little nest in Maida Vale. There was a reason for this.

In those years, 1912, 1913, and the first six months of 1914, the first faint symptoms of a great social change were becoming vaguely, dimly, visible. A new social phenomenon was beginning to appear above the horizon. I shall deal with its full flower of bloom later on, in its proper place. But in those days the seeds were sown. Briefly, Ladies were beginning to ask themselves why the Chorus should have all the fun. I need say no more.

To dull-headed cloth-wits like Plaistow and Bletchley, the new revolution in manners was not visible, and they and their friends continued to be the joy of the florist and the commissionaire. But one or two of us were subtler. We could see perceptible signs that the Ruth Walsh-Aynscots of this life were not always going to be so frigid, and that a somewhat smaller percentage of virginity was likely to grace St. Margaret's and St. Peter's and St. George's in the future. With this enchanting prospect in view, it was only common prudence that we should have drawn in our horns somewhat, as the rather odd metaphor runs. Prowess at one stage-door was a recommendation at all the other stage-doors, but at that experimental period we were uncertain how it would go in the drawing-rooms. We would have, so to speak, to feel our way. We were adventuring into uncharted seas.

It is probable that I was among the original handful who discarded the old, traditional mode of life and began to prepare themselves for the delicious possibilities of the new. For when all is said and done, however enchanting the Beryls, Lotties, and Irenes of this world may be, however flashing their eyes, elegant their black-stockinged legs, soft their bodies, it would never be denied that in moments of stress, whether mental or physical, they were apt to break into most deplorable accents. And a deplorable accent is a jarring note in a sensitive life.

There is a school of thought which holds that any foreign enchantress is preferable to any home-grown specimen, simply for that very reason, that one would not be nauseated by a Provençal, or Lillois, or Limousin, or gutter, accent, because one would never detect it. The sensitiveness which is shocked by the voice of Aldgate would never even notice the vileness of Marseilles or Naples or Barcelona. And certainly that school of thought might have commanded attention in the first years of the reign of King George the Fifth, before the ladies (in the real, technical sense of the word) had fully understood what they were missing. For the plebeian accent was a terrible drawback to the full consummation of moments of ecstasy.

Aphrodite is essentially an aristocratic lady, and those of her followers who drop their aspirates drop a great deal more as well.

But the foreign ladies had their disadvantages too. The butterflies of the night who had first seen the light of evening from a Parisian or a Madrileñan chrysalis were scandalously money-grubbing. And they had a diabolical worldly wisdom which made them very expensive, quite apart from their set tariff. Unquestionably their expert knowledge of the facts of life was a great advantage. No foreign daughter of joy was ever in the remotest danger of requiring the services of Willoughby West, that handy surgeon, however inexperienced or impetuous their temporary employer might be. But—and it is a very large but—they invariably kept their diamonds at the bank and wore imitations, and they seldom neglected the opportunity to run through one's pockets if one happened to drop off into a doze at any time.

So, on the whole, it was better to try to endure the accents of Mile End and Manchester in those days of transition from the daughters of the million to the daughters of the Four Hundred. The foreign enchantresses were so expensive that it was more than worth while to rest upon one's oars, as it were, and wait for the home-grown ladies of fashion to fall into one's lap. The tide of well-born beauty was beginning to flow, and the skilful beachcomber was obviously going to pick up a good many pebbles if he could only be fairly patient.

So I got rid of Lottie, after a few scenes of hysteria, put away her diamonds in my tie-box, and only used Maida Vale as an occasional port of call.

CHAPTER VII

Sir Frederick Smith, M.P., K.C., was an inspiring influence in my life. He was a man after my own heart. A keen brain, a realist, a born fighter, he was to me the beau-ideal of a political leader, and I have seldom regretted that I hitched my political fortunes to his chariot.

It was over the Irish question, of course, that we came together. It was the most magnificent cause possible for a young man, and I went into it heart and soul. While my friends like Plaistow and Walsh-Aynscot and Duncatton were tub-thumping feebly in Dorset or Deptford, I went straight into the heart of things. Smith may have been Galloper to Carson, but I was Galloper to Smith. There is no need for me to recapitulate in detail the history of those stirring days. Suffice it to say the Liberal traitors, Asquith, Lloyd George, the dreadful Haldane, Grey, and the rest, were anxious to disrupt the Empire and betray the Constitution by giving Home Rule to Ireland. Carson, Smith, Joynson-Hicks, myself, and a group of patriotic army-officers at the Curragh, were determined to save Ulster from the maelstrom of Catholic anarchy which must have resulted from such a criminal and catastrophic policy.

There were Cabinet meetings and Round Table Conferences, and secret negotiations, but they were all talk. We few, we happy few, we band of brothers were different. It was with action that we were concerned, not talk.

*

It was on a dark, wet night in the spring of 1914 that I found myself crouching under the wall of a cottage near the small harbour of Larne, in Ulster, waiting for a steamer to arrive from England. It was a proud position that I was in, for I was the intermediary between the Irish Protestant patriots and the secret Ulster Committee in London, and the steamer was packed to the hatches with rifles and ammunition. In my pocket was the signal code, the map with the route on which the arms were to be despatched on lorries to the arranged hiding-place, money with which to pay the lorry-drivers, and the receipt for the cargo which I was to sign after the unloading had taken place to my satisfaction.

It does not often happen to a young man of twenty-five that he is in a position to save the Constitution of his country. To me, crouching with turned-up overcoat collar and dripping hat, and straining my eyes into the darkness for the unlighted silhouette of the steamer against the driving murk of the sky, came a sort of exalted pride in my situation. It was as if the cottage wall was a sentry-box on the North-west Frontier. The Empire was at stake, and of all men in the world it was Edward Percival Fox-Ingleby, Eton and Oxford, by the Grace of God gentleman, who stood like iron in the breach between the Empire and Disruption. On one side of me loomed the grim outline of the Vatican; on the other the redoubtable jaw of Carson. Here was the shilly-shallying form of Birrell, there the group of gay and gallant soldiers who, brave hearts, set the welfare of Ulster high above their trumpery oath of allegiance to the Crown. Yonder was the smoke from the Fenian outrages in Clerkenwell, but high above it rolled—in my swift imagination—the smoke from the burning of Drogheda by great Cromwell and the smoke from the artillery of Boyne Water.

At that precise moment in my high and passionate thoughts, a party of five or six men came round the corner of the cottage wall and asked me what I thought I was doing. It was an awkward moment.

They were quiet, confident men with an unpleasant air of efficiency about them. It was too dark to see whether they were officers of the R.I.C. and there was no means of knowing whether they had had information about the arrival of the steamer or had stumbled upon the fleet of lorries that was waiting in the sunken lane at the back of the harbour. Indeed, in that first instant of crisis there was no means even of knowing which side they were on. They might be loyalists to the Ulster cause, or they might be traitors to the Flag. The only thing which was recognizable about them on that dark, wet night, was that they were quiet, efficient men.

It was a question of making up one's mind quickly. At any moment the steamer might heave its dim bulk into the harbour, carrying with it the honour of Carson and Smith and the British People.

I had to make up my mind. I made it up.

"I am here on Government service," I said, shouting against the wind.

"Which Government?" asked the leader of the party. That was a very awkward question, but when I saw in the intermittent star-light that it was backed by several large Colt revolvers, I understood that there was only one possible answer.

"Ours, you fools," I bawled. "Here are my papers," and I dished out handfuls of our confidential papers to keep them quiet. My ruse was completely successful. The men grabbed the papers and bolted, leaving me alone and safe.

Any other man in my position might have felt that he had sold the pass. My code-word, map, and lorry-route had all been surrendered to an unknown band of desperadoes. On the asset side, I was safe, and the steamer was rounding the point and slowly making for the quay.

Within a quarter of an hour the guns were being loaded on to the lorries, and who so enthusiastic and energetic in the loading as the mysterious men who had held me up with Colt revolvers?

It turned out that they had been sent by Joynson-Hicks—that passionately patriotic Nonconformist—to spy on me, on me, mind you, on me of all people, who was known to the Unionist world as Smith's right-hand man. But do not run away with the natural corollary that Hicks was crazy. Hicks was a solicitor and, as such, simply could not help taking unnecessary precautions.

Smith was a barrister; so was Carson. Hicks automatically put his ordinary watchdogs—the hired sleuths of any solicitor's office—to spy upon the barristers and their right-hand men. It was not distrust. It was second nature.

Consider the matter impartially for a few minutes. Here were three men engaged upon a noble enterprise, an enterprise which was nothing less than the thwarting of the votes of the plebeian multitude, the overthrowing of the ridiculous fallacy that the will of the people means anything at all. Here were three men who were ranking with the aristocratic killers of the Gracchi (if my classical memory serves me), or with those who, in Rome, hounded down the People's Tribune Rienzi (if my mediaeval memory serves me). Carson, Smith, and Hicks were a sort of composite Charlotte Corday, destroying a thing which they hated. In her case it was the dirty Marat; in theirs, the dirty *vox populi*.

But it so happened, by an odd coincidence, that all three of them were lawyers in the two branches of the legal profession, and in the age-long traditions of the Law the solicitor was faintly, but none the less definitely, suspicious of the barristers. At least that is my reading of the incident. The only possible alternative was that Hicks distrusted me personally, which, as Euclid would have said, is absurd.

The arms were safely landed and distributed. Ulster was simmering with excitement. The Red Hand was clenched and ready for battle. The officers at the Curragh were holding fast to their loyalty, and were presenting a united front to the fools at Westminster. Carson was reviewing troops. Smith was galloping furiously hither and thither, and I was playing my part, and Hicks was magnificently appealing to the God of Battles in a series of tremendous speeches up and down England, and it looked as if fighting might break out at any moment in the streets of Belfast.

So threatening did the attitude of the Papistry become towards the loyal Protestants as the summer of 1914 approached that I decided that, if I was to play a useful and active part in the defence of the Union, I must first of all settle my personal affairs. June and July of that year, therefore, found me back at Grantly, putting my estate in order, drawing up lists of the sequence in which my executors were to settle my outstanding debts—I was a little perturbed at the number and size of them, by the way—and steadily refusing Smith's entreaties to return to Belfast. If there was going to be shooting in the streets, and ambushes from behind hedges, no man with any decent sense of responsibility could take the risk, however eager he might be, of charging into the mêlée before he had arranged his worldly affairs in proper form. I was wildly anxious to fight, sword in hand, for Ulster, No Popery, God, the King, and the Right, but not before I had put my estate in order against an early death upon the field of battle.

Those were two happy months. The weather was glorious, and Midhamptonshire was looking its greenest and richest and most idyllic best. It was the last lovely flowering of the country-house epoch, which has gone never to return, at least in our day, and the doors of a couple of dozen crenellated Towers and moated Halls were open to me. North, South, East, and West, parties were being made up for the shooting in Scotland, and I had the choice of a score of Glens, Castles, Lodges, and Straths. The prospective shooting in Ulster seemed very far away, and I must confess that it was with some satisfaction that I could honestly sit back in my big chair in the study at Grantly and reflect that one man, at least, had done his share. The gun-running had been successfully carried out. That was the important thing. All that remained to do was simply to use the guns. That was the business of the two bold barristers and the fire-eating solicitor, and of course the loyal officers of the Curragh. My choice of glen rested, after much thought, upon Invernalyle Lodge in Inverness-shire. It was not that the shooting at Invernalyle was any better than elsewhere, but the hospitality there was likely to be better than elsewhere. The reason for this was that the tenant for 1914, my prospective host, was Sir Lazarus Moselkind, and it was his first venture into Highland hospitality. Recently knighted for "services to the party" by Mr. Asquith—and, incidentally, having at the same time narrowly escaped prosecution on a charge of fraudulent conversion—Sir Lazarus was anxious that his first splash should be a successful splash, and I knew, therefore, that he could be relied upon to hire a secretary who would see that the champagne and the cigars were all according to Cocker.

This certainty of lavish and obsequious hospitality was one consideration which impelled me to select the invitation to Invernalyle out of all the rest. Another was that the Honourable Elizabeth Speight, daughter of Lord Speight, the grocer, was to be among the party. Betty Speight was a tall, well-constructed girl of twenty-two or twenty-three, with a mass of light brown hair, ordinary eyes, ordinary brains, ordinary shoulders, ordinary legs, but with one highly intriguing feature about her. Her arms were touched with those odd, tiny little undulations of skin which look like the surface of the moon seen through a telescope, or like a bird's-eye view of the small sandhills of the Arabian desert. It was almost as if her arms were marked like the face of an iron golf-club.

Now this may seem a trivial, indeed meaningless, detail in the physical make-up of a young woman, but to me, whom comparatively little escapes, it had a very considerable interest.

I have already described how a handful of imaginative and sensitive adventurers into what may be described as the things of the mind, were beginning at this time to consider the possibility of the substitution on a large scale of Belgravia in our clandestine beds for the Chorus. Those of us with vision were, in fact, looking forward to the exquisite time when our mistresses should be drawn from the classes and neither from the masses nor from the Continent. Betty Speight's arms seemed to me to be a direct invitation to prove whether or not our vision was coming near to practical realization. For I had read in the works of an Austrian philosopher, that these strange little patterns upon a girl's arms, patterns that looked exactly like the "pointillisme" of that French school of painters, where each dot is separately dabbed on to the canvas with a tiny brush until the whole pattern is complete, are an infallible sign—so said the learned Viennese—that the possessor of these pointilliste arms is more than ordinarily susceptible to the allure of my fortunate sex.

The opportunity of testing both theories simultaneously, namely, the theory of the growing accessibility of the daughters of a hundred belted earls, and that of the susceptibility of the pointilliste daughter of anyone, together with the opportunity of testing the theory of hospitality as held by the secretary of Sir Lazarus Moselkind, unquestionably pointed to Invernalyle as the scene of my August activities, both on and off the moor.

But of course the war broke out and spoilt everything. Looking back on it now, it seems all very small in comparison with the events which followed, but even to this day I cannot help being sorry that the war broke out just a week too early.

For we were due to assemble at Invernalyle on the evening of the ninth of August. And, from what I heard subsequently from several of my friends, the evening of the tenth, at the latest, would have seen the surrender of La Speight and the complete vindication of the physiological ideas of the Viennese professor.

But the war came a week too soon, and I, for one, mourned its precipitancy. Betty Speight went to Serbia with a Scottish Ambulance and married, from all accounts, a good many Serbian officers. I never saw her again. The whole thing was a pity.

CHAPTER VIII

What is there to say about the war which has not been said already? Blunden, Remarque, Sassoon, Barbusse, Graves, Mottram, and all the rest of them have described it *ad nauseam*. There is nothing for me to add except, as this is an autobiography, a brief account of my own personal contribution to the Allied Cause. It was nothing in itself, but it was a stepping-stone in my journey across the torrential river of life, and so I suppose it must be recorded.

The moment that my own intimate circle of friends grasped the fact that the war was likely to be a pretty serious thing, we held a meeting in my chambers in Albany to map out a course of action. The only absentees were Plaistow and Bletchley, who had let us down without so much as a word of warning, and had rushed off and got commissions in the Coldstreamers, or Coldstreams, or whatever it is called. Neither was St. Etienne-de-la-Fosse present. But that was not his fault. As I have already said, he had been called up to his French regiment and was even then on his way to his death near Compiègne, thereby saving me, you will recall, a lot of tedious bother over a disputed paternity order. But the rest of them were present in my chambers, Gerald Chippenham, Walsh-Aynscot, Hudson and van Suidam, Duncatton, and several others of the *élite* of the town whose names I have long forgotten. Most of them are dead anyway.

The tone of the meeting was excited, electric, nervous, tense. Perhaps out of the dozen or dozen and a half present, I

was the only one who fully kept his head. And how necessary
it was that someone should keep his head was made dread-
fully clear at once by the first remarks. I think it was a youth
named Clayton, a feeble creature with a pale yellow
moustache and red rims to his eyes, who gulped a liberal gulp
of the whisky-and-soda which I had poured out for him,
banged on the arm of his chair with his sovereign-case (an
unheard-of article of jewellery nowadays), and cried above
the rattle of conversation, "Which is it going to be: infantry
or cavalry?" To my astonishment almost everyone present
shouted " Cavalry." You could have knocked me down with a
feather. The stupidity of it was flabbergasting. In the pause
which followed the shout, a man called Cecil Porterfield, a
moon-faced bespectacled youth of no particular charm, but
possessed of a talent for poetry and a position in the banking
world that was nothing short of remarkable in one so
young—he was a director of the Bank of Scotland at twenty-
five—said to the room in general, "What's wrong with the
artillery?"

I give you my word I almost choked. What was wrong with
the artillery? Of all tomfool questions! Cecil was a dear good
fellow, and what he did not understand about bill-
discounting and Baudelaire and foreign currencies was so
insignificant that he was well worth knowing. But the
question gave me a shock. What was wrong with the artillery!
What was right with it? That would have been more to the
point. But before I had time to intervene in this crazy
discussion, van Suidam chipped in.

"Say, boys, how do I get naturalized a Britisher so that I
can join in the fun?"

"My dear van Suidam—" I began in expostulation, but
was interrupted by Walsh-Aynscot, who seemed to have
arrogated to himself the chairmanship of the meeting.

"We are agreed, then," he cried, "that we all apply for
commissions in the cavalry. It only remains to choose

whether we prefer the heavy or the light."

"Hussars," howled the fools, only Cecil Porterfield keeping his thin lips shut. All of them seemed to me to have taken leave of their senses, but Porterfield was the maddest of the lot. They all appeared to have been swept off their feet by those bizarre posters of Lord Kitchener of Khartoum with which a long-suffering country was being placarded, showing that silly old nobleman with his forefinger outstretched and his moustache glistening, saying "Your King and Country need you."

Of course the King and Country needed us. Everybody knew that. In any crisis, whether it be Xerxes marching from Asia Minor, or Turkish galleys driving to Lepanto, or Boney drilling at Boulogne, salvation can only be found in what may be called " the officer-class." There are other names for it, or if you prefer it, for us. It has become the fashion to sneer at the "old school tie. " But substitute the words—as you may legitimately do— "the salt of the earth," and then who will sneer? We were the officer-class, and it was for us to lead the nation as we had led it to Marathon and Lepanto and Waterloo. In August 1914 the Empire was desperately in need of guidance. Well, the guides were there, ready, enthusiastic, and crusadingly prepared for any self-sacrifice. The only difficulty which lay before us was that we had to make certain that our talents were going to be used to the best advantage.

But while the whole meeting had lost its head to the comparatively reasonable extent of voting in favour of commissions in the light cavalry, Cecil Porterfield had gone to the unbelievable length of advocating the artillery arm. It was my duty to bring the meeting back to a sense of realism.

I rose to my feet, amid a babble of phrases like "damned fine polo-team," and "the dress uniform is a winner," and asked for silence. It took a moment or two to get it, and it was not until Charles Hudson had shouted, in boisterous good-humour rather than in good taste or grammar, "After all, it is the fellow's chambers. Give him a chance."

"Thank you, Charles," I said coldly, and then I put the rational point of view to my friends.

What is this talk of infantry, cavalry (light or heavy), and artillery, I asked. It was a classic case of muddled thinking; these were combatant arms of the great national endeavour; were we cannon-fodder? I remember so well my impressive repetition of the phrase. "Are we cannon-fodder?" I exclaimed. And again, "are we cannon-fodder?" Of course we were not. Let the common people die as the common people always have died, in ditches. (In passing, this was a strangely prophetic description of how the common people were destined to die for the next four years—except that the ditches were glorified into the name of "trenches".) But men like us, I went on, were able to serve our country far better in administrative posts than in ditches. We were the brains of the land; this was obviously going to be a long and intricate war, in which organization was going to be far more important than corpses. Where was Napoleon at Austerlitz? I demanded. In the front line? Or organizing victory? Any fool could stand in the way of a machine-gun bullet, but it was not everyone who could supply a fighting division with hay for its horses or with marmalade for its breakfasts. In short, I argued, quietly but, I flatter myself, impressively, that we should not throw away our collective talents in a wild burst of heroism—of which we were all unquestionably capable at any moment when our country's safety was at stake—but that we should offer our services to the administrative side of the Imperial armies, and should try to hammer a tiny section of law, efficiency, and order out of the gigantic chaos which Kitchener was creating.

I was shouted down. Pioneers usually are. We do not complain. It is the ordinary penalty for clear thinking. But I must confess I was a little riled when young Pat Forbes shouted above the din, "White feather!"

Pat was not a bad chap, but he lacked sense, and what is more, he lacked gentlemanliness. He owed me thirty pounds when he was killed on the Somme, and his executors pleaded the Gaming Act and refused to pay up. It was an unsavoury business.

"Pat," I said gently, " I have come straight from the fight to save Ulster's independence, and I don't think your taunt is justified. I didn't see you in Belfast, you know, when men were carrying guns and when we were organizing the defence of the Empire in spite of every hazard."

He had the grace to blush and stutter a sort of apology.

"Say no more," I interrupted. "This is no time for quarrelling." It was agreed in the end, in spite of all my endeavours, that we should all obtain commissions in the Light Cavalry—we had pledged ourselves in advance at the beginning of the meeting to accept a majority decision and all to join the same branch of the Service—and then we broke up. I was profoundly dissatisfied with the verdict, and regretted bitterly the pledge of acceptance of the majority decision. It was, needless to say, my own fault. Carelessly confident of my ability to swing the meeting round to my own views, I had forgotten to allow for the mass-stupidity of the English gentry when it has lost its head through excitement or fear. In this case it was patriotism run mad. A Frenchman would have got more excited, but always with one eye open to the need for cool and daring action. A German would have got excited, with one eye open to the need for organized movement. But these old-established Englishmen simply lost their heads with both eyes shut. And as a result of their folly and my over-confidence, there I was—pledged to service with a combatant regiment, where there would be no scope for the exercise of my administrative ability.

Two hours after my friends had rushed off to their various clubs to draw up their applications for commissions in the

Hussars, I was still sitting in my armchair in Albany, brooding. There must be some way out of the impasse, I felt, if one could only hit upon it.

At first luck ran dead against me. The brilliant notion occurred to me that a British Army in France would have plenty of opportunities of visiting Paris and that there would have to be an A.P.M. (which stands for Assistant Provost Marshal) permanently established in La Ville Lumière. But when I telephoned to Joe Buckley, who was in the office of the London A.P.M.—Joe was up at Oriel in my time, a dear good fellow, but rather stupid—to make enquiries about Paris, it turned out that the job had been filled. I grabbed an atlas and a couple of newspaper-articles by Mr. Hilaire Belloc, who seemed to know all about pretty nearly everything, and tried to figure out where the British armies might be situated. Mr. Belloc obviously was plumping for Flanders, so I applied for the job of A.P.M. in Doullens, St. Pol, Cassel, Hazebrouck, and elsewhere. All had already been snapped up.

That having failed, something else had to be found, and found it was. One has only to think hard enough and any problem can be solved. At about seven o'clock that evening, to me, still in my armchair, came the solution, in the simple word Remounts. Cavalry need horses; horses become casualties; remounts are necessary. By joining the Remount Department, if such a thing existed, or by offering to form one if it did not, my administrative ability would be saved to the country and my pledge to join the cavalry fulfilled. For clearly they would have to give me a commission in a mounted regiment.

That very evening I took the train to Midhampton and before 10 p.m. had struck from Grantly Church I was in the library of Lord Odiham, Lord Lieutenant of the County and Master of the Grantly Meadows pack of foxhounds. He was also brother-in-law of the Inspector-General of Cavalry and had been a Dragoon himself, at about the time of Omdurman or Majuba or somewhere.

The interview was a little tricky at first, for he began by barking at me, "A line regiment. That's the place for you, my boy. Glad to help you to a commission." Suppressing a very justifiable indignation at the double suggestion that my brains, and my seat upon a horse, were only fit for a marching regiment, I steered the conversation towards Remounts, but in doing so made an unfortunate slip. The old boy was notoriously hard-up. He was a chronic over-spender of his income, and his passion for buying horses was famous throughout the Midlands. At that time he must have owned fifty or sixty animals, counting the ones he lent to his numerous nephews and nieces, and he was reputed to be in debt to his corn-chandler to the tune of seven or eight hundred pounds.

At the time what I did seemed perfectly natural and obvious, but looking back on it now with my maturer judgment I can see that it might have been regarded as a little injudicious. Still, it is easy to be wise after the event. I suggested, delicately but nevertheless unmistakably, that if Lord Odiham would use his influence with the War Office to secure me the coveted post of Remount Officer of the Midhamptonshire district, there would be no difficulty whatsoever about the purchase, at the maximum Government price of £70 per head, of as many animals out of the Odiham stables as his lordship cared to part with, without any veterinary examination.

After he had calmed down and had accepted my explanation that my sole motive was zeal to secure as many as possible of the famous Odiham horses for the service of the country, and that my reference to the maximum price was simply to record my conviction that £70 was a ludicrously small sum to offer for such magnificent creatures, the doddering old fool became more reasonable. It is a queer thing how men who are capable of swindling poor tradesmen, as Odiham was, in effect, swindling his corn-chandler, are the first to imagine dishonesty in others where no dishonesty exists or could exist. My suggestion that any Remount Officer who knew the faintest thing about his job would go straight to Odiham, cheque-book in hand, in order to obtain some of the great breed for the country, was twisted into such an ugly-looking insinuation that I narrowly escaped being thrown out of the house by a butler in a cream-coloured nightshirt and two footmen in grey Jaeger pyjamas. In the end the matter was smoothed over, and Odiham promised to see what he could do.

Next morning the young Squire of Grantly paraded his male staff to make war economies and to despatch a selection of the least indispensable to the nearest recruiting office. The first thing I discovered was that eight of them had already joined up, without so much as a word of by-your-leave to their employer. That was carrying patriotism a little too far. There are limits to everything. In a rage I ordered William Bedford to strike their names off my register of servants and to see that they were not reinstated when they returned. To my amazement, the old fool flatly refused.

"Have you taken leave of your senses, Bedford?" I asked coldly.

"Not that I know of," he replied with that irritating geniality which always annoyed me so much.

"Then do what I tell you. Make a note of these men's names. And see that they are not reinstated."

"I won't do any such thing," he declared.

I spoke very quietly. "You've been here thirty-five years, William Bedford. I don't want to have to discharge you now."

" I'm leaving anyway," he said cheerfully. "I was just waiting to tell you. I've got a Government job."

"Got a job at your age?" I cried incredulously.

"Yes. It's a job that none of the decent youngsters want because it doesn't mean any fighting. I'm going to be Remount Officer for Midhamptonshire."

CHAPTER IX

In the end I found my niche in the national scheme of things, but it was more difficult than I had expected. For one thing, not only did William Bedford let me down by accepting the Remount post, but the wretched little George Bedford insisted on joining the Midhamptonshire Regiment as a private. There was nothing to be gained by remonstrating with him. I tried every device to keep him. I told him that I would raise his salary if he stayed and sack him if he went; that the supervision of the Grantly estates was a work of national importance; that someone had got to carry on the work of the nation; that no self-respecting regiment would accept such an anaemic, short-sighted, dismal little swine; and that I was sick to death of both Bedfords, father and son, and that it was a bad day for Grantly when my grandfather brought them into the district.

George listened to all this quite respectfully and at the end merely remarked, "If you care to come over to the office, I can explain the books to you. They're all up to date."

"Then you really are going?" I shouted.

He nodded. "Father will be in the district all the time. He'll always be ready to drop in and give you a hand if you get in a muddle."

I stared at him. "Do you really suppose that I am not going to join up?" I asked icily. "Do you think I'm going to stay here and become a damned estate-agent?"

"I have no idea what you are going to do," he replied, and

with that we parted. But the more I thought about it, the more George Bedford's idea appealed to me.

After all, the care and cultivation of the land was a matter of national importance, and it was not work that could be picked up by anyone. It required someone who had been born and brought up on the soil. Not only that. There was other work in the neighbourhood to be done as well. Men of local influence were urgently required for stump-oratory in the interest of recruiting, and for the organization of fêtes and garden-parties for the Red Cross, and for the general encouragement of the civilian morale. Soldiers might, and probably many of them did, perform feats of great valour in the field of battle, but of what use would they be if they were not supported by recruits, by medical supplies, and, above all, by a cheerful, confident, and self-sacrificing civil population?

My resolve, then, was to devote the opening months of the war to the two tasks of getting South-east Midhamptonshire into a belligerent frame of mind, and of supervising the management of my estates. The former was, as might have been imagined, infinitely the harder of the two. There was plenty of enthusiasm among the womenfolk. But it was haphazard and misdirected, and the place was cluttered up with old dodderers— "dug-outs" as we men of combatant age afterwards used to call them. Odiham was a typical example. Either these old fools used to parade about in khaki as if they really were soldiers, or else they used to ask one in a loud voice, "When are you going to join up, young feller?" The maddening thing was that the women, young and old, fawned upon them. One would have thought that the sudden departure of most of the men of the tennis-playing, dancing, love-making age would have given a chance—not that some of us have ever needed an external piece of chance for the consummation of a conquest—to those who were putting patriotism before self-advertisement and were trying to lick the country into some sort of shape before actually shouldering a musket. But no. The ridiculous glamour of the uniform was sweeping the land, and the feminine sex was falling in swathes before it.

So far did this crazy romanticism go that it even insinuated itself into the ordered routine of my own household. One evening, dinner was five-and-twenty minutes late for no other reason than that Private George Bedford, of the Midhamptonshire Regiment, had bicycled over from the depôt, or whatever it was called, to inspect the work of the local builders who had been plastering up some cracks in the walls of the kitchen and the scullery. It was, one is bound to admit, very kind of him to give up some of his spare time to his old civilian work and to continue his devotion to my interests. But it was coming a bit cool to throw the house-maids and parlourmaids into a state of hysterical ecstasy by appearing in what was, when all is said and done, simply an ill-fitting brown suit of particularly revolting material. For the first time I bitterly regretted the impulsiveness which had led me to send my butler and both my footmen to enlist in the first week of the war. So far as the country was concerned it may have been—indeed it was— the right thing to do. The hour was the hour of self-sacrifice. But it was rather an ironical thought that this very abnegation of self should have led, by way of the confounded prostration of the female sex in front of anyone in an ill-fitting brown suit, to actual positive discomfort for me. Mind you, I was working pretty hard at the time. Up with the lark, organizing, administering, addressing recruiting meetings, making speeches at garden-parties and so on, I found my day's work was no light one, and a little consideration for my digestion was not much to ask in return for service. And George Bedford had the nerve to say that the next time he came out he would not be able to come in mufti, as I ordered him to, because in war-time mufti was not allowed for private soldiers. Military life had, in a few weeks, increased little George's nerve and his face shone rosily pink behind his glasses and he carried himself more straightly. But his sense of discipline was deteriorating already, and he addressed me as if we were equals. The lower orders are always the same. Give them an inch, etc....

But although this feminine adoration was galling to any of us who had had perhaps more than our fair share of basking in its sunshine in happier days, it was followed soon by an even worse phenomenon. We had thought, as we laboured at our desks, or forced our exhausted minds to deliver one more appeal for money or for recruits (funds or fodder, I privately differentiated), that the pyrotechnic hysteria of those first days of the war would gradually fade, and that, to put it bluntly, sex would resume its normal course. That is to say, that the spoils would go to those who most deserved them, instead of to any fool who had taken the shilling or wangled a commission in some twopenny-halfpenny line regiment. Women are not always crazy, we argued to ourselves. Women can sometimes recover their balance. Women can, after however prolonged a period of insanity, put two and two together and make the answer four. Our time will return, we said.

But what did return was officers home on leave from the fighting. In the autumn of 1914 a trickle of officers began, on ninety-six hours' leave, to come home from Flanders, full up to the ears with stories of Plugstreet, Ypres, Landrecies, the Aisne, the brick-stacks at La Bassée, and such-like stuff. If khaki alone slew its feminine thousands, khaki stained with the mud of the trenches slew its tens of thousands.

And the last cruel blow was struck with the institution of the Military Cross.

There was a certain bazaar at Midhampton in aid of the Soldiers' and Sailors' Family Association at which I was to speak in December of that dreadful year, and I looked forward gloomily to the inevitable division of the males present into three classified and distinct compartments. In the lowest compartment would be the civilians who alone were making the successful waging of the war a possibility by their industry, cheerfulness, and devotion to the slogan "Business as Usual"; then would come the Odihams and the Private George Bedfords and the Captain William Bedfords (for they had actually given a captaincy to our Remounting hero) or any male thing in khaki; and then, high above both, there would be the soldier on leave "from the trenches," talking a strange and self-conscious jargon about " crumps," and "Jack Johnsons," and "Jerries." I had wearily reckoned for all this. It was part of the penalty to be paid for self-effacement. But at this bazaar the fourth dimension, so to speak, burst upon me with all its devastating significance. For Lady Little-Westington, tiresome old harridan, turned up with her eldest son, home on leave from a place he called Windy Corner near Festubert, in slightly mud-stained breeches, and wearing the white-purple-white ribbon of the Military Cross. As I watched the fine flower of our county femininity scrumming round the young ass, it came home to me very clearly that this was but a beginning.

The Lord Kitchener of Khartoum had been wrong so often during his life that surely the tide must turn in his favour sooner or later, and why not now? When he said that the war would last for three years, he might turn out to be right, we said to ourselves. True, according to the form of the last fifteen years or so, he must be wrong and the war would last three weeks or a quarter of a century. But form has a way of upsetting itself, and in that gloomy winter of 1914 it was easier to subscribe to the theory that it would last for a quarter of a century than for three-quarters of a month. And a long war meant a never-ending, ever-increasing stream of bumptious young men with medals for valour, returning to our hives of quiet toil and upsetting the balance of decency and virtue.

As I stood in that Village Hall at Midhampton and watched the young women, many of them of good families and, worse still, of desirable appearance, milling round the bemedalled youth with the tired eyes and the receding chin, I realized that an epoch had passed away.

Next morning I took the train to London and applied for a commission in the Cavalry. I also made a short tour of my clubs with a view to discovering which of my innumerable friends were best able to assist me to the exercise of my talents in an administrative post.

It must be recorded that the sacrifice I was making was all the greater because I had only just drafted out a scheme for employing girls, of the upper classes as well as of the proletariat, upon my estate as game-keepers, gardeners, stable-girls, and so on. There would be a treble advantage in this scheme as I had visualized it. The discharged men would go to swell the ranks of His Majesty's forces; an economy in wages at Grantly would be effected—for no one would dream of paying a woman more than sixty per cent of the wages of a man for the same piece of work, and any economy in those days was in the interests of the nation; and thirdly, I can always work better when I am surrounded with a feminine influence.

In this matter of "land-girls," Grantly would unquestion-ably have been the pioneer in Britain, had it not been for the unfortunate circumstance of Lieutenant Little-Westington's Military Cross. The sight of it made me sick, and I decided to join the Army.

Fortunately, though perhaps inevitably, a man like myself does not lack influential friends, and a commission in a yeomanry regiment was soon found for me, accompanied by a berth in the Ministry of National Economy.

CHAPTER X

Khaki suited me. There was no doubt about that. Big, polished boots, spurs, yellow breeches beautifully cut in Savile Row, a perfectly set tunic, the red tabs of the staff-officer, a yellow tie, yellow gloves, a cane, and a hat pulled rakishly down over one eye, put me in a position to compete almost with a Military Cross, and even not to lag too far behind a Distinguished Service Order. Of course, later on, the flying men with their rows of medals, and bars to their medals, and devil-may-care swagger, and wings, and romance, were in a class by themselves. Luckily, however, few of them lasted long. They came and strutted and went, and were never heard of again, which was all to the good. So one did not grudge them their little hour.

The war went on and went on and went on. It is not my intention to bore you with a day-to-day description of my life during those years. I propose to pick out a few salient points. At first I lived in my old chambers in Albany, until the air raids drove me out of London to live in Brighton. No one was ever less afraid of air raids than I was, and no one disliked more my Hebraic companions on the evening express to Brighton. But it was a question of national efficiency. My life or death under a Zeppelin bomb was an infinitesimal matter. My distaste for the Semitic financiers who profiteered all day in the City and bolted like dogs in the evening, was as nothing in the cosmic catastrophe which involved us all. But—and this is the point—so long as the Government which was fighting and winning the war required my services, and were prepared to pay for them, it was my patriotic duty to give my best services in return for my Government's salary. How could my services be the best in the day-time if my night-time had been harried by air raids? No man can spend the night encouraging housemaids to be brave and exhorting ladies of the streets not to lose their heads, whatever else they may have lost, and then arrive at the office in the morning, spick and span and spruce, ready to save the nation a couple of million pounds before teatime.

So I transferred my night life from Albany to Brighton. And I did so with few regrets. As an old "boulevardier" of the stage-doors, I had become increasingly shocked by the growing laxity of morals. Where were the orchids? Where the white kid gloves at dances? Where the courtly bowing from the hips? Where the kissing of white fingers? Where the quiet half-crowns to the commissionaire?

In the place of all this chivalry there was a surging throng of officers on leave, thin, determined fellows, tough, wild-eyed, reckless, mostly drunk, or drunkish, who did not seem to care what happened to the theatre, the town, or the commissionaire, so long as they collared, almost literally, the girl they wanted and dragged her off to the Savoy.

There was no sort of dignity about it. No hand-kissing. No bouquets. Instead there was a scrimmage, a rough-and-tumble, and a disappearance in a taxi. It was deplorable, and all the more so that the girls obviously had become so hardened by war conditions that they revelled in it.

We old-timers shrugged our shoulders and went to live in Brighton. Things had been different in our day, and we did not propose to compete with the "Moriturus te Saluto" brigade. Not that *saluto* was the appropriate verb for what these officers on leave wanted to do to the lamentably willing chorus. But the quotation will serve. They were going to die anyway, and we could take the long view. We were not going to die yet awhile, and we had lovely red tabs upon our lapels and a lovely red brassard upon our left arms, and we were the cynosure of all feminine eyes as we walked swiftly and gracefully across St. James's Park to our offices. We might not be covered with medals for militant combativeness, but we were alive and likely to remain so, provided we caught the Brighton train and not pernicious influenza.

It was at this time, about two-thirds of the way through 1916, just before the ridiculous Somme business began to bury itself in a mass of mud, that I hit upon a most fascinating truth about the feminine character.

It is a matter that is worth some consideration, because, after all, the feminine character is the only real study for a man of intellect and talent, and I do not make any apologies for diverting my readers from the main stream of my autobiography to the sidelights of deduction and intuition which have, from time to time, illumined my humble path through life.

It would almost make a book in itself—an analysis of the attitude of the women of this country to the men who fought in the war. And when I say "the women of this country," I really mean the women of any country, the women of any century, of any hemisphere—in fact, the Eternal Woman.

Consider for a moment the situation in which we were placed—we, the grown-up men and women of a large part of the world.

Death was at our very doors. Death was literally brought home to us. The Casualty Lists were, of course, terrible, and especially terrible to me who had so many gay and gallant friends killed so soon, mown down in untimely death; but the bomb which fell at the Gallery Entrance of the Strand Theatre while Fred Terry and the divine Julia Neilson were playing, came home to me and mine even more vehemently. I remember, on hearing the news next morning in the Metropole at Brighton, thinking aloud to myself in bed,

"Thank God, it wasn't the Stalls Entrance."

A bomb in the Strand! How many hundred times had we not seen the newsboys racing from the printing presses with posters shrieking "Bombshell in Local Government Board Estimates," or "Bombshell in Herzegovina," or "Bombshell in Actuarial Circles." How little did we think that we would actually see the hole made by a real bomb in the Strand—and so near Julia Neilson too.

To return:the masculine populace—or at any rate the part of it which really mattered, the Four Hundred, so to speak—had been transformed overnight into heroes, or potential heroes. A regular cloud of glamour enveloped us. Even the dullest, ugliest, and stupidest of them became romantic. And naturally the women of the country were thrilled, as the women of a country at war always have been thrilled down the ages. But women are not entirely swayed by their emotions. They have a wonderful knack of recovering their intellectual poise in a short time.

To take a small but significant example of what I mean. If you make love—in the physical sense—to a woman, let us say in the middle of the afternoon, and you have a business appointment at five o'clock, and the woman has an engagement to play bridge at five o'clock, you will invariably find it necessary to smoke a cigarette and drink a whisky-and-soda before proceeding from the Courts of Venus to the market-places of the money-changers. It is essential for the recapture of common sense, for the return journey from Paradise to Monotony. But your woman needs no artificial soothing. Within a couple of minutes she is patting her hair and replacing her lips and strolling about the room in all the careless elegance of perfect stockings and a well-balanced mind. The truth is, I suppose, that men are poets, whereas women are commonplace, in the sense that they are all exactly alike in their attitude to the outer world. They are all completely matter-of-fact. Men are dreamers. Men are visionaries. Women are prosaic. Women live only for the moment.

Now apply this small example to the bigger, but essentially similar, problem of women's attitude to military men.

At first they are swept off their feet. Uniforms, spurs, boots, medals, a centuries-old tradition that they are being defended by heroes, and a primitive excitement at the very idea of violence, throws them back ten thousand years. But after a time they go even further back—say twenty thousand years—to the twin instincts of self-preservation and race-preservation. They begin, as it were, to pat their hair and stroll about the room thoughtfully in their stockings, wondering about next week's rent and the bill from Schiaparelli.

A lover, home from the trenches in the Ypres salient with a D.S.O. or whatever the ridiculous thing is called, is very nice and emotionally glamorous. But if he goes back to Ypres and gets himself killed in the pursuit of a bar to his D.S.O., of what use is he then? Is a husband with a Military Cross and one leg better or worse as a husband than a husband with two legs and no medals? Of course he is incomparably worse. And so it comes back to the final logical question—and women are far more logical creatures than men—is a crippled V.C., home from Ypres and condemned for years to live in a hospital, worth more than an O.B.E. in the Ministry of National Economy? Is Glamour a better protector in the stern battle of life than a Settled Job with a Fixed Income?

Women began returning to earth in about the autumn of 1916 and asking themselves just these very same, identical questions. The answers were painfully obvious, and the heroes gradually slipped into the back seats. The front seats were soon occupied by those of us who had the full possession of our physical faculties, and were on the spot, and were in command of an income.

Being on the spot all the time was an immense advantage, and within about two years of the outbreak of the war the women of the country had grasped the truth of this. A regular, week-in, week-out administrator is an improvement as a lover upon an intermittent, and probably non-recurrent, hero. He may not be so spectacular, but at least he is handy. From the autumn of 1916, then, the war became a great deal more tolerable for us. Indeed so tolerable did it become that I gave up Brighton and returned to Albany—the waste of time and energy in the double train journey, at each end of a long day's work, making serious love-making impossible. Looking back on it now, I cannot help taking a little credit to myself for my nerve in returning to the very heart of the bombed area. But I suppose it was not really an outstanding act of courage. The atmosphere of war-time keys one up to a higher tension, and a correspondingly higher capacity for self-sacrifice, than is possible in the humdrum atmosphere of peace. And, curiously enough, one does not think anything of it. It was with almost complete indifference that I supervised the sandbagging of the walls and floors and ceilings of my chambers in Albany, arranged for an emergency exit into the basement, and negotiated with the newly-formed Transport Ministry, which had taken over the railways as a measure of National Emergency, for a refund of the unexpired portion of my season ticket to Brighton.

At Christmas time 1916, I could not help feeling at peace with the world. My captaincy had been gazetted, my superior officers in the Ministry were satisfied—as well they might have been—with my work; I had won the C.B., the Serbian Medal for Valour, and a Russian decoration; and a number of my investments, especially my shipping investments, had soared to such an extent that they more than counterbalanced my losses in German shares and the monstrous income-tax. I remember one of these shipping companies very well. My holding was small—a couple of thousand at the outside—and the company's failure to pay a dividend during the three or four years before the war had been only a minor irritation. In the first year of the war it paid seventy per cent on its ordinary shares. In the second it paid a hundred per cent, and, just before the Christmas of which I am speaking, I had received a circular from the Board of Directors announcing that the entire line of steamers had been torpedoed and sunk with the exception of one, and that, if and when this last survivor was torpedoed, it was proposed to wind up the company and pay back five pounds to each holder of a one-pound ordinary share. (This will give you some idea of how colossally profitable it was to own merchant shipping during those years.) At that particular moment I was being badgered for an attractive but exorbitantly expensive pearl necklace, and the prospect of a windfall of ten thousand pounds was very pleasing. How I prayed that that last surviving tramp steamer would be torpedoed very, very soon. And on Christmas Eve my prayers were especially fervent, for, on that very afternoon, I had been driven almost to the point of yielding over the necklace (she was that maddening type of girl who works on the "if you won't, then I won't" principle; it's a mystery to me why I stood her so long), and another couple of days would have probably done the trick. But happily my prayers were answered and the ship was torpedoed and sunk with all hands off the south coast of Ireland on Christmas morning, and I got my ten thousand pounds. I gave the girl a bangle in the end, if my memory serves me, for, of course, the necklace was out of the question. No girl, however adorable, was worth a pearl necklace in those mad, but free-and-easy days.

This success in the shipping world went a long way to diminish my anxieties about another investment of my father's. For he, bucolic soul that he was, had been so ignorantly reckless that he had invested no less than twenty-five thousand pounds in the French iron and steel concerns in the Briey Basin in Lorraine.

At the first onset of the war, the Germans overran the Basin and took possession of all the mines, works, and ore, in which my money had been invested. I was harassed by this unfortunate circumstance. I was distressed. No one could be readier than I to sacrifice cash in the cause of Country. But to throw that amount of money into the Teutonic maw, without any chance of return, was a nightmare to me, and it is one of the secrets of the war, now revealed for the first time, that I took an active part in the subterranean negotiations by which the French artillery was ordered not to bombard our property in the Basin. There were short-sighted persons who said that we were assisting the Germans by allowing them to exploit the Briey iron; who said that we were putting our own cash interests before the patriotic interests of the Allies. Could anything have been further from the truth? We were taking the long view. A French artillery bombardment would have destroyed an immensely valuable property—ours, incidentally—and would have left a chaos. Does any sensible shareholder in any concern want that concern to be reduced to a chaos by an artillery bombardment? Of course he does not. He wants his property to be conserved, and to be returned to him intact at the end of hostilities. And so did I. And that is why I will never hear a word said against the Comité des Forges, which collaborated with me in my successful struggles to save the iron in the Briey Basin from the French artillery. That we also saved the iron for the German armament-makers is entirely beside the point. That was an accident of war.

So, as I say, Christmas 1916 found me at peace with the world. But peace seldom lasts long. However much one may deserve a little tranquillity, however hard one may have laboured to earn a little quietness, it is not often that deserts are rewarded and earnings paid. Especially, so it has often seemed to me, is this the case with those who have worked the hardest.

On my return to the office in the New Year, I became

conscious of a faintly jarring note in the smooth routine. For more than a year my department had been run—though I say it who shouldn't—with a purring, whirring rhythm which was the envy of the rest of Whitehall. My male staff, which consisted of half a dozen anaemic youths ineligible for military service (I can vouch for their ineligibility, because I attempted, over and over again, to force them past medical boards into the Army, the Navy, and even into the mine-sweepers, always without success), arrived at my office every morning at ten o'clock sharp. They were a useless crew, but they had to be put up with. So long as they did not attempt to think, they were just tolerable. Every Monday I used to call them together and say, " Gentlemen" (which was in itself a ludicrous overstatement), "please do not think. I will do all the thinking which is required." My female staff came to the office earlier. The charwoman started work, I believe, at 7 a.m. ; the telephonists sat down to their switchboards at 8.30, and the typists removed the jackets of their machines and began to fiddle with carbon papers at 9 a.m. precisely. Thus the routine was in full swing when I seated myself at my desk at 11, or, in moments of real national emergency, as early as 10.45.

This was the set-fair barometer of my daily war work. But almost imperceptibly, the tide of official prosperity began to ebb. The first hint which I received of this strange new influence of the moon upon my fortunes was a chit from some other department, asking for the date of my birth. I answered it, with careless and thoughtless abandon, truthfully. I was born, and not ashamed of it, in 1889. For a week nothing more happened. Then came a chit from another department—I rather think from the Ministry of National Service or some such weird institution: it was one of the Ministries which seemed to have been created to give employment to a platoon of gentlemen called Geddes—and this chit enquired whether there was any physical or mental disability which prevented my "proceeding overseas" to my regiment. I replied, naturally, that I certainly had no physical disability, and that, so far as I knew, my worst enemies—if such existed—had never suggested that I had any mental disabilities, but that any idea of my "proceeding overseas" was out of the question.

Eagerly though I longed to exchange blows with the hated Teuton, I wrote, my place was on the administrative side. Bayonet-thrusters were many; executive talent was rare. Fatheads were more plentiful than Carnots, and Victory in 1916 required its Organizers no less than Victory in 1794.

I thought nothing more of the matter until, in April 1917, I was suddenly ordered to appear before a Medical Board. Stung by this outrage, I demanded an interview with my Chief and lodged a dignified protest. He took my side at once, and declared in the strongest terms that the idea of removing me from Whitehall was preposterous. But there was something in his manner which disquieted me. In spite of his brave words, he steadily refused to look me in the eye. He fidgeted. He fiddled irritatingly with an elastic band. It was impossible for him to do anything else but protect me against ill-treatment, for he owed me five hundred pounds which he could ill afford to pay back. From that point of view, my security and my power to assist the country to the maximum of my capacity were assured from external interference. And then a horrid thought impinged upon my consciousness. What if he was playing a sort of financial King David to me as a financial Uriah, with the five hundred pounds as a sort of Bathsheba? Suppose that the treacherous old brute—he had got the medal for Lord Roberts's march to Kandahar in the 'seventies—was actually trying to draft me to the front to get me killed, so that he would escape repayment of the debt. The idea gave me a bit of a shock. I suppose when one is naturally disposed to take the most benevolent view of the characters of one's fellow-creatures, it is always a shock to stumble upon evil. It hits one between the eyes, as it were. And so it was in this case. There was the old fool, a Brigadier-General by right of senility and of nothing else, wriggling and squirming in the consciousness of his own perfidy. It was time to be firm.

"I must make it perfectly clear, sir," I said very gently, "that if I am sent off to be uselessly butchered, just as if I was of no greater value than anyone else, I am perfectly ready to go. My affairs are all in order, and my solicitor is in possession of all my papers, with a full record of all that I owe—and am owed."

"My dear boy," he exclaimed fulsomely, "you know that I would hate the very idea of losing you. You are indispensable to the working of the department. But," and he lowered his voice and looked round furtively, "I am very much afraid that someone in the Establishment Department of the War Office is after your blood. Do you know a man called Hereward, Captain Hereward?"

"Never heard of him, sir."

"It's he who signs all these chits about you."

"All these chits, sir? There haven't been more than two, have there?"

The dotard pushed across a file. "More like twenty," he mumbled. I suddenly felt quite sick. If anyone had taken the trouble to send twenty separate chits to my Chief in order to try and get me into the trenches, it meant that somewhere or other I had a very serious and dangerous enemy. I cudgelled my brains for a Hereward in my life. The name was faintly familiar and yet was unplaceable. And then a vision came back to me, a vision of a tall, shambling, pasty-faced youth, reading for the Church and attached to the principles of Tolstoy, whose general flabbiness had so annoyed me on a winter's afternoon in Oxford that I had playfully cut him across the face with my riding-crop. Cyril—yes, that was the name of the wretched creature—Cyril Hereward. And now after all these years, he was still nursing a vendetta in his chicken-heart and subordinating even the welfare of his country to the gratification of a petty revenge. It was a grim thought that this despicable character was an Englishman, bearing a celebrated name (if, indeed, it was his own). It is hardly an exaggeration to say that from that moment onwards Hereward spoilt the war for me. He never called a halt in his persecution. He manoeuvred and wire-pulled and intrigued against me unendingly, and I had to expend a great amount of energy and time in counter-intriguing in sheer self-defence.

At first I made the mistake of enlisting the help of a couple of important drawing-rooms to hoist Cyril Hereward with his own petard and have him sent back to France. Unfortunately it turned out that he had lost an arm in some particularly foolish engagement near Loos, and three dowagers and the mistress of a Lieutenant-General turned on me peevishly for wasting their time.

Then I tried to have him removed from the War Office, but once more luck was against me. For it turned out that his immediate superior—by a most unhappy coincidence—was old Lord Odiham, now a full Colonel, with whom I had had the silly misunderstanding about remounts in August 1914. The only result of my bold, attacking manoeuvres was that Hereward was made a Major instead of being dismissed. How he reconciled it all with his Tolstoyan principles was a thing which I could not profess to understand. Is it true, I wonder, that elastic consciences make for happiness and contentment in this world? It is difficult to believe that this should be so; yet such men as Hereward seem outwardly, at any rate, satisfied with themselves and their conduct. But it is a question that can never be personally resolved by me, whose conscience has always been pathetically rigid and even strait-laced. After these two failures in attack, there was nothing for it but to fall back upon defence and try to avoid being outflanked. Taking as my model, therefore, the splendid defence which A.P.M.s were putting up all over Flanders, I settled down to entrench myself in the best style of France and Flanders.

It was a long and wearying business, very bad for nerves already at full stretch from air raids, from the difficulty of getting taxis after the theatre, and from over-work. Time and time again Hereward almost had me, and only intensive campaigning in Mayfair saved me. Once I thought of Willoughby West, the brilliant young surgeon whose gratitude to me over the matter of debts at his—our—club, might surely have been reckoned upon in such a grave emergency, and I wrote to him at the hospital near Boulogne in which he was working. His answer was one of the most painful and staggering blows which have ever come my way, and Heaven knows I have met with some cruel injustices in my time. West, now a temporary Lieutenant-Colonel in the R.A.M.C., wrote that he was never so delighted to get any letter as he was to get mine; that my simple, as it seemed to me, request for a medical certificate of unfitness for service overseas was a flat violation of the Defence of the Realm Act; that my very mild hint that failure to furnish the certificate would be followed by a writ against him for my money was blackmail; and, finally, that if I did not at once return him his I O U he would send my letter to the appropriate authorities. It was, I suppose, my innocence that was to blame for ever sending the letter and for trusting so implicitly in Willoughby West's sense of gratitude and decency. The fault was, in a way, mine. I had trusted a scoundrel and reaped the consequences. There was nothing for it but to send him back the I O U and to hope that his hospital would be well and truly bombed.

In the autumn of 1917 Hereward was nearly up to me. His breath was hot upon my neck. My chief, and protector, had been removed on the ground that a four-hour day, which was all the dear old boy was fit for, was not long enough, and his successor was a civilian, a hard-faced, unpleasant man with four sons in infantry regiments in France and two already killed. He was a rich man too, and apparently quite free from decent human weaknesses. After the first twenty-four hours, it became sickeningly clear that I must do something drastic. I could almost hear the rustle of the papers in the now enormous file of interdepartmental documents about me, as Sir Timothy Venn—for that was the name of my new chief—scrutinized the hostile activities of Major Cyril Hereward. The messengers in the office were laying six to one, and no takers, that I would be out within a fortnight. (The messengers had a strange knack, not unassociated with skeleton-keys, I fancy, of discovering the contents of private files.) My subordinates were wearing the hungry look of men and women who see promotion looming.

It was, in fact, a grim crisis.

There has always been something about the Inglebys which comes out magnificently when the game seems to be utterly up. I claim no credit for it. Heredity is an attribute over which there is no control. But when lesser, ordinary men are throwing up sponges and in towels, you will always find that the Inglebys are buckling-to.

And so it was now, in this autumn of 1917. I was in deadly danger. Hereward, the dirty renegade Tolstoyan, was at my heels; in front of me were the swamps of Passchendaele. And beside me was the national work which I, and I alone, could do efficiently. Quick thinking was required, and quick thinking was achieved. One evening, in a late October fog, to me, walking slowly across St. James's Park from Whitehall to Albany, came the incandescent light of solution.

Lady Ursula Cloppin was the solution, and to Lady Ursula's dismal but opulent mansion in Belgravia I hastened.

Lady Ursula was rich, fat, passionate, spiritually lonely, influential, and very much attached to food. About fifty years of age, she had experienced in her time all the sensations of love—at least so she herself said—without tiring of any of them. She had plumbed the depths and scaled the heights, without a buzzing in the ears and without vertigo. She had, to put it briefly, lived. But—and here was her trouble and my opportunity—she had outlived her companions in life. One by one they had folded their tents—or, in modern language, checked out from the Cavendish Hotel or the Piccadilly—and crept discreetly away to younger and less disillusioned companions. For Lady Ursula was fifty and the daughters of the belted earls were gradually leaving purdah and coming out into open competition. So the Lady Ursulas of this world, no less than the *papillons de nuit* of Jermyn Street, were finding it necessary to bestir themselves if they wished to retain their clientèle.

It was not a very pleasant régime to which I voluntarily subjected myself. Twenty-eight years of age, a red-tabbed Captain, thrice decorated, tolerably good-looking, with an unquestionable attraction for the fair and frail sex, and rich, and a landed proprietor, I found it galling, and even slightly undignified, to have to make love to a woman of fifty. But needs must when the devil, in the shape of Major Cyril Hereward, drives, and Lady Ursula had great influence with a Ministry which had been set up some time before, but which was only now beginning to assume its paramount importance in the lives of the civilian population.

It says a good deal for my foresight that I was one of the first people to deduce the ultimate importance of this Ministry, and to see that, if my cards were properly played and a footing could be obtained inside its all-important walls, Major Hereward and his like would be simply wasting their time, and the country's, in their officious attempts to de-barnacle the hull of the Ship of State from such as me.

Lady Ursula's husband was a weak, small, fussy, walrus-moustached Civil Servant. I despised his weakness, his smallness, his fussiness; I laughed at his moustache, and I mildly respected him for his general good-breeding. But I profoundly respected him for the new position to which he had been seconded from the Local Government Board. For Sir Josiah Cloppin was Chief Under-Secretary of the Ministry of Food, and Lady Ursula, his lady-wife, was passionate and fifty, and was suffering from that inside competition.

So I became Lady Ursula's lover, and Sir Josiah's private secretary. For Lady Ursula was so enchanted with my elegant technique that she very quickly coerced the poor little rabbit-like Sir Josiah into getting me transferred from the National Economy Ministry to the Food Ministry. And once in the Food Ministry, as private secretary to the Chief Under-Secretary, my position was entirely secure.

Where was your Cyril Hereward now? Where were your thoughtless rounders-up of cannon-fodder? Where, in fact, was Passchendaele?

In one brilliant stroke I had outflanked them all. Consider my new position. Every day German submarines were sinking our food-ships. In theory I found this deplorable, now that I no longer had any financial interest in the torpedoing of our mercantile marine. But in practice, every sinking strengthened my position in Whitehall, in the London Command, and in the hearts of the ladies. Food became scarcer and scarcer. A system of rationing had to be introduced—as I had foreseen—with sugar-tickets, and meat-tickets, and so on. No one had enough of anything, except those who had a friend in high places. And who was in a higher place than the private secretary of the Chief Under-Secretary of the Ministry of Food? Innumerable meat-tickets and sugar-tickets were in my gift. Husbands might sneer and think nothing of such a position. Wives knew better. Their sons were coming home for the holidays,—little beasts, but very useful little beasts—from preparatory schools and public schools, underfed, pale, anaemic, and clamouring for steaks and chops. What happened? The children are whining for meat and sugar. The husband can do nothing. The mother wrings her lovely hands in despair at the misery of her adored offspring. Suddenly, out steps the *deus ex machina*—the handsome young secretary with an illicit handful of meat cards, and the Kensingtonian mansion resounds with his praises, mostly in an adoring feminine voice.

In a very short time I had built such a fortress out of coupons round myself that I could snap my fingers as gaily as any A.P.M. in London or in Flanders.

Yes, on the whole, taking it all in all, Lady Ursula was well worth it. She had drawbacks, but so, from all accounts, had Passchendaele. I suffered, but from all accounts the troops suffered in their engagements on their dismal slopes and contours at least as much as I on mine.

There was, so I gather after comparing my own experience with the war experiences of the fighters at Passchendaele, this difference between us. Their long, undulating slopes were denied to them. They could not reach the climax of them. Mine were not denied to me. Perhaps posterity will say that they were the luckier. I think I will say so too, although at the time I fancied that they might be envying me. God help all sinners. There were moments in Belgrave Square when I could almost have wished myself in the front-line trenches, firing hand-guns and throwing stink-bombs, or whatever the technical terms were. But all the time, whether in that canopied Victorian bed or out of it, there was the one buoyant thought, the one consolation which made up for almost everything, that each kiss upon those soft but somewhat middle-aged—to put it generously—lips, was another sock on the jaw for the gallant Major Hereward. The more I kissed, the safer I was. Kissing a woman at any time is a fantastically beautiful pastime, but when it saves one's life as well, it becomes a gift from the high angels.

Lady Ursula, then, was my reply to Hereward. His

memoranda were answered with food-tickets; his manoeuvres were met with veiled threats against not only his own ration-supply but against that of his sisters and his cousins and his aunts. I won, of course, but it was a wearing business, and I was genuinely thankful when the Armistice brought the whole nonsense to an end. That trivial incident at Oxford, lasting perhaps a fraction of a second, had given me the best part of a year's struggle and toil.

CHAPTER XI

The Armistice found the world tottering insanely; it found me perfectly balanced. Austrians, Bulgarians, Germans, and the rest of them, might have been caught unawares. Edward Fox-Ingleby was caught in full possession of his faculties.

At 11 a.m. on the 11th of November 1918, I listened to the bells and the guns which signified that I must return to civil life and that my small part in saving the country had been played, and before Big Ben had struck the half-hour, I had explained gently but briefly to Lady Ursula that our idyll was over. She protested, in the rather stupid way that women are apt to protest in such circumstances, but I quietly over-talked her. "We have had our romance," I murmured, "and all things must end sooner or later. You have enjoyed me," I said, "and I have enjoyed you [God pardon me], and now let us go our ways."

There might have been an undignified scene, with a tiresome squabble, if I had not had the commonsense to walk out before she was fully under weigh with her contralto invective. It was not till several hours later that I remembered that I had left a flowered-silk dressing-gown, a pair of embroidered bedroom-slippers, and three pairs of silk pyjamas with hussar-facings, behind me in the old lady's bedroom. I wrote half a dozen times for them but got no answer, which seemed to me rather ungrateful, considering all the sugar and meat which I had smuggled through to Lady Ursula at imminent risk of my job. But there! I was never one to complain. And there was always the consolation that the shrimp, Josiah, must have looked a perfect ass in my pyjamas, whereas I could have looked nothing less than a hero in his bed.

So the Armistice came. And in my opinion, it did not come a moment too soon. For I was bored with the war. The whole thing had become hysterical. All notion of values—and I mean values in the real sense of the word—had melted under an avalanche of madness and high explosive. There was no reason left in the world, outside Whitehall. Pantaloon and Harlequin and Clown, armed with machine-gun and bomb instead of strings of sausages, dominated the international circus, and the few surviving brains of cool balance were in deadly and imminent danger of being compelled to jump through crazy hoops at the point of the Stokes gun. Up to a point the war had been a good thing. It had had its bad moments, it is true, but it had also had its good moments. The terror of air raids was, on the whole, more than off-set by the spirit of comradeship which toil in Whitehall engendered. It was not in vain that we welded ourselves into a real band of brothers the like of which has probably not existed since Agincourt. The prosecution of the war was our paramount duty, and we prosecuted it. To that extent, that we could face the world afterwards with clear, unsullied consciences and the knowledge of hard duty sincerely done, the war was an enviable experience. It set the irremovable stamp of manhood upon us. Whatever the future had in store, nothing could take away from us the memories of the past. We were as one with Caesar and Themistocles, and Old Bill and Napoleon, Rifleman Harris and Corporal Trim, and Cervantes and Aeschylus, and the Hero of Inkerman and Goethe who was at the cannonade of Valmy. We had fought, each in our own way, and we had won.

But it was time the tragic farce came to an end. It was time that the constructive brains which still survived should have a chance to construct the world anew, nearer to their heart's desire.

The peal of bells on that November morning found me, then, in happy mood. There was a sufficient shortage of the essential foodstuffs, for several months after the Armistice, to make my chances of very early demobilization rosy. The war might be over, but dowagers and their grandchildren had to live from day to day and I was still in control of the all-important coupons. But in spite of that advantage, there was an awkward decision to be made by people like myself in those bewildered days immediately after the Germans had crumpled. On the one hand, there was the responsibility of feeding a harassed and almost anaemic nation; on the other, there was the crucial necessity of returning to mufti before the stampede began.

For it was obvious that in a very short time the soldiery would be compelled to realize that the halcyon days of big pay, and field allowances, and ration allowances, and fuel-and-light allowances, and lodging allowances, were over, and that London and Manchester and Glasgow and the rest of the big industrial cities were ready to absorb young men who would wear bowler hats, say "Sir" to the boss, live in bungalows, and work five and a half days a week for a small wage.

There was the choice before me: either to continue feeding the civilian herd, or to jump back into civilian life ahead of the military herd.

After the most careful and objective consideration I decided upon the latter course. I say "objective" because it is true to say that my own welfare did not weigh a straw in the balance. It was simply a choice between two different ways of serving the country.

Was it better, from the national point of view, to continue feeding the mass of semi-starving, rickety children, or was it better to become a civilian before a thousand Generals were let loose upon an unfortunate land which they, the whole thousand, collectively and individually, were perfectly convinced that they had saved by their tomfool manoeuvres and cock-eyed capers far in the rear of the belligerent areas?

I could feed the rickety children just as ably as I had fed Lady Ursula. But that had become a matter of routine, thanks to my organization, and anybody could carry on the system which I had created. But who was to save England from a thousand demobilized Generals?

That was a very different kettle of fish.

On the evening of November 11th, 1918, I gazed in pensive mood out of my chambers in Albany at the wild mob which thronged Piccadilly. A great surge of despisement went through my heart as I watched: these were the citizenry to which we had given a large measure of our lives. Swaggerers in khaki, I exclaimed bitterly to myself and painted harlots. That is the meaning of Armistice Day. Shall I labour to the bone, I mused, to feed your lickspittle jaws and your lip-sticked lips, or shall I give up salary, uniform, red-tabs, position, and all, to try to give you a better world to live in when you have returned to your senses? Shall I, in fact, feed you or lead you?

I decided to take the long view and become a leader. Once the decision was taken, the rest was easy. A last final magnificent distribution of food-tickets in the right quarters enabled me to leave His Majesty's Service on the 16th day of November 1918 with a handsome, but by no means over-handsome, gratuity for my services. As I left, for the last time, the old familiar office in Whitehall, and spoke sharply, for the last time, to the girl-commissionaire who had, as usual, offered me the wrong British Warm off the row of pegs, I could not help feeling a glow of satisfaction. The long day's work was done, as Shakespeare or someone said, and two tremendous victories had been registered. Mr. Lloyd George had annihilated the Kaiser, and I had outmanœuvred Major Cyril Hereward.

So let us build an imaginary Arc de Triomphe for the double victory and pass on to my post-war civilian life.

CHAPTER XII

In any case I would have been demobilized at a very early stage in the post-war reconstruction. For, as it turned out, I need not have bothered to play that high trump— the meat-coupon—in the lightning sprint (if I may mix my metaphors) for demobilization. For hardly had the thunder of Armageddon's guns died away on the various fronts from Dunkirk to the Vilayet of Mosul than Mr. Lloyd George decided to hold a General Election. The House of Commons which had, in a manner of speaking, waged the war, was tired and outmoded. There had been a time when it was alert and youngish, but that time had passed. The strain of thinking had proved too much for it, and Mr. Lloyd George, the Organizer of Victory, wanted new blood.

A few days after the Armistice, a telegram was brought to me in my office. I opened it and, I confess, a thrill of pride and justifiable cock-a-hoopness passed through me. For the telegram was nothing less than an invitation to contest my own local seat, South-east Midhamptonshire, the very one which I had longed for five years before. "Will you contest South-east Midhamptonshire for us," ran the wire, "at the forthcoming election please reply to John Robinson Bank Buildings Midhampton Reply paid."

John Robinson was a totally strange name to me, but I wired back, "Delighted to contest South-east Midhamptonshire for you stop which side interrogation mark message ends reply paid."

The answer was satisfactory, for it simply said, "Coalition Conservative Robinson."

The election itself was child's-play. My planks were three in number: Hang the Kaiser, naturally, was the first; the second was Life Pensions for all us war veterans; and the third was Down with Ireland.

My opponent was a Liberal, who cut his own throat by insisting that the Kaiser could not be, and would not be, hanged, and that Ireland would inevitably get Home Rule. The man was crazy—it jumped to the eyes—or at any rate a remarkably poor politician, and by the first week in December 1918 I found myself at St. Stephen's, Westminster, a Member of the Mother of Parliaments, with a thumping majority.

I had a good many acquaintances in that first post-war House of Commons, but very few friends. They were, as Mr. Maynard Keynes so shrewdly remarked, a lot of hard-faced men who looked as if they had done well out of the war. I had come into contact with many of them in the course of my work in the Ministries, and I am proud to recall that I had made a good many enemies amongst them by my rigid refusal to allow the placing of food contracts to be influenced in any way by financial or social considerations. It has always been my conviction that, in England at any rate, honesty is the best policy, and, in the long run, the safest policy. In America, the use of graft is sometimes unavoidable and is almost always defensible, and moreover, if one is found out, there is practically no comment except for a few whispered condolences. But in England things are different, and the consequences of discovery are too serious in our country of high public morals to make the risk worth while.

This inflexible attitude did not endear me to the sort of hard, grasping manufacturers and middlemen who were now thronging the lobbies. Nor did the soldiers who had returned from the battle-fronts to win constituencies, or had won them while actually absent on war service, show the slightest gratitude towards those who had made their victory possible by maintaining the country on a war footing. Indeed I was the innocent victim of one or two rather unpleasant scenes with some of these fellows. My former friend Eddie Duncatton, for instance, publicly called me a "shirking embusqué" in the Library of the House. Eddie had transferred in 1915 from the Hussars to a line regiment and had come back a Lieutenant-Colonel, to win an industrial seat in Staffordshire. I ignored the insult. I could afford to. For Eddie's political career was not going to last. He would lose his seat in the rising tide of Socialism at the next election, and he was not rich enough to buy himself a nice safe seat like South-east Midhampton-shire. As for the glamour, such as it was, of his temporary lieutenant-colonelcy, it would soon turn out to be as temporary as his rank. So I gently patted him on the shoulder, and was not in the least ruffled when he shook my hand off rudely and flung out of the room. Shell-shock accounted for many strange actions in those days, as we who had been through the hell of air raids very well knew.

Of the rest of my old friends, de-la-Fosse and Bletchley were dead, and as Plaistow had lost every cent he had in the world, all his wealth having been invested in Russian oils, he had dropped out to a great extent; van Suidam was dead, and thus my long-hoped-for entry into the Society of Newport News was indefinitely postponed; Charlie Hudson had gone back to America to control his father's American Zinc; and only Gerald Chippenham and Walsh-Aynscot of the old crowd were left, and somehow one saw very little of them. Chippenham's father had retired from his position in the Conservative Party machine, so the only real reason for intimacy with Gerald had disappeared, and I must confess that I found Walsh-Aynscot rather a bore. He was doing fairly well in the coal trade, but not well enough to make him outstanding.

It will be seen, therefore, that in those early days after the Armistice I was a lonely man. Somehow or other my talent, or genius if you prefer it, for friendship was becalmed in a backwater. It was, of course, only a period of transition, and it was natural that one who had survived his own generation and was out of tune with both the earlier and later generations should pass through a time of loneliness.

I concentrated grimly on my work and waited patiently for things to change.

That immediate post-war period was one of the strangest in our British history. At home there was the perpetual reflux of demobilized soldiers, men like Eddie Duncatton, each one thinking that, on the strength of some music-hall songs about cheering them, and thanking them, and kissing them when they came back again, they were entitled to sit down and be pampered and petted by the civilian population, by the Treasury, and especially by the ladies, for ever and ever. There was also the unbelievably intricate business, which we politicians had to face, of resettling the country upon a peace basis, and of gradually infiltrating the munition works with the idea of pacific manufacture. Abroad there was the reconstruction of Europe, Asia, and a good deal of Africa; the restoration of world finance; the inauguration of the League of Nations; and a thousand other things.

You will not be surprised that I was busy. Not even my worst enemies could say that I am not a realist, and I rather think I was among the first to drop the ludicrously impracticable idea of trying to hang the Kaiser, and also the ludicrously uneconomic idea of trying to provide pensions for all war veterans. There was no need to feel any qualms about dropping these two major planks in my electoral campaign in South-east Midhamptonshire, because my majority had been so large that there was nothing to fear. A few protesting deputations were easily swept aside, and one or two of my richer Coalition Liberals, feeling conscientious doubts (as Liberals are always apt to do at the most unexpected and irritating moments), were brought over with some rather nice dinner-parties. One little enclave of Liberal stalwarts who were dubious about the wisdom of my policy of realistic broad-mindedness, was successfully tempted with the prospect of meeting Mr. Balfour at dinner, and although Mr. Balfour did not turn up—no surprise to me who had his courteous letter of refusal in my pocket—three magnums of Ayala '04 made a more than adequate substitute for the veteran sceptic and his conversational doubts. (As they came from the backwoods and the coverts of the hunting Midlands these dubious politicians-of-the-local-machine did not detect that the Ayala of 1904 was just a trifle the worse for age. They revelled in it, while I drank a capital Berncastler and made the management of the restaurant deduct twenty per cent from the price of the Ayala for selling me an ageing wine.)

Another deputation of Conservative working men, representing several thousand voters who had thought, sweet, naïve souls, that Reparations would mean a lump German sum into every worker's pocket, was more cheaply entertained. Beer and sandwiches saw me through on that occasion, and after that hurdle had been safely dealt with, I was able to recline on my back bench without fear of electoral worry for at least four years.

But reclining on my back bench is only a figure of speech. Few private Members took so active a part in their own specialized line of politics as I did in mine. From the very start I made it my business to specialize in Irish affairs. Had I not fought—or nearly fought—in the Ulster display of patriotism in 1914? Had I not galloped beside the Galloper? Had I not—unforgettable occasion—held Carson's hat and stick while he thundered, on the Distillery Football Ground, against the menace of democracy and the scandal of the Constitution? Ireland was my spiritual home.

It was not long before I was making a considerable mark in

the House by my assiduity in defence of Sir Hamar Greenwood, the Irish Secretary, and his policy of "getting murder by the throat". The Auxiliaries and the Black-and-Tans had a strong and vigilant champion in the member for South-east Midhants. No one applauded more vociferously the tales of Auxiliary heroism which Sir Hamar used to tell so often to the Chamber, or booed more grimly the cowardly ambushes of the rebel dastards. On St. Patrick's Day my buttonhole of shamrock was even bigger than Sir Hamar Greenwood's. I was, indeed, the first Member to get shamrock specially sent over by aeroplane from Belfast for the occasion.

But although politics occupied a good deal of my time between 1919 and 1922, I by no means neglected my social duties and responsibilities. I had plenty of money at this time. Shrewd investments in Argentine railways, the torpedoing of our ships, the sale to the Government of agricultural produce from my estates by means of a friend in the Ministry of National Defence (though I shall never forgive him to my dying day for exacting from me a commission, blackmailing me is the nearer word, to the tune of ten per cent in the hour of his country's travail), all these had substantially increased my capital. It was with no difficulty, therefore, that I reopened Grantly on the grand scale in 1920. Old William Bedford had retired from my service with the rank of Major in the Remounts, and I must say it was with a good deal of relief that I accepted his resignation. For he would have had to be discharged anyway, and I have always had a sensitive dislike of discharging anyone from my service. But that business of filching the Midhamptonshire Remount Service from under the very nose of the Young Master in August 1914 was quite unforgivable. I could not overlook it and retain my self-respect. So when honest old William came to me and resigned, I made no demur. I even went so far as to settle a pension on him of two hundred pounds a year for life. If I had discharged him, which was fully within my rights, there would have been no obligation to grant him a pension at all. So on the whole he came well out of it, and had no reason to regret the thirty-eight years of service which he had given to the Fox-Ingleby family. In fact he was pretty lucky in that his employer bore him no resentment for an action which was, to say the least of it, tricky.

So William Bedford retired into Midhampton with his pension and his savings, and his son George would have reigned in his stead as estate-agent at Grantly if George Bedford had not flatly and unaccountably refused to reign.

It was a case of swelled head. George had enlisted as a private and had risen, far above his station, to be a Major with a row of service decorations. He had, apparently, displayed some sort of knack in the dispositions of trench-warfare and had earned the commendations of his seniors. Naturally no one grudged him the laurels which rewarded this sort of knack. We all applauded his successful ingenuity. I went so far as to begin tentatively to organize a supper of the tenantry and the employees in his honour, with a dance in the village hall to follow, with all the village dance's bewildering sequences of D'Alberts, Veletas, Paul Jones's, White Sergeants, and so on. But I was deterred by a most unfortunate experience.

I had made an appointment with young George to discuss the whole range of Grantly affairs in the winter of 1918—a few days after the General Election—for there was a vast amount of arrears to be settled and cleared up. It was my first meeting with George since 1915. Somehow or other the picture of him in my mind was still that of a weedy, thin, steel-spectacled, pasty private in a line regiment, paying his due respects to his employer with a cross between an obsequious touch of the hat and a doubtful salute, and it was in a moment of pure thoughtlessness and carelessness that I travelled down to Grantly in my captain's uniform.

George Bedford was waiting for me on the steps of the Hall. He was not obsequious, but he was respectfully civil. But he too was wearing his uniform, and Captain Edward Fox-Ingleby, C.B., M.P., Squire of Grantly, landowner, Justice of the Peace, found himself compelled to salute Major George Bedford, D.S.O., M.C.

It was a grim moment. The instant that military punctiliousness had been satisfied, I pushed past him into the house and re-emerged a few minutes later in a suit of flannels. The perspective was restored, but that compulsory salute was unforgettable, and it was with a feeling of profound relief that I heard George also offer his resignation. He was off to Kenya.

It was a curious phenomenon of these years—the drift to Kenya. One would have thought it was the lost land of Ophir instead of a corner of Africa where the coffee-bean can be unprofitably cultivated. Scores of young men were flocking to this unpromised and unpromising land, and Nairobi was becoming the New Jerusalem. Well, George Bedford wanted to go, so let him go, and God-speed. No Majors were wanted around the estates of Grantly so long as the Squire was only a Captain. So George went and cultivated the coffee-bean, and disappeared from my life.

My one regret was the amount of money which I had disbursed on his agricultural education at Oxford, and when he offered to pay it back by instalments out of his profits in Kenya, I naturally accepted his offer. But either he made no profits or else he cheated me, for I never saw a halfpenny of my money. In fact I lost an additional sum in employing a scoundrelly lawyer in Nairobi to report to me in about 1925 on George's situation and to advise me whether or not to sue George for my money. The lawyer, clearly bribed by George, reported that legal action would be quite useless and would merely be throwing good cash after bad, and then he sent me in a thumping bill of costs for his enquiry and advice, a bill which in the end I had to pay.

Another estate-agent took George Bedford's place—a temporary Captain from the Sherwood Foresters—a man of no private means and thus entirely dependent on his salary, and Grantly went smoothly on. There were many changes, of course, both in the farms and in the jobs, but so far as possible I kept to the old hands and, if the old hands were dead, to their children. Attachment to the soil is a great virtue, and a good landlord can easily convert, by his own personality and methods, what might easily be serfdom into a brotherhood of service.

That was our ideal at Grantly, to achieve a brotherhood, and I think we can honestly say we succeeded. Wages were raised and so were rents, and everyone was happy.

*

My first year in Parliament was dominated by the negotiations in Paris about the treaties. I must confess that they bored me. While our own flesh and blood was being assassinated by cowardly Irish-American blackguards (for there was not a single gentleman among the whole crew, and very few who did not hail from the Bowery or the lower quarters of Chicago), being shot at in ambushes and treacherously waylaid in traps, it was very difficult for me to take an interest in the fate of Syrians, Jews, Smyrniots, Bessarabians, and all the rest of the dagoes who clutter up the map. Besides, Curzon and Balfour and the Foreign Office crowd had refused to take me with them to Paris, even though I volunteered to pay all my own expenses, whereas Smith was always glad to have me working for him over Ireland. So naturally the whereabouts of Teschen, the massacre of Armenians, the native land-laws of a place that was called, apparently, Tanganyika, and the deaths of a million or so refugees from Russia left me cold. Those of us who had come through the war found it difficult to be really moved by any tragedy except those on our own doorstep. We had won the war; now let the politicians get on with the peace. That was our attitude. They would make a bungle of it, true. Politicians always do bungle everything they touch, but we were too war-weary to care. We all of us had, I suppose, shell-shock in probably its acutest form. So the European catastrophes—the Greek rout in Asia Minor, the migration of typhus-ridden Poles and Jews from captivity to their destroyed homes in Poland, the starving millions on the Volga, the rickety children of blockaded Germany, the Czecho-Slovak prisoners cutting their way home from Siberia—meant very little to us. The only detail of those post-war international politics of the world which moved us to any sort of emotion was the League of Nations, and the only emotion to which the League moved us was laughter.

CHAPTER XIII

But home politics and international politics were not the only games to occupy strong and lusty young men in those years. We had our duty to our country, our never-ending duty. But we also had a certain duty to our own youth, to our own springtime—delayed for five grim years—and to our own splendid strength. England had been shattered, been pulverized, been left metaphorically in ruins. Her young men were dead and her young maidens were sad. So we, who were the survivors of the Apocalypse, had a double responsibility. We had to restore a political order in England, on lines which would have pleased Pericles and his old Athenian friends, so long ago; and at the same time we had to delight, in our spare hours, all those young and lovely ladies who had been deprived by Armageddon of the husbands which they had been entitled to enjoy, and taught in their youth to expect.

England wanted governing, and the women of England wanted loving. And a bare handful of young men had to try to manage both tasks. We did our best.

Let me turn aside for a moment from the central theme of my story to recapitulate my personal position in 1920.

I was thirty-one years of age; tolerably good-looking, with a black moustache, and a head of black hair that showed no signs of thinning; a veteran soldier of the biggest war the world had ever seen; the recipient of several foreign decorations. I had an intact body; I was a rich landowner; a Member of Parliament; and not totally deficient in attraction for the fair sex.

Looking round at my surviving contemporaries, could I honestly say that a single one of them possessed such a string of qualities as I possessed? Honestly I could not. Some had this quality; some had that; some had the other one; and some had a different one altogether. One was brilliant and ugly; another was a golden Apollo without a syllable of conversation; a third was handsome and gay, and as poor as a church mouse; and a fourth relied upon some desperate military exploit to cover a stammer and hare-lip and a wall-eye.

Of course, among my dead friends there were, I am sure, many, or at least several, who would easily have outshone me at every point. But the Great Reaper had done his work, and the gaps were wide and deep. One must always give credit to the men who fought in the war and survived. But it would be dishonest to posterity to write down on paper that the survivors were, taken all in all, anything else but a pretty poor lot. It is always so in a war waged by a true democracy. The flowers of the forest perish, and only the weaklings, fortunately with a few exceptions, survive. The burning explosion of patriotism which swept us into khaki in 1914 in the desperate hour of imperial need, did not even singe the dismal whiskers of the conscientious objectors and the shirkers. It required Derby schemes of attestation and, ultimately, conscription, before the wrigglers were swept into the national net. Nor did they cease from wriggling even when they had reluctantly been thrust into the uniform which we others had been wearing for so long. A vast number of them survived the war and returned as heroes, yes, as heroes, to their villages, slums, and—I must say it, though it makes me feel ashamed of my caste—to their mansions.

The few of us who were left could not be expected to carry on, except with Mormonic or Mahometan principles of multiple procreation, the future of the race. We were prepared loyally to do our best. But there were still the old conventions to hamper our loyal efforts. And monogamy continued to hold the legal field, in spite of the crisis in the national birthrate.

Yet the race had to go on, as the race always has gone on. It was a strange situation, but it was one that has invariably and logically arisen at the end of any important war. And when I say important, I mean a war in which a great many men have been killed or irremediably wounded on both sides. Exactly the same thing happened after the Peloponnesian war between Athens and Sparta in the fifth century B.C.; and after the Napoleonic wars; and after the World War, which is so often and so stupidly called the "Great War." (As if there could ever be anything "great" about a war, except the unquenchable spirit of the men who organize its conduct and who fight in it.) The flowers of the forest are cut down in untimely death, and most of the survivors are neurasthenic or maimed or unattractive.

What happens? The same thing always happens. An immutable, eternal Law of Nature comes into force with steady, inexorable pressure, and before this law men are as toys, as playthings, as puppets. We have no voice in our destinies. We, the lords and masters of the earth, have no control over our lives. Battered, shaken, trench-weary, noise-racked, nerve-strained, we return to civil life and are confronted with the most powerful influence on this planet of ours—the Life Force. What chance has the returning warrior ever had, all through the ages, against the Life Force?

None.

History, psychology, and physiology prove that this is so, and always must be so.

Let me explain.

The male sex has never been, as a whole, passionately interested in the continuation of the race. There always are, of course, a certain number of doting fathers. But you will find that almost always they dote upon their sons and not upon their daughters, and then only for the reason that they themselves have been distinguished at some footling game or other, and are pathetically anxious that their sons should follow in their athletic footsteps. But these are not really fathers. They are only games-mad vanity-bags.

The ordinary, sane, balanced man is not essentially a father. Indeed, to judge from the experience of myself and my closest friends over a longish period, our attention has been concentrated in exactly the contrary direction, with a considerable percentage of success. For when you come to think of it, paternity means the sowing of a crop of screaming brats, enormous bills, ruined furniture, angry landlords, sleepless nights, and resignations, owing to the necessity for economy, from gay and jolly bachelor-clubs.

The children themselves are intolerable nuisances until they are about twelve years old, and they become independent and impertinent bores when they are about seventeen. So all that a father gets in the way of paternal enjoyment is a maximum of five years between the nuisance and the boredom, and those five years are probably spent in a forlorn and frantic attempt to stave off bankruptcy by working sixteen hours a day. And to set against that doubtful possibility of five years of enjoyment, one must put the absolute certainty of at least twenty years of self-sacrifice and toil.

No. Men are essentially lovers by nature, not fathers. They were created for women—or rather they were created to be amused by women—and not to be amused by children.

Women are different entirely.

The Life Force is tremendous within them. It makes them centre all their lives round the continuation of the race; it makes them ready—even glad—to sacrifice father, brother, lover, or husband, to the welfare of the child; it gives them superhuman patience at four o'clock in the morning when the sweet little pestilential angel is yelling the roof off; and it enables them to suffer discomforts and endure pains which might test even our endurance and fortitude.

We cannot understand this mystic Life Force, but we have got to reckon with it, for it can play the very devil with our lives, especially the lives of those of us who have survived a world war.

The outward manifestation of this damnable Life Force is very simple, absurdly simple, but it always works.

The moment that the war is over—in any period—there is an instantaneous and calculated decline in feminine standards. The race must be preserved. The men are in a daze. So the men must be jerked out of their daze. Short skirts, burnished stockings, low-cut gowns, dazzling shoulders, and smouldering, volcanic eyes, are only preliminaries. They are only the skirmishers in the battle. The main mass of manœuvre—as Napoleon would have called it—is always concealed behind these light tirailleuses, so to speak. But it is always there, inexorable, ready to pounce, and, men being what they are, irresistible.

In times of long peace and sunny prosperity, the altar takes precedence, in the feminine mind and in the feminine routine, of the bed. But after a war, the manœuvre must be changed and the bed becomes the falconer's voice to lure the tassel-gentle to the altar.

And so it was in those mad post-war years after 1919. The women of England wanted fathers for their children, and they knew exactly how to set about getting them.

They knew that a thousand thousand million pounds had been blown into the air in four years and a half and that therefore the young men would have less to spend. So, without a twinge, without a pang, they turned in a single day from champagne to Chianti, from Cartier's to paste, from the Ritz-Berkeley-Carlton-Savoy-Claridge's to grubby little places in Soho, and from orchids to violets.

They travelled in tubes instead of in Daimler hires; they went to the pit instead of to the stalls; they accepted with delight the new artificial silk stockings; and they never, never kept a man waiting more than ten minutes for an appointment.

And, as I say, whenever it was necessary to clinch a campaign, they went to bed.

There were two advantages and one disadvantage in this revolution in feminine manners. The first advantage was that this primaeval instinct for race-continuation completely ousted tradition, propriety, prudery, and convention. Professionalism was almost driven from the streets and the public places by the overwhelming pressure of outside, amateur competition. The daughters of joy were no match for the daughters of the aristocracy. Jermyn Street, and Sackville and Air and Albemarle and Bond Streets, seldom saw a wandering male after 11 p.m. except elderly manufacturers who were up for a couple of days from Burnley, Bolton, Sheffield, Bradford, and such-like dens of cotton and woollen atrocities. No longer was there any necessity to shudder at terrible accents or to struggle with one's public-school French. The ladies were in the field at last in force, and our youthful pre-war dreams had been realized beyond our rosiest hopes.

The second advantage was that these girls had brains and knowledge, both highly developed by the forcing-house of the war. No longer was the Fair Sex content to rely upon our chivalry and our skill in the affairs of the Courts of Venus, to escape any unlucky consequences which might follow upon these affairs, and it increasingly took the responsibility for its own safety into its own fair and fragile, but competent, hands. This was an especial advantage to me. My treacherous friend Willoughby West had risen to heights beyond the range of my influence, and I had always found the exercise both of chivalry and of skill in these matters excessively tedious. The new style of practice, therefore, enchanted me and I was always loud in my commendation of the new feminine wisdom.

The drawback was the shadow of the altar. Women now seemed to think that the wages of sin were marriage lines. As, fatally too often, they were.

CHAPTER XIV

It was in the summer months of 1920 that I first met Diana Marston. She was tall, beautiful in an aloof, modest, innocent way, with a firm chin, a mass of dark golden hair, a magnificently opulent figure, and an earl for a father.

In pre-war society she would have had a certainty of surrendering her virginity on a well-found marriage-bed with a satisfactory arrangement of marriage settlements. In other words, she would readily have been sold in the Marriage Market by her old hag of a mother, Lady Marplesdon, to the highest or noblest bidder. But after the war, she suddenly turned, as all marriageable women suddenly turned, at the same moment, from marketable goods into a primaeval savage. If you had seen her, at those post-war dances in the West End hotels, and in the Mayfair drawing-rooms, in the days when hosts were forcing their scandalized wives to provide cider-cup and claret-cup instead of champagne, you would have said that, in the circumstances, as all the men were dead, she was eternally doomed not merely to spinsterhood but to virginity as well. For her modesty, her gentle diffidence, her retiring nature, were not, you would have said, of a worldliness sufficient to cope with the hard conditions of life. She might be superbly voluptuous in figure, but that alone is not enough. Without a yielding disposition, a superbly voluptuous figure might just as well not exist, except in the eyes of dispassionate creatures, and of what use to anyone is dispassion?

But if you had seen Diana Marston, and had thought all that stuff about her diffidence and unworldliness and so on, you would have been utterly wrong.

For she was the Life Force Incarnate. She was a Menace. With all that modesty and innocence, she was—I do not wish to overstate my case but I must speak the truth—she was Hell.

I am a wiser man now—at the age of forty-nine—than I was at the age of thirty-two. I can see now exactly the mistakes that I made then, and the subtle trap into which I fell headlong.

But you must remember—and I plead it in extenuation of my stupidity—that my background was one of careless conquest. In our halcyon days, we had gaily and lightly commanded, and the fair sex had ecstatically obeyed. We had been the young, handsome lords of creation, and, as Napoleon said, they were invented to be our slaves. It had gone on so long that it had become part of the routine of life. So when I automatically told Diana to come here and go there, and to do this and not to do that, and she obeyed me in exactly the same old style of all the old years, I did not even think it was wonderful or flattering or strange. If I thought anything, which is doubtful, I thought it was the normal run of my experience with women.

It was this blind confidence in a long-established rule of society which brought me down. For the rule was dead. The Life Force was at work, and the rule of feminine obsequiousness and submission was no match for the Life Force.

It was in this spirit of blind and stupid and ignorant self-confidence that I accepted a reckless wager at White's Club one evening. Diana and I had been seen out together a dozen times in a month, at restaurants and theatres and night clubs. Tongues were beginning to wag. The handsome, wealthy, young squire, landowner, Member of Parliament. And the magnificent, tall, blonde, ivory daughter of a peer. Of course, people talked and journalists wrote.

But to me it was all a faint joke until I was offered six hundred pounds to four hundred pounds by a small syndicate at my club that I would not have seduced her within a month. After some thought I accepted the wager, it being agreed that my bare word as a man of honour was to be accepted as proof of my failure or success.

Considering that I knew nothing whatsoever about this devilish Urge which was sweeping the women of the war-stricken countries, and considering that outwardly Diana was a cold and statuesque marble goddess, I think you will agree that I was pretty sporting in accepting those odds. Don Juan himself would not have undertaken the job at worse than even money if he had had one cool glance at the objective, and Lothario would have insisted on fifteen to two against.

But I trusted in my own personality and my own technique, and took six to four in hundreds from the syndicate.

It was madness, of course, utter madness. I do not mean that the taking of the odds was mad. It seemed to me to be easy, and pleasant, money all the way. But the whole enterprise was mad. I will explain why in a moment, and you will understand.

The bet was six hundred to four hundred that I would not have seduced Diana Marston within thirty-one days. I did not need the money. I was rich. Stocks were rising in England, and in America, where I had invested the bulk of the fortune which I had acquired by shrewd speculation during the war, they were soaring in brilliant rockets.

I did not need the kudos to be won by seducing an aristocratic iceberg. In fact there would be no kudos in the feat, if I brought it off, for I positively insisted that my five friends who formed the syndicate against me should swear themselves to secrecy. They were good fellows, all five—in fact they were friends of mine, which is the same thing—and they readily agreed to keep silent about the whole business. Therefore if I won the bet, only six human beings in the world would appreciate my exploit—myself and the five members of the syndicate. No. I am wrong. It would be seven. I had forgotten Diana. But my point is that the whole silly affair meant neither money nor fame to me. At the best it meant a quiet laugh at the club, and a pleasant hour with Diana.

At least, that is how it seemed to me at the time, and that is how it still seemed to me at the club on the twelfth day of the stipulated month, after the pleasant hour with Diana on the night before. It was just another conquest and, as she was in shape opulent, so much the more voluptuous a conquest. At noon on that twelfth morning of our wager, the gallant five members of the syndicate arrived at the club, for I had convened them by telephone.

They came to the club, the gallant five, and the moment they entered the smoking-room they could see that they had lost their money. Mind you, there was no suggestion of triumph on my face. A gentleman is one who has schooled himself to be a generous winner as well as a courteous loser. Another might well have greeted the vanquished with a gentle smile or even a glance of self-satisfaction. Not so I. Rather was it the magnum of Pol Roger which stood in a pail of ice upon the table, and the half-dozen glasses which were arranged round it, that gave them the clue to the situation. We discussed that magnum, and another after it, with gusts of laughter and a lot of conversation in subdued but none the less hilarious tones.

Please do not run away with the idea that the hilarity was in any way vulgar. My friends were picked friends. They were reliable. They were gentlemen. They had pledged themselves to secrecy on the matter of this bet, and it was a lovely thing to reflect upon, that there was still a small corner of England left in which a spark of chivalry still glowed, unquenched even by the flood of filthy water when the sluice-gates of morality were unlocked in 1914.

These five men, my friends, could laugh at the circumstances in which they had lost six hundred pounds. But they would sooner be tortured to death than reveal to the world what those circumstances were. No woman's name had ever been bandied about the town by any one of the six of us, nor would it ever be, save only the name of such a woman who had become, by her own fault, and more often by her own intention, a byword and a common scandal. So I took my cheques for the six hundred pounds (and sent my valet round in a taxi to the bank with them) and glowed reminiscently at the memory of Diana's beauty, and tilted my hat at a slightly jauntier angle, and bought a new gold-topped ebony stick, and bore myself for a day or two as if I were Tamerlane or Genghiz Khan or Alexander, and then forgot all about it.

Pebbles on the beach; fish to fry; there were plenty of both.

How wrong I was! My God, how wrong I was!

And yet it was no fault of mine. A hundred thousand of us fell by the wayside just as I did.

On the fourth day after my victorious morning champagne party at the club, I received a note in a strange writing, delivered at Albany by hand. The exact words have escaped me after this long lapse of years, but, in effect, they ran: "Edward darling, are you ill? Why have I not seen you? You know what you mean to me. All my love. Diana."

For a moment I was flummoxed. There must have been a time—roughly speaking, between the Diamond Jubilee in 1897 and the battle of Spion Kop—when parents were pretty keen on the name Diana. Personally I have never understood why the Virgin Goddess should have been popular at any time as a fairy godmother. However, that is by the way. But one consequence of this singular lack of originality among the young married folk of the Boer War period was that, in about 1922, one was rather cluttered up with Dianas, and it took me several moments to marshal my array, so to speak, and to deduce from various details of evidence that this *cri de cœur* was from La Marston, *fille de* Marplesdon. The moment I had grasped the identity of my charming correspondent I sat down in a quiet corner of the club, called for a glass of sherry, and put in half an hour's serious thinking.

It is, you will agree, characteristic of the masculine sex that, even with this plain warning in front of me, my thoughts should have concentrated not upon my own personal imminent danger but upon the broad philosophical principles involved. But, as I have said, men are essentially philosophers, dreamers, spinners of visions. We are cursed with the spirit of poetry.

So I sipped my sherry and reflected upon the psychological difference between men and women, as revealed with such clarity by Diana's note.

In this tiny incident in the affairs of the world there were two people, two human souls, involved, and no one else. On the one side there was a man, myself, and on the other a woman, Diana Marston.

Our paths in life crossed on a Friday. On the following Monday week she surrendered to my ardent and, though perhaps it is not for me to stress the point, strategically conducted wooing. And on the Tuesday, as I have related, I bought the magnum of champagne and collected my six hundred pounds. The business was over. The transaction was completed. The sponge could be slipped backwards and forwards across the blackboard. The slate was clean. Another incident could be recorded in the celestial books, and one could begin to look about for something fresh.

That was my idea. That was the masculine philosophical idea. But it was not Diana's idea. She was, as I found out later to my cost, a woman.

That twelfth night was to me—at that time—the signal and splendid conclusion of a whirlwind siege. To Diana, as it turned out afterwards, it was the first step in a slow and methodical siege. To me, they were a dozen days, isolated from past and future eternity. To her they were the beginning of a continuous period of time. I had besieged Diana impersonally. She meant nothing to me except a delirious hour, a warmly conscious glow in my self-esteem, and six hundred pounds, and—perhaps—a capital story whispered in the corner of my club.

But to Diana the whole thing was different. I was not a seducer, nor a rich young ex-officer, nor a fairly handsome Lothario, nor one of the recognized wits of the town, but a person. She was a person and I was a person. That was all.

So when I thought the little piece of nonsense was finished, Diana thought that the serious relationship between two Persons had begun.

I do not believe for a moment that she really regarded it as a love story. In my opinion, women never regard any story as a love story. Cleopatra liked Antony only because she could not get Caesar, and there is no record of Helen's dissatisfaction with life in whomsoever's arms she lay. Ninon and Diane de Poitiers and Lady Hamilton are written down in books as great lovers, but it would be more accurate to say that they were careful only to be loved by the great.

And so it was with Diana Marston—*la Diane de nos jours*. Love in the abstract, as men know it, ideal, self-sacrificing love, counted for nothing. Everything was personal. The world might be rocking on its ankles, but it would not matter so long as Diana was not rocking on her lovely ankles. I might be on the point of plunging out into the uncharted oceans of wild and wonderful experience, but that desire to plunge must be instantly suppressed, until Diana could make quite certain that I was plunging entirely, absolutely, exclusively, and madly for her sake and for her sake only.

Men live on vast, sweeping, magnificent generalizations. Women live on a word of praise. Oh, the disillusionment of it all!

We scale the precipices of Heaven, and all that we are asked when we return is, "Did you do it for me?" or, alternately, "When you got there, were they wearing Paquin models?"

We fight with angels and with devils, and our battles are rewarded with a casual permission to tie up a shoe-lace.

For the angels and the devils are part of a mighty Cosmos, circling round a God, inexplicable, inexhaustible, vast, and so, to women, they are simply a bore. But the shoe-lace, and the tying up of it, are part of the life of the woman, and so infinitely more important to her than all the rings of Saturn or the sweeping, nostalgic curves of the eternal comets.

"What's Hecuba to him, or he to Hecuba?" said Shakespeare.

"What's Heaven or Hell to me, provided that I am the centre?" says the woman.

We men think of the world as a place controlled, or at least supervised in a vaguely benevolent way, by an elderly man with a big beard who has only recently given up a nasty habit of popping out from behind rocks in the Eastern Mediterranean. We may not appear on the surface to give him a great deal of attention. From time to time, if there is no reasonable way out, and it is a really wet day, we attend a village church and sing some very odd songs in his praise. But—and this is the point—when we chant about India's coral strand, and the mysterious pilgrims of the night, and the child she-bear—we men do really and genuinely believe in the existence of one divine central controlling-power.

Women only believe in themselves as the central controlling-power, and expect us to supply the belief that they are divine.

143

So they allot to themselves the centre of the world, and to us the privilege of doing up the casual shoe-lace and, of course, as a corollary, the privilege of paternity.

Anything which touches us, touches nothing. Anything which touches them, touches the mainspring of the universe.

And yet how seldom it is that we men understand this fundamental truth. Ninety-nine per cent of us go through life not merely without understanding it but without even knowing that it exists to be understood. Even I myself, who had long known vaguely of the existence of it, had been content with a vague knowledge. Even I had not followed the matter to its logical conclusion. If I had, my life would have been a very different affair. If I had in 1922 employed that remorseless method of analysis which has become almost second nature to me in more recent years, the significance of Diana's note to me at the club could not possibly have escaped me.

As it was, to my half-blurred, absurdly cosy, sunny vision, it was just another feminine invitation to a repetition of a dalliance that had been enjoyed. It had happened a score of times before; it would happen a score of times again.

The mistake I made was in confusing Diana Marston's cool, delicate poise, and her air of thinking always about the glow of volcanoes upon Sourabaya or the shadow of palm-trees upon coral-fringed lagoons—in confusing all that with the full, red lips and kohl-fringed eyes of my war-time play-mates. It was a foolish blunder, you will say. Ah! just remember. During four years of military glamour and several years more of glory as one of the conquering heroes, everything had been easy. Every adventure had run in the same design. Every siege—or almost every siege—had ended in the same delicious surrender. Can you blame me for getting into the frame of mind in which all lips seemed full and red, and all eyes seemed a standing invitation?

Careless, you say? Well, yes, careless. But I have always

found—at least ever since the idealistic worshipping age of sixteen to twenty had passed—that careless confidence is vastly more effective than gentlemanly diffidence. D'Artagnan would have cut out Cyrano as a lover every day in the year. The silent knight, alone and palely loitering, deserved everything he got from La Belle Dame, and you may take it from me that she was not "Sans Merci" until she had him in thrall. By the way, that is another—less important but interesting all the same—quality which is universal in women. The moment the knight starts to get pale and go loitering about the place, alone and silent, you may lay every penny you have in the world that his exquisite and delicate lotus-bud of a Ladye Fayre will take a running jump at him and come down on his ear with a pair of nail-studded hockey-boots. And what is more, she will remain on his ear, marking time, as we used to say on the parade-ground.

If they get you down, they will keep you down, and the more you like it, the less they will. For the *belle dame* has always despised the pale knight who accepts her brutality, and because she despises him she is soon bored with the business of jumping on his ear. But she won't stop doing it, though. Not she. Thraldom and *merci* do not go together in the feminine breast.

That is why careless confidence is incomparably the best card to play against a woman's virtue, and to keep on playing. But in the matter of Diana Marston I overdid the carelessness, and confused her, in my shell-shocked, war-exhausted mind, with all the other soft companions of forgotten hours.

When I got her note, I automatically thought that her calm grey eyes were fixed upon my bed; that they might be concentrated upon the altar never crossed my bamboozled mind.

It was like muddling Freya of the Seven Isles with Becky Sharp, or Diana Vernon with Madame de Montespan. Now, of course, related at this distance of time, the story must appear almost grotesque in its stupidity. But make allowances, reader. You have not, let us hope, lived through what we lived through in those grim days when only Haig stood between us and the rape of our mothers and our wives and our sisters. You have not known the horrors of meat-cards and sugar-cards, nor learnt from the sound of sirens that death may soon be coming down from the air, nor experienced a shortage of petrol so acute that one could hardly use one's own private car for more than a couple of hundred miles a week.

We were not really normal. The habit of quick and clear thinking had been bludgeoned out of us. So bear with this record of stupidity and try to understand us. For in 1920 and 1921 there was precious little masculine wisdom going about and a precious deal of feminine wisdom.

It took me only twelve days to get Diana into bed. It took her little more than a year to get me into church.

At this point I must make one thing perfectly clear. It would be unfair to myself to allow the readers of this autobiography to impute a lack of chivalry to me because I discuss so frankly my relationship with my first wife. An autobiographer has got to tell the whole truth, so it seems to me, about himself, or else he will be giving a totally false impression. He must be fearless in speaking out. He must not hesitate to face facts, at whatever cost to himself. There are those who would say that a man is at fault if, in an autobiography, he so much as mentions his wife in any other way than that of fulsome praise. My reply to that is— "Why write an autobiography at all in that case?"

What is the point of telling a story and leaving out the most important part?

You may say, perhaps, that Diana may be hurt by this frankness. My reply to that is— "Mind your own damned business." After all, one is a gentleman, and a gentleman can be trusted—and must be allowed, if you please—to regulate his own affairs, and the affairs of his womenfolk, in any way that he may see fit.

Whether Diana dislikes or admires my courage in coming so fearlessly out into the open with the story of my intimate life is no affair of anyone except myself.

I am not apologizing. I am explaining.

The six months between my ephemeral triumph and Diana's more lasting one are like a vague nightmare in retrospect. It is hard to remember any particular details. Nobody notices the stages by which a glacier advances, but it gets to the end of its journey all the same. Diana was the glacier, and I was the end of her journey. But until she reached it, or me, she was femininely brilliant at avoiding all semblance of frigidity. There was no ice-maiden—in any sense of either of the two words—about her. She was as exciting as anything that ever went bowling up to Maida Vale in the old days in a hansom-cab, with a benevolent cabby beaming down through his trap-door and murmuring "Boys will be boys."

The critical moment in those six months was when she suggested off-handedly that I might care to dine in the bosom of her family. (Incidentally, it has always been a problem to me, of which no solution has ever presented itself, why Edwardian families, usually the dullest and starchiest and dreariest of folk, should be allowed by dictionary-makers and phrase-coiners to enjoy the same word as that exquisite part of the feminine body.)

All unwittingly I accepted the invitation and went to dinner. The sixth Lord Marplesdon was an elderly card with a thin yellow face and a preoccupied manner—even when I was talking to him—as if he was perpetually wondering exactly what it was that the numerous companies did, of which he was a guinea-pig director. Lady Marplesdon was hawk-like and formidable, and she played an excellent game of bridge. She was a massive woman, a rugged rock-like version of her softly curved daughter. Her skill in evading the payment of small debts, in borrowing pound notes to pay taxis and forgetting to return even the change, let alone the pound itself, and her economies on such things as the quality of the sherry or of the kitchen bacon, were all notorious. I did not find them out until later. One seldom does find out feminine qualities until later.

But alas, the Life Force was not operating through the withered old fool or the monumental dame, but through their voluptuous and calculating daughter.

On April 14th, 1922, I became their son-in-law.

CHAPTER XV

We honeymooned, as happily as could be expected in the circumstances, in Sicily. It was a quiet, dignified honeymoon. I resolutely put out of my mind the picture of the smoking-room in the club and my five friends winking at one another and asking the time-hallowed question, "Why buy a book you have already read?" and answering it with the time-hallowed answer, "To lend it to your friends, of course."

We visited Palermo and Girgenti and Taormina, and divided our time pretty evenly between admiring the dark yellow temples and avoiding the puce-coloured Englishmen and their puce-coloured wives who have settled in Sicily ostensibly for their health, which "will not stand the cold and the fogs, my dear," but actually in order to dodge income-tax. We dutifully examined the quarry at Syracuse, the fort at Epipolae, and even hired a car to drive to Segesta. Indeed it would be right to say that "dutifully" is the adverb which correctly describes all my actions during our honeymoon. By some mysterious sequence of events, over which I had not had the slightest control, I had become a married man, and it was my duty to make a success of the affair. Diana's attitude was what ordinary men would describe as inscrutable but which to me was transparency itself. Gone was that modestly admiring flash of her blue eyes with which she used to accompany her laughter at my little quips before dropping her eyelashes demurely again. Gone was that appealing little gesture of laying her slender white hand upon my coat sleeve when I was describing some especially hazardous feat in the hunting-field, or some exceptionally narrow escape during the war. And gone was that trustful dependency with its gentle air of saying, "I am out in a cold, hard world, but so long as you are standing four-square to the winds and I can shelter behind your god-like strength, then I know that I am safe and I do not even need to bother about thinking for myself."

All that had disappeared, and in the course of a few weeks of honeymooning. But I never was a fool about the smaller actions of women. I have always been able to make a fairly accurate guess at the darkly tortuous little thoughts which are passing through their pretty little heads. In the major things of life they have over and over again betrayed me, ill-treated me, cheated me, bespattered my dreams and trampled upon my heart. They have done all that to me. Well—I am not complaining. They were the queens and I was the drone. But at least they have never bamboozled me. If grief and disillusion have come my way, they have always found me with my eyes open. It has not been ignorance that has so sadly exposed me to feminine ill-treatment, but rather it has been an old-fashioned chivalry and an excess of sentiment which has prevented me from turning to the greatest advantage my knowledge of the twistings of their minds.

And so it was with Diana. There was nothing mysterious, to me at any rate, in her sudden change. I had simply witnessed the age-old, immemorial transformation which takes place in a single moment in the presence of a minister of religion or of a registrar, the transformation of a woman who has not got her man into a woman who has.

Why should she not so become transformed? It is perfectly natural. I, who understood, have never dreamt of blaming her. When we go out fishing, we sit or stand in perfect silence upon the bank; we take infinite precautions; we use a delicate rod and the particular dainty fly which we think is the most suitable for our occasion; we exercise all our experience and guile. But the moment our fish is gaffed and cannot escape, it is only natural that our manner should relax somewhat. We wave a hand to the other less successful fishermen down-stream, and we whistle a careless tune, what time we make absolutely certain that our fish will not slither back into circulation while we are not watching.

No, my only complaint against women is that in this, as in so much else, they are inartistic. They are so blunt, so direct, so deliberately unconscious of the finer shades of feeling, so stubborn in their knowledge of what they want, and so callous in the methods by which they strive for what they want, that they inevitably rasp the sensitive souls of those of us who are their victims. We are ready to be enslaved, to be padlocked to a chain, but it would make our captivity a little more gentle if the captor were not so arrogantly casual.

Diana, like all the rest, made no effort to ease the change from adoring submission to casual arrogance; she did not allow the word " imperceptible" into her vocabulary of life. She took me as a lord and master into a church at half-past two on a spring afternoon, and took me out at a quarter-past three on a chain.

The only thing that makes tolerable the recollection of that indignity after all these years is that I knew precisely how low an indignity it was. At least one lamb in the world had known the slaughter to which it was being led.

It is the unconscious lambs who are to be pitied and, of course, despised.

Please do not think for a moment that Diana was not deeply in love with me at this time. I would be grossly unfair to her if that impression was allowed to filter through my words. She was most certainly deeply in love with me, and had, I know, the sincerest intention to make me a good wife. Like all women, she could gaff her fish and love it. She might, as the type of the submissive mistress, think that its wriggles, being the wriggles of a male, were undignified; but as the eternal mother she would think that its wriggles needed comforting.

Love made Diana feel, as it makes all women feel, both adoring and victorious. It was fortunate for me that I had been endowed with sufficient understanding to know this, and to make allowances for it, and to adjust my life to it, for love made me feel, as it makes all men of the finer metal, humble and reverent.

There was little else of interest about our honeymoon. The only incidents which return to my mind after all these years are the insolence of a guide in Palermo whom I engaged for a day and then dismissed with a couple of lire after ten minutes because he smelt so abominably of garlic; the monstrous inefficiency of the British vice-consul, to whom I went for assistance when the rogue of a guide took the matter to the police; and the delicious black eyes of the chambermaid in the hotel in Taormina with whom I dallied once or twice when Diana was spending a couple of hours lying down in her room. I can see them still, those lustrous Oriental eyes, against the saffron-dark skin of her body.

I was sorry to leave Taormina. There is also a Greek Theatre there which is generally much admired by tourists. I had not time to visit it. There was so much else to do.

Sicily is an enchanted island and I could have wandered there for a long time, but affairs were calling me and we could not linger too long among the lemon groves of Catania or on the slopes of Etna.

Political crises were flaring up at home, and my place was in my constituency and in the Carlton Club.

CHAPTER XVI

It was becoming clear that a Tory revolt against the Lloyd George Coalition was boiling up towards the end of 1921. The Irish Treaty had planted an ineradicable bitterness in the hearts of those of us who had fought so long and so patriotically for the cause of Loyalism, and there were many other reasons why right-thinking men should be distrustful and afraid. For myself, I had determined that I would oppose with all my power any truckling to the Irish Junta of traitors which was headed by De Valera, Griffiths, Collins, Cosgrave, Fitzgerald, and the rest of the scoundrels, and it was not easy for a man of conscience to reconcile this determination with my loyalty to Smith, soon to become the Earl of Birkenhead. Smith, my old companion of the pre-war Ulster days, had thrown himself in with the negotiators and was willing to "shake hands with murder". What was I to do, torn as I was between loyalty to my principles and loyalty to my friend?

It is always a desperately difficult choice. But for a man of sentiment there can, in the end, be only one answer. Idealism, and the devotion to principle, are noble things and probably I have suffered as much for my ideals and my principles as most men.

But there is—for me—one thing which outbalances and always has outbalanced principles, ideals, sentiment, and everything else, and that thing is Friendship. That is the only thing which really matters. So when I had to choose between the Loyalists of Ireland and my friend Smith, I chose Smith, and I came down with all my weight and influence upon the side of the Treaty.

The Prime Minister was delighted, and even went out of his way on one occasion to address me in the Lobby as "Foxy"; under the impression, I suppose, that the Fox part of Fox-Ingleby was my Christian name.

Naturally, I did not correct him.

But I took the obvious and sensible course of letting one of the deputy assistant Whips know that in the event of the Tory revolt simmering up to the boil, he could count on my support to the last ditch for Mr. Lloyd George.

"You won't catch me stabbing in the back the man who won the war," I said to the Whip, and he said no, he didn't think he would ever catch me stabbing anyone in the back, which I thought was a pretty fine compliment. "As for an Under-Secretaryship," I went on, "I am not an ambitious man, and I have no real talents at all for public work, and no qualifications whatsoever except for a sort of natural gift for departmental organization."

The Whip gave me a most illuminating and penetrating look, and we parted on those terms.

I have never regretted the choice I made when I offered my allegiance to Mr. Lloyd George and Smith. The rats were already getting ready to desert the ship, as it turned out afterwards, but I and a handful of others stuck to our posts in the Coalition. So simple-minded were we in our devotion that we never even noticed that the Coalition ship was sinking. It never occurred to us. Indeed, it was not until the Government had three times in four months—twice in November 1921 and once in February 1922—failed to implement its side of the unspoken bargain between us and did not give me an Under-Secretaryship, that I began to see that something was up.

You see, when I offered my lifelong allegiance to Mr. Lloyd George and the Coalition, the Whip's sympathetic look had been, to my ingenuous mind, the promise of an Under-Secretaryship. Then when nothing happened and men were promoted over my head, I began to wonder. And I came to the conclusion that there were only two possible explanations of his behaviour. Either he was deliberately withholding from me the due reward of party fidelity—in which case he was a common or garden rascal—or else he was taking a very subtle way of telling me that the Coalition ship really was foundering, and that it would be a fatal mistake for me to accept office as a sort of Under-purser, or some such rank, just as the waves were closing in above the binnacle, or whatever it is.

Either he was a double-crossing knave or a circuitously kind gentleman. I did not know at the time which it was. For within a few weeks the celebrated Conservative Party meeting took place at the Carlton Club, and I was forced to make a decision between my old leaders, Lloyd George and Smith, and the ones who wanted to lead me in the future, Bonar Law and Curzon and Baldwin.

It was a painful position. On the one side was my old chief, the great Galloper; on the other was a world in which Smiths no longer galloped. Here was the Welsh Wizard, who had won the war but who was losing grip; there was the sweeping tide of Conservatism. In the one pan of the balance was all I had clung to in the past; and in the other was all I hoped to cling to in the future. Was I to remain a Coalitionist when the Coalition was dead? Could any intelligent man go on giving his allegiance to a thing which was lying upon a mortuary slab underneath a sheet? Can a realist worship a ghost? Of course not. The thing is ludicrous.

So I voted at the Carlton Club meeting against the dead Coalition and in favour of live, vital, resilient, bounding Conservatism as personified by Mr. Bonar Law.

And when a fellow-member came up to me in the smoking-room of the National Liberal Club and had the blasphemous audacity to call me "Judas" to my face, I was able to explain that I had acted throughout consistently and with the highest motives, and that he was a howling ass. I then had the satisfaction of reporting him to the committee of the Club for blasphemy in the smoking-room, and, when the committee refused, snobbishly, to take action against him, I had the satisfaction of resigning from that massive marble edifice. I marched out, in fact, with bands playing and colours flying. As a matter of strict fact, I was bound to have resigned anyway after my conscientious decision to leave the niminy-piminy Coalition and to stick to my party, come rain, come sun. But it was nice to be able to resign from that weird edifice of marble and whiskers on high moral principles. All my life I have been strongly in favour of high moral principles.

CHAPTER XVII

I was now thirty-four years of age, with every reasonable expectation that the world was at my feet. Rich, married to a beautiful wife who adored me, popular everywhere with the right people of both sexes, a member of Parliament with a safe seat, regarded with approval by the high authorities in the Conservative Party, with a record of four years' service in the army, I was entitled to think that by means of my own talents and my own exertions I had brought myself within range of ministerial rank, and that the Cabinet did not lie very far ahead over my horizon.

But although I held my seat with an increased majority during the General Election of 1922, the Under-Secretaryship did not come my way at once, so I devoted my main energies during 1923 to social and domestic affairs. The drudgery of the backbencher's life was intended for dull pedestrian hacks and not for eagles.

Diana's baby was due to arrive in September 1923, and this circumstance naturally occupied my thoughts a good deal. It is a commonplace to laugh at the notion that the husband suffers more than the wife on these occasions, and probably there do exist callous brutes for whom childbirth is nothing but a peg on which to hang vulgar stories, and an excuse for accepting rounds of drinks from other callous, and maudlin, acquaintances. But even the ordinarily sensitive man goes through great anguish during the four or five months before the birth, and it is no exaggeration to say that

157

the hypersensitive man suffers torture.

Consider for a moment what he has to endure. His aesthetic sensibilities are frayed by his loved one's appearance more and more gratingly as the weeks go on; his physical life is suddenly transformed—perhaps for the first time for many years—by an enforced chastity, unless he is such a cur as to insult his poor wife by seeking amusement elsewhere during these months oftener than is necessary; his nerves are incessantly jarred by the unreasonable snappishness—almost shrewishness—which the expectant mother so often displays; if he is not a rich man, he is worried by the dilemma whether to jeopardize his material position by booking the most expensive gynaecologist in London, or whether to jeopardize his own peace of mind by relying upon a cheaper article; and he is haunted by the fear that a premature birth might catch him alone in the house, perhaps in the depths of the country, without a doctor or nurse within call.

All these agonies except the financial dilemma I suffered, while Diana went on her quiet routine unruffled, tranquil, without a care in her head. No. There could be no real comparison between our pains.

But it was impossible to bear all these agonies for nearly half a year. There is a limit to human endurance, and after a month or two of nervous strain I insisted that Diana should leave London and go down to Grantly at the beginning of May and await the event in the country. It would be quieter for her, healthier, and, when the summer months came, infinitely pleasanter. By remaining in London myself and attending to my Parliamentary duties, and filling in my spare time with a very charming American girl from New York, I would be removing by one manoeuvre three of the stresses, aesthetic, physical, and mental, to which, as I have said, impending paternity is subjected.

Diana at first protested that she wanted to stay in London, that she would be lonely in the country, that she did not mind the heat, and that she would be much happier with me than without me. To be happy during these months, she added, was of great importance to the character and health of the infant.

I pooh-poohed, very lightly and gently of course, all these objections, taking each in turn.

"You will not be lonely, sweetheart," I said, "because your mother has promised to stay with you all the time, and although your mother and I do not exactly see eye to eye on a number of things [she was a damned old harridan as a matter of fact] you know that you get on fairly well together."

"But for nearly five months," she objected. "Nobody could stand mother for nearly five months."

"Your father has stood her for about thirty years," I pointed out. "It's true that those thirty years account for the state of wandering senility to which he has been reduced, but there it is. As for the heat, it's easy enough to say that you don't mind it when an icy April wind is still blowing. But you'll hate it when it comes."

"Then I'll wait in London till it does come."

I swallowed my rising impatience and went on, still gently but now firmly, "Diana, it is sweet of you to want to stay with me, and there is nothing I should like more, as you know. But we must not think only of ourselves. There is the little babe to be considered as well. My son and heir must be given every possible chance, and I am of the opinion that you ought to spend the next five months in the healthy air of Grantly. And, Diana," I wound up, "let me make it perfectly clear that I don't propose to discuss the matter any further."

I only mention this incident as an illustration of the casualness of certain women towards their responsibilities. Diana was not thinking for a moment about the baby, but only about herself and her own comforts. There is unquestionably—it is not a pleasant thing to have to record but nevertheless it is true—a selfish streak in the feminine character. Even when it was a question of her first-born, Diana was stubbornly anxious to take the risk of extra months in the hectic, unhealthy atmosphere of London. Fortunately for the health of some new-born babies, the father sometimes exercises his masculine authority and ensures that mother and child shall have the fullest advantage of the vitally important period of pre-natal tranquillity, instead of whirling together round the floors of filthy cigar-smoky night-clubs.

Diana went down to Grantly with her mother in the second week of May, and it was agreed that I was to spend as many week-ends with her in Midhamptonshire as could be spared from my political duties, and, of course, the Easter and Whitsun recesses.

My domestic arrangements being thus satisfactorily settled for the summer months, there was leisure to turn to social entertainments.

Probably historians will write down 1923 as the critical year of transition between the dazed, groping, sad, post-war years and the beginning of the dawn of a new generation. Society was settling down a little, finding its feet among sands that were not shifting quite so crazily as before. One harvest of the fields had been reaped and another was already ripening.

But what of us? What of our handful of survivors? We were the last forgotten gleanings of our crop, and we were too old to be even noticed by the splendid young successors.

A new morality had arisen, and we had to accept it with as gracious a dignity as we could maintain. We were too young to retire upon the shelf, and yet we hesitated from descending into the antics of the Bright Young Things.

What a weird crew they were. The title was of their own choosing and seldom has a title been so inapt. They were not Young in the real sense of the word—for they had none of the flowering grace and charm of youth, nor its unself-consciousness, nor its radiance. They were shrill and haggard and unhappy. Nor were they Bright in the sense that we had been the life and soul of London before the war. These poor mummers were deadly dull. In fact the third word in the title, now that I come to think of it, did accurately describe them. They were Things. Men like myself could have no association with such a troupe.

There remained for us the spirit of the quiet discreet romances of the dear, dignified old days, and it was for us to adapt that spirit to the altered mechanics, so to speak, of the age.

The main alterations were three: firstly, as I have already briefly explained, the excitement which always surrounds the armed camp throughout the ages had during the war turned every woman in the land into a potentially willing recreation for the warrior. During this process of conversion women gradually discovered, greatly to their surprise and not a little to their discomfiture, that what had begun as a sacred duty to heroes who were about to die was in reality often a pleasurable affair. The Victorian mammas, physically battered by the bearing of a score of children in a score of years and mentally bruised by the selfish callousness of whiskered, ignorant, domineering, Victorian papas, had built up an image of the matrimonial couch that had succeeded only too well in terrifying Georgian daughters from any experience of it that was not strictly necessary. And in those days Virginity was elevated into a jewel of such rarefied and transcendent value, was whispered about with such reverential voices as the most precious of the feminine possessions, was, indeed, almost translated from maidenhead to godhead in so many pre-war households, that many a young woman who had been brought up in those households found it difficult to understand, at the critical moment, what all the fuss had been about. I will go further. One young woman of my acquaintance—I will not put our relationship any closer than that—told me, years ago, after I had known her for some time, that she was a virgin. I laughed in her pretty face. There were sound reasons for my laughter. She persisted. I laughed again. It turned out that, although I was obviously right in my derisive laughter, she had a certain amount of justification for her persistence. In her own words, "I never thought for a moment that what they all made such a fuss about for twenty years could be taken away in such a trivial manner." Feeling, not for myself, but as a man on behalf of men, I disliked intensely the use in the circumstances of that word "trivial." For myself, of course, it was nothing. For my sex, I resented the implied insult.

But the attitude of that girl was the inevitable reaction against the bad old attitude. And it was a good reaction. All that nonsense was now finished, and such phrases as "enjoying her favours" and "she gave herself to him" were quickly discredited when it was appreciated that the favours were mutual. The result of this, as I have said, was the inevitable decline of Jermyn Street, Piccadilly, the Burlington Arcade, and Bond Street, the decay of Maida Vale, and the complete desertion of the stage-doors by all save the elegant young gentlemen who sent bouquets of flowers to the elegant young gentlemen of the chorus.

No longer was it necessary to instal the lady of the hour in her own apartment or villa. Either she lived in the parental mansion with a latch-key of her own, in which case all that was required was a one-roomed *pied-à-terre* in a central situation, or else she lived in a flat of her own. In either event she was less expensive in so far as the overheads were concerned. Of course orchids and dinners at Claridge's and suppers at the Savoy increased the total outlay, and scent now had to be nothing less than the best or it was detected at once. For, in 1923, the women of the land were gradually winning the battle. They were getting us down. They were securing their mates. The campaign was not yet completely won, but they could well afford to add two inches to the length of their skirts, and add an inch and a half to the height of their "corsages," and cut down their daily output of fascinating vivacity. They were not at this time in a position to insist upon champagne, but they could be bold enough to turn up a dainty nose at anything but a really good Berncastler, where two years before they had been humbly accepting iced lager. Soho was by now out of the question, except as a picturesque, bohemian joke, whereas before it had been "heaven," and a bunch of lily-of-the-valley, so adored, so cooed-over, so endearingly snuggled against the soft bosom in 1921, was glanced at in a markedly cold manner in 1923.

But, all the same, the woman of 1923 who was riding inexorably to conquest of everything that she wanted, was cheaper than the girl of Maida Vale in 1913. For in addition to the saving in overheads, there was the important saving on what might be called the retaining-fee. For these high-born ladies passionately maintained their amateur status.

The second alteration in the mechanics of the social round was the motor-car. Roads were being adapted for motor-traffic and the bad old days of dust had been practically eliminated; cars were improving in quality, and breakdowns and punctures were becoming rarer. The week-end in the small country-hotel was on the point of being elevated into the social institution which it is to-day, and I can with all modesty claim to have been one of the pioneers. It is true that, with a few rare and notable exceptions, the country hotel-keepers of 1923 had not grasped the fact that their entire trade was being revolutionized by the motor-car, and their staple food was still tough roast beef, their staple floor-covering was worn, brown linoleum, and the staple odour in every room was very old cabbage. But with a little enterprise I discovered one or two which were remarkably comfortable, if perhaps a little primitive, and it was to one of these that I made the first of many happy excursions, in company with my new little American friend, as soon as I had allayed my anxiety about dear sweet Diana's health by packing her off to Grantly.

And this brings me to my third point. It was in these years that we became actively aware of the existence of the American woman. During the latter part of the war we had met a large number of American men, diplomats, business-men, soldiers, and sailors, but the feminine invasion naturally did not come until later.

The colossal prosperity which munition-making had brought to the United States, the cutting-off of Europe as a tourist paradise during the war years, the desire to see St. Mihiel and the Argonne forest and Château-Thierry, where the doughboys of America had won the war, the distaste for prohibition, the desire to be presented at the Court of St. James's, the passionate, if rather vague, ambition to buy European antiques and so become the leading culture expert in Omaha, Nebraska, or Grand Rapids, Montana, all these were factors in the rush of the American woman to Europe.

From the very first I found the American woman a fascinating study for anyone interested, as I have always been, in the varying types of humanity which we see around us. She is like no one else. She has a type all of her own.

I am not referring, you will readily understand, to the swarm of middle-aged, plain, dowdily-dressed women who all seemed to come from Kansas City and St. Louis and St. Paul, and who buzzed drearily in great black clouds round our picture galleries and museums at this period. They did not come under my microscope. As a type, of whatever nationality, middle-aged, plain, and dowdily-dressed women have never interested me very much.

Instead of trying to give you a composite picture of the sort of American woman who did fascinate me, it would be simpler, perhaps, to describe Violetta Starrett as she was when I first met her in the spring of 1923, because she was, in essentials, characteristic of all that I mean by "the American woman."

Violetta was the wife of Winslow Buddington Starrett, a well-to-do stockbroker in New York City. Like many other American brokers, he had been earning a fair but unsensational income in 1914. By the time Wall Street had handled the innumerable War Loans, and Liberty Loans, and Victory Loans, and all the rest of the staggering financial operations of the next four years, and by the time that the New York Stock Exchange had handled the investing transactions of all those who had profited by those staggering operations, Mr. Winslow B. Starrett, like many other American brokers, was a rich man, and in 1922 he had come to Europe to have a rest and to pick up a few art treasures, about which he knew nothing whatsoever. He brought his wife, who was an art treasure in herself, and he knew precious little about that either.

Violetta was about five-foot-eight, with square shoulders, a full bosom—none of your flat-boarded modern-girl nonsense about her—and long graceful legs, and long white fingers. Her forehead was broad, with a mass of brown hair swept back from it; her cheekbones were just high enough to emphasize the curve of the cheeks down to a determined chin; her nose had a faint and unexpected tilt which only began at the very end, and her mouth was small. But the most wonderful thing about her beauty was the contrast between a dazzlingly white skin and a pair of black, deep-set eyes. And the perfection of the technicolour of Paris, London, and New York dressed her and painted her finger-nails and her toe-nails, and waved and tinted her hair, and plucked her eyebrows, and all the rest of it.

Violetta was, in effect, the American woman.

Well read, a vivacious talker, amateur of the theatre and the concert hall, an admirably fluent linguist, with the same

New England accent in all the languages she spoke, she had already in her thirty years of life listened to ten times more monologues on the trend of the stockmarkets than an English wife has to put up with in sixty years, and she was monumentally bored with Winslow Buddington Starrett, his face, his conversation, and his love-making. Fortunately, perhaps, like the wives of almost all rich Americans, she had to endure vastly more of the first two than of the third. Rich Americans, for some reason, are seldom too tired for conversation. Their faces and their conversation are eternal, but, from all accounts, their love-making is only intermittent.

The worthy Winslow was stoutish, fiftyish, with a large flabby face, several chins, and two smallish eyes of nondescript colour, a mind which moved very slowly, and inexhaustible good-humour and kindness. At least I thought, until our acquaintance ripened, that they were inexhaustible.

We met at a dinner-party, I forget where, and the two memories of it will never fade from my mind—Violetta's cool, confident radiance, and, after the ladies had left the room, Winslow's two-cigar dissertation on the influence which the Yangtse floods of two years previously might or might not exercise upon the price of silver and on the consequent lowering of the purchasing power of the Indian rupee. At least it was something like that. It may have been the consequent raising. It was one or the other.

Never did two cigars seem so interminable, and never did human mind work more slowly, or human tongue move more slowly. At last it was over, and by cleverly pushing past my fellow-guests on the way to the drawing-room I contrived to secure the chair beside the lovely American.

That was the beginning of a whirlwind campaign. The very next week-end saw me driving my big Isotta-Fraschini, not to Grantly Puerorum to visit my dear lady-wife in order to console her in the first week of her sequestered life—after all, she had her mother with her—but through the New

Forest with Violetta Starrett by my side. Honest Winslow had gone to Liverpool to discuss cotton bales or wheat margins or something.

My baby turned out to be a girl, and that was a bore. When they are of a suitable age, attractive in appearance, and reasonable in their ideas, other people's daughters are capital. But to have a daughter oneself is tedious.

One is all in favour of the theoretical equality of the sexes, but it is only natural that a big hereditary landowner should desire to have a son to carry on the tradition.

However, I was careful not to allow Diana to see my chagrin, beyond dropping the casual hint that she was certain to have better luck next time, and that the sooner we tried that luck the more advantageous it would be all round.

The baby was healthy and fat, and looked no more and no less like a raw beetroot than any other baby, thereby completely vindicating my insistence upon pre-natal country air. The godparents were Diana's brother, young Tony Marston, a school friend of Diana's called Sophy Spink (a very plain girl), and Violetta. Diana objected strongly and for absolutely no conceivable reason to my choice of Violetta, and also to my choice of Violetta as the baby's second name after Anne (all baby girls were called Anne at about this time), but I insisted.

After the christening, Diana and the infant remained at Grantly, while I returned to London, where once again a political crisis was in the air. This was October 1923. But this time there was another crisis as well, and a more serious one.

CHAPTER XVIII

If I have not touched very much upon my financial affairs so far, it is because they had been in the position of those countries which are happy in having no history. In my gay gilded life between Oxford and Whitehall there had been moments, as I have said, when my expenditure had largely outrun my income, but the fortunate circumstance of the war soon restored an equilibrium. My shipping gains, and one or two fortunate investments in American munition companies, made on the strength of some confidential documents which passed through my hands at the Ministry of National Economy, had added a good deal to my fortune. There are many men in my position who would never have admitted to their profits from the torpedoing of British ships or from the use of secret State information, but that has never been my way. In the first case the torpedoing was not done by me, and in the second it was only out of sincere patriotic motives that I made use of the information.

There is no need to defend myself, because there is nothing to defend myself against, but, in view of the slanderous rumours which were in circulation about me at the time, a simple statement of the facts is perhaps permissible. In the middle of 1915 it was common knowledge at the Ministry that an order for a million shells for the eighteen-pounder gun had been placed with the Nazareth Steel Company of East Pennsylvania at a price of sixteen dollars a shell. Everything had been settled except the actual signature of the contract by the Minister and the Nazareth agent, and that formality was to take place as soon as the Head Office in America had telegraphed its final approval. Unfortunately for the Nazareth Company, and fortunately for Britain, the Head Office delayed its approval for nearly a week, and during that week I happened to obtain two crucial bits of information. These were no less than the news that the Nazareth Company was largely dominated by a German group in Pittsburg who would certainly see to it that our shells would be defective, and that the Galilee Company of Western Pennsylvania, a passionately pro-British firm, could and would provide the million shells more quickly, more reliably, and far more efficiently at the special cut rate of sixteen dollars and fifty cents a shell.

What was I to do? Picture my position as a loyal Englishman in his country's crisis. It would take too long to persuade the Minister to cancel the Nazareth draft contract. It might be a fortnight before he would grant me a preliminary interview, let alone take the necessary action for cancellation. On the other hand, was I to sit back and twiddle my thumbs while our Treasury was milked and our brave men supplied with defective ammunition?

It was a cruel dilemma. I solved it with what I may be allowed to call characteristic boldness. I drew up a duplicate contract, identical save in the title of the firm and in the amount of the cost per shell. I then informed his Lordship, the Minister, that the Nazareth agent was sending his deputy to sign in his place, and I told the Nazareth agent on the telephone that the Government had postponed its final decision for a day or two, and then brought the Galilee man to the signature ceremony. It all worked smoothly. There were dozens of contracts to be signed, and his Lordship, never a statesman of outstanding alertness, signed them all without even glancing at them. This was in any case the usual custom of the Ministry until its absorption into the Ministry of

Munitions, when an officious staff of accountants, mostly Scotch, insisted on checking every figure on every document in a most tiresome way. But that was later. All that remained after the Galilee man had got his contract signed was to tell the Nazareth man that his contract had been cancelled, and that if he wished to have a chance of getting a cut at the forthcoming heavy-howitzer contract he had better keep his mouth shut and not whine. Being a wise man, and accustomed to American ideas, he kept his mouth shut. He whined a bit, but only in private, which did not matter.

The Galilee Company, greatly to my embarrassment and surprise, afterwards insisted on my accepting a large block of their Ordinary shares to commemorate their first transaction with the British Government. And just for the very reason that it was their first war transaction and that many more followed, the shares which I was given appreciated very sharply in value.

I suppose that I was unwise to allow myself to be bullied into accepting these shares. But at the time I regarded them, and still do, not as a personal present to myself, but rather as a memento—a piece of silver plate, as it were, or a commemorative plaque upon a wall—of an occasion that was to prove of great value to my country and its gallant defenders.

But the world is full of malice, and a man like myself is always bound to have plenty of yapping enemies. Curs never pay any attention to the heels of nonentities. So it was no surprise to me when stories began to drift up and down St. James's Street and backwards and forwards in Pall Mall, to the effect that the gift of Galilee Ordinary shares had been offered to me before the signing of the contract and not after, and that the American citizen who had offered to me the information that the pro-British Galilee could supply a better shell, and more reliably, than the pro-German Nazareth, was the very same identical citizen who had told me that the Nazareth Corporation was pro-German and unreliable.

That is the whole story. My choice was between dud shells for our artillerymen and good shells. I chose good shells, and was the victim of slanderous rumour for several years as a consequence of my patriotism. It is unnecessary for me to add that I took no action in the Courts, although strongly pressed to do so by a number of influential friends, among whom were several famous lawyers.

But I was too old a fox for that sort of thing. What riled them all was that I had actually got the money and they wanted it. Any of the lawyers would have acted for me and taken his cut off the joint—Galilee Ordinaries having risen three hundred and forty points since my happy discovery of the Teutonic tendencies of the Nazareth crowd—and any of my best friends would have given evidence on my behalf for a sum down (or against me for a larger sum down). But I was not to be caught.

I left the money in America, and at the end of 1921 I was a much richer man, even allowing for the huge income-tax and super-tax, than I had been in 1914.

A change came over the financial world in 1922. There was an old Greek—was it Heracleitus? a vague smattering comes to me over the ages from those tom-fool days at Eton—who said that everything moves and that nothing stands still. He was right, absolutely right, whoever he was. And that is why you will find in this humble little book of reminiscences an incessant use of such words as "change," and "alteration," and "newness," and "modern". Everything moves. Nothing stands still.

I have never complained about the spread of new things, even of new ideas. One must take the rough with the smooth.

Thus, when the great slump overwhelmed us in England, after the artificial boom of those years immediately following the war, it came as a great shock to men of less equable temperament than myself. Literally hundreds of my contemporaries, or older men, lost their heads, and their fortunes, in the crash, and for years bemoaned, in a most un-British manner, this new thing which had befallen them.

To me it was also new. But to me there was something else new, and that was the unparalleled prosperity of the United States, where so much of my liquid property was by now carefully invested. It was the old story—swings and roundabouts. In England I lost heavily, in the United States I gained prodigiously. With consummate coolness, when all Lombard Street seemed to be cracking like the China orange to which it is proverbially linked, I stood firm and made only one gesture in recognition of the strange age in which we lived. I transferred all my American business into the hands of dear old Winslow Buddington Starrett. I felt it was the least I could do for the poor fellow. Heaven knows, he was due to get something from me. I had got something from him. Rochefoucauld would have made an aphorism upon the charm of the situation, where a broker's commission is balanced against a wife.

The crisis at home, however, was sufficiently serious to warrant the reduction of my establishment at Grantly to a mere skeleton. I sold off the farms, cut down the beech-wood (the one which old William Bedford had made such a fuss about on the occasion of the heath-fire years before) and sold the timber for a lot of useful money, and discharged all my employees except the indoor staff and the gardeners, dismissed the estate-agent, the "temporary gent." whose servility I had never liked at any time, and made all arrangements for the building of a model village on the green, wooded hill on the north-east side of the Grantly Estate, a hill which was called Lovely Mount.

Here again I was one of the pioneers of a new movement. Now that I come to think of it, how often was I a pioneer in movements which have subsequently enthused the whole of the kingdom! And how little thanks did I ever get from anyone for my pioneering work!

Lovely Mount was a beauty spot, one of the most famous in Midhamptonshire. It was a steepish hill, covered with oak-trees, with three gentle valleys forming a triangle below it, full of primroses and wild hyacinths and aconite and dog-roses, enclosing the hill. My father had planted the meadows in the valley with an immense number of daffodil bulbs and had scattered fritillary seeds in them and had strewn wild cyclamen under the oaks, and the whole scene was enchantingly beautiful in spring and early summer. In the late summer and the autumn there was the splendour of greens turning gloriously into reds, and of reds turning sombrely into browns, and of browns giving way at last to black bare branches. Yes, Lovely Mount had been rightly named by some old Midhamptonshire worthy of long ago.

It was this beautiful spot that I had dedicated in my mind to the service of my neighbours who were less fortunate than myself. True, it had been in my family for three generations. But was not that an additional argument, I asked myself, for letting someone else enjoy now what we had enjoyed for seventy years? Was it not someone else's turn to pick the fritillaries and quote Wordsworth to the daffodils? Why should the Mount be lovely only to a grandfather, a father, and a son? Why not to a whole village?

With these thoughts animating my mind, I called for plans from four firms of auctioneers, surveyors, and architects in Midhampton for the construction of a model village. And such was my naïveté, my inexperience in the ways of the world, that I made no secret of my intentions. I told a lot of people, casually, in the ordinary course of conversation, of my scheme to assist local housing, on my own estate and entirely at my own expense.

The folly of being so simple was soon evident. To my astonishment, shrill screams of protest split the quiet welkin of Grantly Puerorum. Letters, mostly ill-mannered and all ungrammatical, appeared in the county newspapers, between the accounts of whist-drives at British Legion Clubs and the prices of pigs, denouncing my proposals. Quaint bodies like Rural District Councils passed resolutions. A public meeting was held in Midhampton. Several of my landowning neighbours wrote personal letters appealing to me to preserve the Mount, but I was happy to note that these were all old ladies, either widows or spinsters, and, of course, it was unnecessary to pay any attention to their twaddle about wild flowers and Roman Camps. Not one of the big men in the district took a hand in the campaign of abuse and pressure. Men in general, and certainly the excellent type which owns land in large quantities, have a very just feeling that a man is entitled to do what he likes with his own, and they do not interfere with him. If a neighbour wishes to preserve fritillaries and celandine on his estate, that is his affair; if he wishes to build a model village, that is his affair too. And that, in my opinion, is the true tolerant spirit of Christianity. Besides, every right-thinking neighbour knows that his turn may come next, in these days of heavy taxation, death-duties, and the ever-increasing responsibilities of a good landlord, and he knows that he may want at any moment to part with some of his land to be split up into small building-lots. And, although it is obvious that to split up one's land and sell it to the jerry-builder for profit is a very different thing from building a model village for the benefit of the overcrowded dwellers in horrid little insanitary Tudor cottages, yet my neighbours felt that when their sad day did come, they would be in a less uncomfortable position if they had not interfered in my private affairs. For, in that case, if I were so minded, I might easily interfere in theirs.

Locally, therefore, except for the middle-class protests from Midhampton and the occasional old cat in bombazine and cameo brooches, there was nothing to fear. You can, then, imagine my fury when busybody societies in London actually had the nerve to poke their pasty noses into the estate of Grantly Manor. The first intimation I got of this scandal was a visit from two young women and a middle-aged man, who alleged that they represented a circus called the Council for the Preservation of Rural England. The man was a fool and the girls were plain, so I had them thrown out by my indoor staff.

The Wild Flower Society came next. Apparently a number of rare wild flowers had been in the habit of growing upon Lovely Mount even before my father scattered his seeds and planted his bulbs. The deputation this time consisted of two middle-aged ladies in pince-nez and button-boots. I gave them my assurance that every flower of any interest would be transplanted into my own wild garden, and had them thrown out.

Then an Archaeological Society came and blethered about the Roman Camp on the top of the hill. I told them that the proper housing of the poor mattered more to me than all Caesar's camps, Elizabeth's beds, and Cromwell's church-stables in the country, and I had them thrown out.

By this time my temper was rising, and its rise was not cooled off at all by indignant—and palpably manufactured—letters in *The Times*, or by an impertinent question in the House put by the Bolshevik member for a neighbouring constituency, or by an interminable series of alternative suggestions put forward by another London body, which operated under the title of the Town and Country Planning Advisory Council (my last word to them was that they could advise anyone in the world from Lenin to Jack Hobbs, if they wanted to, but they could not advise me), or, last straw of all, by a Society for the Preservation of Ancient Buildings.

That was the final insult. This Society wanted to stop me from pulling down the little pre-Tudor cottages, on the ground that they were perfect specimens of the rural architecture of the period. One in particular had an architrave or a king-post or a linch-pin, or some such rubbish, which was unique in the Midlands. There were only three others in England and they were all in Devonshire or Dorset. At least so this egregious Society said. Furthermore, they had the nerve to suggest that I should present my one to the nation as a National Monument, and, failing that, that I should maintain it in good order at my own expense.

So here was a fine situation. One group of busybodies was trying to stop me from building fine, good cottages on my own property, and another society of busybodies was trying to stop me from pulling down dirty, insanitary old cottages also on my own estate. And they call this a free country.

It is on the family records, so far back as they can be traced, that the outstanding quality of the Inglebys—on the male side at least—has always been their equanimity of temper. Probably I am no different from the rest.

But on this occasion an old berserker streak came out in me. An ancient Viking strain—for the Inglebys are almost certainly descended from the Karl Thorsefne who discovered America, and so enabled me to discover, later, my divine Violetta—made my temples throb furiously.

That I, the Lord of Grantly Manor, the last of the Inglebys, should be harried by out-at-elbows architects, and spinster agrarians, and dotard mediaevalists, was utterly intolerable.

I determined to strike a blow that would teach them all who was the controller of the destinies of Grantly Manor.

The plans of the four firms of auctioneers, surveyors, and architects were thrown into the fire. (They demanded compensation for their trouble. They did not get it.)

A new set of designs were drawn up for me by an impoverished young architect, whose chief, indeed only, recommendation to me was his poverty, and a firm of Kettering builders was imported to do the work. The designs were, in accordance with my instructions, faintly reminiscent of Tudor cottages but in the form of bungalows, and each was different from all the rest. Thus, one would have an old-oak-beamed verandah and hideous gabled windows. Another would have painted bricks and painted beams upon a concrete front and a rustic-woodwork verandah. And so on. Plaster, and deal, and paint, and fretwork, and olde-worlde ideas were the main ingredients.

It may sound brutal. Perhaps it was brutal. But remember that I was in a flaming temper, and that also I was striking a stout blow—in a rear-guard action—in the defence of individual liberty. Lovely Mount was mine, and the unique pre-Tudor cottages were mine, and in doing what I liked with them I was maintaining the age-old heritage of the Englishman, of whatever walk of life or of whatever state in this country—to be free from outside interference. So I cut down the oaks on Lovely Mount (and made a nice thing out of selling the timber to the jerry-builder whose contract I had accepted for the bungalows), and I dug up the three little valleys, and I planted a mass of bungalows all over the place. I then completed the lesson which I was teaching to the loathsome busybodies in London by tearing down the insanitary pre-Tudor cottages. (I sold the beams and bricks, the jerry-builder having refused to touch them even as scrap, to an architectural association in Daventry which seemed to set some store upon such junk. Imagine my anger when I discovered, years later, that the bricks were of that rare, thin, mellow, fifteenth-century shape which makes them a prize for connoisseurs, and that the association had cheated me out of at least a hundred pounds.)

Once the bungalows were up, and the cottages were down, nothing remained but to transfer the inhabitants from the latter to the former and then to sit back triumphantly, having shown the serried societies of London that you cannot, even in these decadent days, tamper without risk with the liberties of the individual in this our land of England.

One final thrust I delivered. You may call it spite, or jumping on a fallen adversary, or sheer high spirits. I know what my own phrase for it would be, and it would be the third of these three. I could not forget or forgive the visit of the button-booted ladies of the Wild Flower Society, and I named the bungalows by such names as "Fritillary View" and "Celandine Cot" and "Daffodil Vista" and "Cyclamen Grove" and "Crocus Bed" and "Snowdrop House."

As each pestilential building went up, I had a name ready for it that would strike terror into the hearts of those button-boots.

Incidentally, it turned out afterwards that by substituting this haphazard, pepper-pot scheme of cheap bungalows for an ordered and designed and expensive model village, I had added about fifteen hundred pounds a year to my income.

Which just shows that there is Justice in this world for those who know how to deserve it.

CHAPTER XIX

I celebrated my victory over the massed nosey-parkers of the country with a small dinner-party at the Ritz, to which I invited young Captain Skellington-Green, a promising young Member of Parliament who had won a solid Nonconformist stronghold in the South-west from a Liberal in the 1922 election; a charming and pretty intelligent girl whose name I cannot remember; and, of course, the Starretts.

I only mention this dinner-party because it was the ultimate cause of a great deal of unhappiness to me. It was the first time that my wife met Charles Skellington-Green. The girl whose name I cannot remember was typically English. She was wonderfully unlike Violetta. She was brown-haired, and beautiful, and admirably turned out. But she lacked the American poise which, translated into terms of social action, so often shows itself in a desire to please. Violetta answered my quips with quips that were almost as shrewd, but when I spoke seriously she listened attentively, indeed admiringly. This other girl had not the same cosmopolitan *savoir faire*. She was ready to exchange joke for joke, but any sort of monologue, however interesting or well-informed, quickly brought a far-away look into her slate-grey eyes. Perhaps it was due to the restless impatience of the age, or just to an innate laziness of mind. I don't know why I have mentioned her, except perhaps to point this contrast to Violetta. She was, essentially, a silly miss, but she had the fresh radiance of youth, so much could be forgiven to her.

Diana was a disappointment to me at that dinner-party. It was her first appearance as a hostess since the birth of Anne Violetta Fox-Ingleby, and while I had never expected any approach to wit and vivacity from her, it was rather annoying that she should have chosen this evening of all evenings, the celebration of my triumph over the nosey-parkers, for behaviour that was not far removed from sulkiness. Fortunately there was a woman at the table who was *simpatica* and could sense intuitively my chagrin. Dear Violetta made the most gallant efforts to save the party, and the more deeply that Diana withdrew into her shell, the gayer and lighter became Violetta's talk. I was intensely grateful to her for being so understanding in my difficulty, and between us we maintained a sparkle of wit and exchange. Dear old Winslow was a little quieter than usual and hardly delivered more than half-a-dozen lectures on the interlocking of currencies to the far-away English beauty on his right. I fancy the poor fellow was a little depressed at the thought of his impending departure to New York. For I had entrusted him, in addition to the profits of my war investments, with the very considerable moneys which had accrued from the sales of my farms and from the happy little excursion into rural rehousing at Lovely Mount, and I had impressed upon him the importance of hastening across to America immediately to use my money to my best advantage in the ever-soaring stock market. I felt, in doing so, a warm glow of superiority over King David. At least, Winslow was not going to be killed. In fact, so far was he from death in the forefront of the battle that I was actually putting money into his pocket. Uriah had an infinitely worse deal than Winslow Buddington Starrett. But if I felt superior to King David, I could not help a quiet giggle to myself at the idea of *le mari cocu* hastening away all unconsciously to make money for his supplanter on a commission basis. For I had insisted on Winslow taking his normal commission. Half the gentle fun would have been missed if I had accepted his generous offer to act for me as one friend to another. That he was, so to speak, a paid servant of mine, added subtly to my amusement.

"I agree with you, my dear old boy," I remember saying to him with a hearty clap on the shoulder, "that we should deal as one friend to another. But I insist upon a basis of Give and Take."

And I think that Winslow's depression may also have been partly due to the fact that Violetta had set her heart upon being presented at Court, and was to follow by a later boat.

Winslow was the sort of American who pays attention to his wife once in six weeks, but is melancholy-ridden if he thinks that she is occupying the intervals to her own satisfaction.

Anyway, whatever the reason, and I have no doubt there were several, dear old Winslow was not a gay jester at the party.

Charles Skellington-Green laboured gallantly throughout dinner to entertain his hostess, but I could see out of the corner of my eye that he was having an uphill task. It was, in fact, anything but the triumphant feast which I had planned.

That evening when we got home, Diana and I had our first real row.

The moment we were in the library—it was about midnight—I turned to her and said, very quietly:

"And now, will you kindly explain?"

"I'm very tired," was her feminine subterfuge.

"Not so tired that you can't listen," I retorted. "What the hell do you mean by disgracing your husband in front of his guests?"

"I didn't feel very cheerful," she said.

I groaned in despair. "How often have I told you that it doesn't matter two straws what a wife feels like when she's out with her husband? She's got to be gay even if she feels like the devil."

"It isn't always easy, Edward."

"It very often isn't easy for me," I replied, "when I'm tired after a long day in the House, or looking after my affairs and making certain that you have enough money to spend on your trinkets and fal-lals, but you don't see me sulking like a silly school-girl."

"You find it easy enough to be gay when you're with Violetta," she said with some spirit.

"What exactly does that mean?" I asked quietly.

"Exactly what I said."

"And you imply—?"

"Nothing is implied beyond—"

"Beyond what?"

There was a moment's pause and then Diana said in a low voice:

"Beyond what is common property."

That was a bit of a facer. It had never occurred to me that Diana would hear anything. It was always a cardinal axiom among the young bucks in my early days that the husband is always the last to learn. The ignorance of the husband had been a consolation to us on a good many more occasions than once. And we had automatically assumed, although of course we did not know in those early days, that the same applied to the wife.

But I had forgotten the infernal frankness of the modern generation.

However, there was nothing for it but lofty denial.

"I don't know what you mean," I said coldly.

Diana sighed in that intentionally offensive manner that all husbands know, and then said:

"I wouldn't have minded so much if you hadn't flaunted it, Edward. But you don't seem to have tried to keep it a secret. That is what is so insulting."

"Of course I did," I blurted out angrily, and saw that my attitude of lofty denial had gone by the board. I seized another attitude.

"It's so like a woman to say you wouldn't have minded so much if this, if that, if the other thing. It isn't sense. And it isn't true."

She nodded slowly. "I didn't mind so much the other times, when you were a little more careful."

"You've been spying on me, damn you!" I shouted.

"During the last six months?" she asked, with a wan smile. "That would have been difficult. I have been rather tied up with Anne. But a good many people know you by sight, Edward, and there is always a kind friend who will pass the news on to a wife, especially if she is down in the country with her mother, and is likely to be bored to tears if she has to spend weeks on end without an occasional bit of gossip. And all one's best friends understand that there is no real gossip like gossip about one's husband. You were seen with the Dickson girl at Bury St. Edmunds," she went on carelessly.

"Damn it," I exclaimed, "I did think Bury St. Edmunds would be safe. How could I possibly have any friends in such a ghastly hole?"

Diana laughed slightly and went on, "And you were at Ludlow last August with a pretty little blonde. You were doing well in August, Edward—unfaithful to me and to Violetta at the same time."

"I will not be talked to like this," I cried furiously. "If you are going to do anything about it, for God's sake go and do it. But I won't stand being lectured."

"No one is lecturing you," Diana replied with infuriating gentleness. "I am only telling you that I am not such a fool as you think."

"Well, what are you going to do? Divorce me?"

"I haven't thought it out yet," she said slowly, gazing into the last embers of the fire.

"You don't mean you seriously mean to divorce me?" I exclaimed.

"I'm not sure."

I was beginning to get alarmed.

"But, darling," I said urgently, "sweetheart, just think what would happen to my political career if you make me figure in a divorce suit. Those sanctimonious swine up there would have me out of the seat in no time. They'd force me to resign. It would ruin me".

"Yes, I suppose it would," she murmured, resting her chin upon her hand.

"And if you cited Violetta, think of the scandal for her."

"I wouldn't think of it for two seconds," said Diana vigorously, turning on me with flashing eyes. I hastily dropped the subject of Violetta. It did not appear to be a popular theme.

I returned to easier ground, although just at the moment hardly any ground looked very easy. It was clear, though, that the situation called for charm rather than bluster—perhaps charm with the latent threat of bluster in reserve. I had no wish to be dragged through the divorce courts. Quite apart from the harm it would do to my political career, there were my constituents to be considered. For myself it did not matter very much. There were other careers, more lucrative and less arduous, open to me at any time. But the Conservatives of South-east Midhampton were in a different position. They had pinned their faith on me, and twice had been led to victory. A new Liberal candidate was nursing the Division and making a good deal of headway with his un-scrupulous pledges and his typically Liberal cloud of nebulous half-truths, and if the popular young Squire of Grantly was submerged in a scandal, the seat might easily be lost. In those days the Liberals were still pretty strong and this candidate, a certain Spencer Crump, was a glib, plausible fellow who not only learnt his figures and facts before he distorted them, but had succeeded in covering his own personal tracks so well that my agents could not discover a single discreditable episode in his life. To look at his record as it appeared in my office, you would think he had never told a lie, drunk a whisky-and-soda, seduced a girl, or borrowed a pound note in the whole of his life. I could not let such a dull, middle-class frump of a creature represent my lovely South-east Midhampton.

So I turned on the charm-tap and knelt on the rug beside Diana's chair. I hated doing it, but it was, in common decency, the only thing I could do. My constituents who had trusted me could not be let down. Fortunately the rug was a thick bearskin.

"Darling," I said, or words to that effect, "I know I'm difficult sometimes, but it is my temperament. Mother was Irish, you know, and temperament is not a thing that anyone can help. I didn't mean to hurt you, sweetheart," and a good deal more in the same strain. Mother was not Irish, of course, as she came from Macclesfield and was born Fox, but a little poetic licence can always be excused when the cause is good.

At the end of it, Diana turned her great, mild eyes to me and said, "But do you love me?"

"Of course I do," I replied vehemently.

"More than you ever did?"

"Yes, much more."

"How much more?" (Was there ever such a tomfool question?)

"Oh, lots and lots."

"How am I to believe that?" I groaned inwardly but kept my patience.

"But can't you see it for yourself?"

"I suppose so."

There was a pause, during which I wondered if the game had been won and I could safely get up and have a drink. The bearskin, though thick, was not thick enough to sustain the knees of a prolonged beleaguer. Then Diana went on, "And you'll give up that woman?"

"Yes, darling, I swear it."

"And never see her again?"

I hesitated over this, and she hardened instantly.

"Well?"

"You see, sweetheart," I explained, "that's a little difficult to promise. You see, Winslow is my stockbroker and looks after my American affairs, and it's a little difficult to refuse to meet the wife of one's man of business."

"I don't think Winslow will mind," Diana said drily. This remark upset me a good deal.

"Good God," I cried, "you don't think that he—" I broke off. There are some things which a gentleman does not discuss with his wife.

"Besides," I added, "he's only an old fool."

"Do you promise you'll never see her again?" Women's persistence can be maddening. There are times when their minds seem incapable of sticking to the point of a discussion for more than ten seconds without diving down side issues and irrelevancies, and then there are other times when they are utterly incapable of doing anything else but stick to the point. I do not know which is the more infuriating.

"If I do, will you promise not to divorce me?" I asked, becoming a little sulky, and Heaven knows I had reason to be a little sulky.

Diana had the nerve to refuse, and even hinted that I was hardly in the position to make terms.

"But think of Anne," I pleaded. "You don't want to bring disgrace upon the poor little creature's life. Just because I've had an idle fling or two, you aren't going to ruin poor little Anne."

"Let's leave Anne out of the discussion," said Diana coldly.

At that I must confess I saw red. Probably it was foolish of me, but there are moments in all our lives when generous impulses surge up and cannot, will not, be suppressed.

I rounded on Diana. "Leave Anne out?" I cried, leaping to

my feet, overjoyed at the chance to save something from the wreckage of my cartilages. "How can you be so heartless as to leave her welfare out of all this? How can you settle your life without giving the faintest consideration to hers? No, don't interrupt," I swept on. "Let me tell you this. If you've forgotten your own daughter, I haven't forgotten mine. You can bring her up under the stigma of the divorce court if you like, but if you do she will never, never forgive you, and nor will I."

"You're twisting what I said—" she began.

"Backing down already?" I interrupted with sarcasm. "I don't blame you."

Diana wrapped herself again in her cloak of heavy inertia and returned to a study of the fire.

After a moment or two, during which I poured myself out another drink, she said:

"Do you promise?"

"Promise what, in Heaven's name?"

"Not to see that woman again."

"Oh, all right, all right," I shouted furiously. "Damnation, I'll promise anything for a quiet life. Though how the devil you expect me to struggle all day and half the night at my job in the House while you nag, nag, nag at me all the time, I simply don't know."

"I'm sorry if I nag you," she said sedately, which, I suppose, is as near an apology as one is ever likely to get from a woman. What an incomparably pleasanter place the world would be if women were, so to speak, gentlemen.

I patted her cheek. "Don't worry, sweetheart," I said, "your husband isn't such a bad chap as you might think," and with that I went up to my dressing-room and went to bed.

Next morning I sent a note round to Violetta by hand saying that we had better not meet for a week or two, and that if she would meet me in the lounge of the Mayfair Hotel at noon I would explain what had happened. Just as I was leaving the house to stroll through the Green Park towards Piccadilly Circus, a messenger arrived with a dozen orchids for Diana. A card was attached, "With very many thanks for a delightful evening. Charles Skellington-Green."

"What a nice fellow…charming manners…old-fashioned courtesy…"were casual phrases which went through my mind as I selected a hat and cane, and then a queer notion came to me suddenly, so that I stood wrapt in a brown study and gazing at the magnificent Richard Wilson which hung in the hall. The butler recalled me to myself after at least a couple of minutes had passed, with a cough, and I woke up to see a curious smile on my face as it was reflected in the glass of the Wilson picture.

"Call up Captain Skellington-Green, Jobling," I said to the butler, "and ask him if he would care to drink a glass of sherry with Mrs. Fox-Ingleby and myself this evening at six o'clock. And have his answer waiting for me in the lounge of the Mayfair Hotel in half an hour."

Green accepted, and at half-past five that evening I had to telephone from the House to Jobling to instruct him to present my apologies to Charles. An important division was expected shortly and I could not leave. But I hoped, I added, that he would find adequate entertainment without me.

CHAPTER XX

The whole world knows how Mr. Baldwin, as he then was, rushed us into the General Election of 1923. It was a hideous bungle from start to finish, as any moderately clear-sighted man could have foreseen. But there was nothing for it but Party Loyalty and Hope for the Best. A small group of us, perhaps a little more endowed with courage and with political vision than the remainder of the herd, made no secret of our conviction that a serious blunder was being committed, though for obvious reasons we did not push our resistance to the extent of jeopardizing our chances of promotion later on.

We said, in effect, "We think Mr. Baldwin is wrong, but such is our loyalty to him and to the Party that we will follow him, and it, to the death."

With these brave sentiments we marched out to battle for Tariff Reform. My majority in 1918 had been ten-thousand-odd, a figure vastly inflated by the hysterical circumstances of the "Khaki" Election; in 1922 it was round about five thousand, of which I reckoned that three thousand was the normal Tory majority, with the other two added for the personality and popularity of the sitting member.

I stood for the whole Party programme of course, for I am nothing if not a good Party man, but I concentrated mainly upon "Buy British," "Save the Union Jack from the Kremlin," and "Fair Play for Agriculture."

My opponent, the Crump, strung together the usual fandango and fantasy of irredeemable pledges which one expects from a Liberal candidate. On this occasion there was no Labour man, and Crump and I had a straight fight. At least it was straight in the sense that we alone were in the ring. It was straight in no other sense.

Crump descended at once into the slime. He dragged out the fact that my three cars were Isotta-Fraschini, Delage, and Buick. "Is this how to Buy British? " the reptile screamed.

"Italy, France, and the United States were our allies in the war," I replied with crushing weight.

Crump made cheap gutter-play with my housing scheme at Lovely Mount. It is true that by a mismanagement on someone's part the old cottages were torn down before the new ones were built, and some old folk had been evicted forcibly in a March wind and had died of pneumonia owing to lack of shelter. But it was not true that I had said that old folk were better out of the way in any case; or at any rate if I did say it, it was not meant to be repeated. And in any case, I can hardly recall having made the remark. The old story of the stables, which were too damp for my hunters and had been converted into cottages for the poor, was brought out, and even my letter of commendation from the R.S.P.C.A., which I circulated as a leaflet, failed to make good the leeway.

The cutting down of my staff at Grantly during the slump, the wages (perfectly fair living-wages) I paid on my estates, the sale of my land, all these were unscrupulously employed.

As for Crump's war service, you would have thought that the fellow had fought the war single-handed, what with all his D.S.O.s and M.C.s and Legions of Honour and Médailles Militaires and Russian Crosses and Palms on his Croix-de-Guerre! It need hardly be added that the fellow wallowed alone in his filth. His opponent did not go down into the sewers with him. No. Not I. I did not even parade my war record against his, and his personal character was unassailed on any platform of mine. Besides, as already recorded, my agents could not find any point in his personal character upon which it would have been possible to assail him. He was a sort of dirty Galahad.

He had not a chance from the word "Go." Liberalism was dying. Free Trade was dead. He was a carpet-bagger. His opponent was the sitting Member, a local landlord, a local personality, a rich man, and, though I say it, who perhaps should not, a not altogether unpopular man. Crump was poor and earnest, both severe handicaps in a Midland constituency. The Tory majority of five thousand at the last election might be reduced by the three thousand rats who are so often liable to waver or to be stampeded, but the other two thousand, which I might call my own two thousand, were staunch and stout. The thing might be close-run, but I was a certain winner all through. That is how I calculated it out.

But by God! The fellow got in. Sneaked in by ninety-three, after two recounts.

It was not that I cared two straws about being defeated. If Eton taught me anything, it was the idea of accepting defeat with a courteous bow and a gay smile. Politics interested me a good deal. Any decent citizen ought to be interested in politics a good deal. Politics is only another word for taking an interest in one's fellow-citizens, and in the condition of life in which one's fellow-citizens live. But politics were not the be-all and end-all of my life. There were other fish to fry. But the deadly wound which was dealt me in the 1923 Election was the thought that South-east Midhamptonshire did not want me.

It was the ingratitude that seared my soul. For six years as their Member, and for twenty years as the Squire of a large part of the constituency, I had toiled in their interests, and they had thrown me out for a Crump.

It was a carpet-bagging Crump, a wretched namby-pamby Liberal, who proposed the customary vote of thanks to the Returning Officer after the declaration of the result, and it was an Ingleby of Grantly, a true-blue Tory Squire, who had to suffer the ignominy of seconding the vote.

It is hardly worth adding that the Crump creature kept meticulously within the bounds of election law, and no amount of quiet investigation by my people could unearth the smallest peccadillo in his methods, the least inaccuracy in his accounts, or the faintest trace of bribery. There being, in consequence, no chance of unseating the fellow on a petition, I accepted my defeat like a man and went back to London, more hurt than angry, and more concerned at the depths of human ingratitude than at the loss of my seat.

Nor did it afford me any pleasure to discharge a gardener before returning. It was an unpleasant necessity. But the man's wife, daughter of a local temperance fanatic and herself a bigoted Evangelical, had displayed a Crump leaflet in her parlour window. The man had voted for me—or so he maintained—but he had not prevailed upon his wife to remove the disgusting red poster. "Brook," I said to him sternly, when he was brought before me, "I am master in my house, and I advise you to be master in yours. There is no room here for hen-pecked husbands. We are all men at Grantly." He said nothing, but went.

It was not till after he had gone that it came into my mind that his name was not Brook but Grigsby, which only confirmed me in my wisdom. A man who cannot even stand up for his own name is of no use to me.

Charlie Skellington-Green lost his seat too, at which I was pleased, for this reason. A really keen young politician has very little opportunity for the fripperies of life in London, and I was anxious that Charlie should have a good time before he became immersed in the affairs of the world.

Whereas a young man in London with money and leisure often finds time heavy on his hands and is glad of diversion, the wife of a keen young politician also requires diversion in her long hours of loneliness. When the General Election was announced, I had hoped that Charlie might fail to take his hurdle, simply for the reason that he seemed to me to be the sort of man who would make an ideal companion for a friend's wife when the friend was busy on the affairs of the nation. Charlie was two years younger than I, moderately good-looking, chivalrous, entirely platonic, and a pleasant if not brilliant talker. Of course when I hoped that Charlie would have the leisure during the next two or three years to entertain Diana, of whom he was very fond in that charming way which is so flattering to a husband's vanity, it did not occur to me that the rats of South-east Midhamptonshire would turn their miserable little teeth against their champion and benefactor and that I too would lose my seat. Fortunately, not much harm was done, because the new Parliament, as you will remember, only lasted for eight months.

Charlie lost his seat in rather curious circumstances. It was a Midland manufacturing town, dependent to a great extent upon a continuous supply of raw material at the cheapest possible prices. This made it profoundly suspicious of Tariff Reform. On the other hand, the mass of middle-class and well-to-do residents, who were the backbone of Charlie's majority, were equally suspicious of Socialism. Charlie came out hot and strong for Baldwin's programme, but at the last moment an Independent Tory stepped in and stood for Free Trade, Toryism, and anti-Socialism. He was a good speaker and a nice handsome lad, and he polled eleven hundred votes, which was just enough to dish poor Charlie and let the Socialist in by twenty-two. The lad forfeited his £150 deposit, but that was only to be expected, and when I guaranteed his election expenses I had budgeted for the loss of the deposit. He was a promising youth and it afforded me a lot of pleasure to be able to give him his first chance of electioneering experience. It was poor luck for Charlie, but one must learn to accept the rough with the smooth in this world. He took his defeat pretty hardly, it seemed to me, so I thought it prudent not to mention my indirect connection with the affair. He was in such a mixture of temper and depression when I met him at the club, that he would not have appreciated my motives in trying to help the promising young lad. He had not even the common decency to condole with me on my defeat, which was a blow to the Party incomparably more serious than the loss of his trivial seat. But I said nothing. I stood him a drink and despatched him round to Diana for consolation.

So far as the active affairs of the world were concerned, I was rather at a loose end in 1924, after those crawling creatures in my constituency had voted for the dismal Crump. My personal life, of course, was lively, as it has always been.

But it is not possible to spend the entire twenty-four hours in each day in the exact position in which one would naturally like to, and so I toyed at this time with the idea of looking round for some occupation outside politics which would fill in the spaces, so to speak, between the feminine enchantments. Intellectual stagnation is always death to those who have been born, through no fault nor to any credit of their own, with a sort of dynamo whizzing round inside their heads.

Many and many a time have I wished that I was like so many of my friends—contented cauliflowers without a thought in their heads outside the daily routine of night and day. It must be a pretty enviable life if you don't have to think from morning till night, like those fellows in the Brigade or the hunting set in Leicestershire, or the winter-sports crowd in Switzerland, with their fixed smiles and their baggy trousers and their quaint, unreasoning self-consciousness. You see them in every club—except the Savage and the Savile, which are, it appears, full of literary cards and such-like riff-raff—and at every ball and every meet of hounds. You see them at Ascot and St. Moritz, on the grouse moors and at Cowes, all, male and female alike, looking like flat-fish. But for those of us who have been cursed with brains—oh, well! —we would not have had it otherwise.

My first idea was to follow the footsteps of so many of my friends and join the Stock Exchange, but drawbacks to this course soon became very evident. For instance, my initial ignorance would put me in a position subordinate to my partners, always a repugnant thing to a man of sensibility; then, when my ignorance had been overcome, in the course of a few months, my partners would draw their share of the profits accruing from my talents, and no individualist could tolerate such a thing; again, their blunders would involve me in troubles that were none of my making; and finally, and perhaps most weighty of all these considerations, partners would expect me to be regular in my attendance at the office, whereas I might want to go to Paris for a week with—say— Violetta, or to Cannes for a fortnight with—again say— Violetta.

These were insuperable obstacles. No one could put himself in such a low and equivocal position who had been accustomed from his teens to command. The alternative was to launch out on my own, in a quiet way at the beginning, of course, as a financial expert, and I was just considering the pros and cons of this line of action, when my political sense, which has always been tolerably keen, told me that Mr. Mac-Donald's Government of 1924 was not going to last very long. In a few months, I felt, I would again be representing the worms of South-east Midhamptonshire, and I decided that I would do well to postpone my single-handed raid into the markets until I had consolidated my political position and won my long-deserved Under-Secretaryship.

So I temporarily retreated—*reculer pour mieux sauter*, as the French say—from finance, and spent the rest of the MacDonald administration concentrating upon Violetta, for the darling was still in England. She had contrived to postpone her return to America over and over again, sometimes for this reason, sometimes for that, and although poor old Winslow fretted a bit, he was too busy to make a fuss about it. He was probably too busy, in fact, to give a passing thought to his wife oftener than about once every three weeks, and then only just before he fell off into his laboriously earned slumber. Oh, those American business men. What men! What sub-men!

It added to my contentment at this time that Diana seemed to have laid aside her unworthy suspicions after our scene of the previous year, and, apart from the mortification of my electoral defeat, 1924 went for me as merry as a marriage bell. Money was plentiful, Violetta beautiful, and my home-life, or rather what little I saw of it, was peaceful. And Charlie Green was most assiduous in his platonic devotion to Diana. I was delighted with the way he amused her. After all, a husband cannot amuse a wife all the time, and if he has a spark of decent feeling, he will always be delighted if a cheerful and amiable young man comes along and entertains her. I watched them both with a paternal benevolence.

Towards the end of the year the MacDonald Government vindicated my political judgment and made a collective set of asses of itself, and another General Election took place. I stood again for my contemptible South-east Midhampton, and it went bitterly against the grain to have to fawn upon them for their filthy reptilian suffrage. The new Fascist régime in Italy was getting seriously to work at just about this period, and many a time during the election, as I made some unfulfillable promise to some boorish clod, or kissed some revolting baby, or addressed a mothers' meeting on the price of lard (which, facially, they all so closely resembled), I prayed devoutly that we could have some sort of system of government over here on Italian lines which would preserve the theory of democracy without any of its workings. Heaven knows, I am, and always have been, a friend of the People, and a democrat of democrats, but that has never prevented me from detesting and execrating the People at the same time with all my heart.

The People to me have always been a great problem. It contains lots, I am sure, of very nice individuals. I have, in fact, met several charming proletarians in my various contacts at Grantly and during my elections. No one could be nicer for a few minutes. But when they are all lumped together in a mass, however charming they may have been as individuals, they become abominable.

Thus the ordinary British workman is a capital fellow if you get him by himself. A mug of beer will enchant him. And if you get ten British workmen and give them ten mugs of beer, you will enchant them. But if you get a hundred thousand British workmen and start offering them a hundred thousand mugs of beer, you find you are up against a Trades Union, and they all leap to their rickety feet and bawl that you are a dirty capitalist. That is why we Tories, fundamentally, dislike the Trades Unions. Our appeal to the working man is not the appeal of the rascally demagogue on the soap-box or the blasphemous howl of the sergeant to his platoon, but rather the quiet, persuasive, condescending charm of the gentleman to his valet. It is notorious that in the war the private soldier, who was glorified into a hero by a uniform and the imminent prospect of death, where before he had been the scum of the earth, would infinitely sooner follow a gentleman rather than a valiant warrior from his own Limehouse Causeway or Hackney Marshes.

We, the Conservatives, the Tories, the—if I may use the word—gentlemen, depend upon our man-to-man influence. When the mass-influence comes in, we go out. Personality is everything to us. Slogans are everything to the Liberals and

Labourites, who have neither education, in the real sense of the word, nor personality. Well, you can choose. Personality on one side, and slogans on the other. The common folk usually choose rightly.

The Election of 1924 was, you remember, a terrific victory for us. I am sufficiently broad-minded to admit that we had much in our favour. Mr. MacDonald's troupe was well-meaning, but it incessantly missed trapezes and fell ignominiously into the rescuing Liberal net below. At last it took an over-confident bounce and found, to its mingled indignation, astonishment, and pain *au derrière*, that it had bounced once too often and that the Liberal net had been withdrawn.

Probably the Liberals withdrew the net at that particular moment because they wanted to catch a temperance minnow with it, or a sprat that was trying to escape from the League of Nations.

Anyway the Reds, or Near-Reds, or Pinks or Puces, or whatever you like to call them, missed trapezes and tumbled on to the hard ground.

That was a help to me. The Election was half-won before it was half-begun. The Zinoviev Letter completed our Austerlitz. If I thought that I was writing for a reasonably intelligent and even semi-educated citizenry, I would not do more than refer, simply, to the " Zinoviev Letter."

But times are different. Memories are short. So I will explain that the Zinoviev Letter was a document which came from nowhere and was written by no one and was received by no one and was read by everyone. It explained exactly how the Union of Soviet Socialist Republics was to win Britain, and it resulted in the Conservatives winning the Election. I often wonder what Baldwin would have ultimately become if it had not been for the timely production of a letter which apparently was not written by Zinoviev (whose real name was Apfelbaum) or by anyone else.

If it had not been for this mysterious emanation from the spirit-world, via the *Daily Mail*, Mr. Baldwin might easily have had to devote his declining years to the study of pigs, after all. A strange finish for an ironmaster.

But I can afford to be fair-minded about the famous letter. It won many seats for many of my friends. Hundreds of them in fact.

But I needed no Apfelbaum in South-east Mid-hamptonshire. Not a single member of the dreaded Comintern was required in our gossamered meadows or in the shadows of our honeysuckled hedges to sway a single bucolic vote. For everything had been arranged, months before the Kremlin poked its scarlet nose into our meadow-sweeted and herb-willowed lanes.

For this is what had occurred.

Another promising young man had come to my notice. This time it was a young Socialist.

Now I am nothing if not broad-minded. The fact that Daniel Smithers was a Socialist did not handicap him in my eyes. The career open to the talents is my idea of service.

Smithers was young, eager, honest, and, luckily, poor. How could I, middle-aged, disillusioned, rich, stand in the way of rushing lovely youth? The lad wanted to stand for Parliament. He had no money. Why, I shouted to myself in my Belgravia library, "And so he shall stand for Parliament!"

I paid all his expenses, and he neatly split Crump's vote, and I strolled back into Parliament for my old constituency and my old constituents—to hell with it, and to hell with them for their treachery!—without any necessity for fetching in any forgeries from the *Daily Mail*.

Baldwin had to have the help of a colossal figure, as Zinoviev was then, to bring home the bacon.

All I needed was a humble Smithers.

CHAPTER XXI

Charlie Skellington-Green got back into the House too, and we both got our Parliamentary Secretaryships in the new Government. Charles went to Civil Aviation and I to the new Ministry of Fine Arts. It was with mixed feelings that I weighed up the advantages and disadvantages of Charlie's promotion to Ministerial rank. For his sake I was delighted. He was a dear, good fellow, full of charm and a sort of modicum of brains, and very ambitious. He had set his heart upon a political career, and he saw no reason why he should not attain to the highest possible rank in the hierarchy of Government. Those of us who were accustomed to the assessing of men's values through long experience and, perhaps, a little more than our average share of psychological insight, did not rate Charlie quite so highly as he rated himself. We never believed that he had it in him to rise right to the top. But as things turned out neither he nor we will ever know which was right. I admired his sincerity, and his incapacity to tell a lie, and his unselfishness. But he had no worldly sense. If you gave him a piece of bread he had no idea on which side to butter it.

The disadvantage which at first seemed to attach to his promotion to Ministerial rank was that his duties took up much of his time, and I feared that he would be a less frequent visitor at 29 Belgrave Gardens. And it was most important to me that he should not be allowed to slip out of our orbit. Violetta, now firmly entrenched in London in spite of poor Winslow's intermittent entreaties, was more adorable than ever, and I felt that at any moment my wild love for her might make me do something foolish, and precipitate a crisis with Diana. Ever since Diana's half-expressed threat that she might divorce me, our relations had been quiet with the quietness of a dormant volcano. She had said nothing more about Violetta, and it was tacitly assumed between us that I was keeping the promise which had been so unfairly extracted from me by menaces.

It is, I believe, a point in law, and is, I know, a point in chivalry, that promises extracted by menaces are not binding upon anyone, even upon a gentleman. But the menaces were still in the background. Diana, like all women when they think that their dignity is being touched, was utterly implacable and utterly unscrupulous. It was impossible to trust her appearance of placidity.

So I was anxious to reinsure myself against volcanic upheavals, and the best way to effect that insurance was to inveigle Charlie round to Belgrave Gardens as often as possible. Not that he needed inveigling. Diana, although nearly twenty-eight by this time, was still sufficiently attractive to allure a youngish man who was not accustomed, I suppose, to insist upon the best and nothing but the best.

Ministerial work was a great thrill to me. I had wielded authority ever since my father died, ever since I was eighteen, but it was hereditary authority. It was a power which I had not earned for myself. The lives of men and women had been put into my hands by the exertions of parents and grandparents. It was very pleasant that the lives of men and women should be in my hands. I liked it. Who wouldn't? There are few things more satisfactory than the power to make or break.

But until I was thirty-five years of age, that power had been inherited.

Ministerial rank altered all that. It was by my own talents and my own capabilities that I was adopted as a Parliamentary candidate; it was by them that I was elected; by them that I became a notable backbencher; and by them that I was appointed Parliamentary Secretary for the Department of Fine Arts.

I would be the first to agree that my grandfather and father made it possible for me to approach the ladder at all, and I piously applaud them for it. But it was by my own individual exertions that I was able to put my feet upon rung after rung, until I reached the Ministry of Fine Arts.

It was a new Ministry, and obviously the Minister and the Parliamentary Secretary had to be Old Etonians. The quickest way to form traditions for any new institution is to put it in the hands of people who have been brought up in the midst of traditions. You may say that it would have been better to have given the new Ministry to Old Wykehamists, who are even more deeply rooted in tradition than we are. But the answer to that is, that Old Wykehamists know little of the Arts. They are admirable fellows at the classics, and as administrators they carry out instructions faithfully and loyally. But when it comes to individuality, or independence of judgment, it is my experience that Old Wykehamists are lost. Never having been trained to think for themselves, they are bewildered in emergency. Once precedent has been left behind, they have no idea what to do. It is different with us. Probably the perfect Administration would be one which was directed by a couple of Old Etonians, manned by a permanent staff of Old Wykehamists, and with the floors swept and the ink-pots filled by Old Harrovians.

My chief at the Ministry was Henry Pettinger. He was the ideal man for the job. He had always been keenly interested in anything connected with Art. A great reader, a connoisseur of claret, a collector of paintings by such famous men as Tadema, Landseer, Leighton, de Laszlo, and other household names which escape me for the moment, an amateur of embroidery and himself no mean exponent of the art of needlework, an enthusiast for all forms of wood-carving, he was, in addition, a first cousin of the Duke of Hampshire, his mother having been Lady Hermione Peacehaven before her marriage. It will be seen, therefore, that the Prime Minister made a sound choice when he gave the new Ministry to Henry Pettinger.

We made a pretty good team. Pettinger was a worthy soul. He had served the party with a really wonderful loyalty for nearly thirty years, having inherited a safe family seat on the South Coast at the age of twenty-five. He was one of those politicians who try to make up for a mediocre intelligence and a narrowness of vision by assiduity, by fidelity, and by an unfailing readiness to sit on dreary committees, to appear on the platforms of other fellows' constituencies, to obey the mandates of the Whips, and to entertain his own salt-encrusted and sea-blown constituents to huge spreads of strawberries on the Terrace in summer.

But underneath all this modest exterior and unnecessary quietness there lurked an intense political ambition. Very few people had sufficient psychological insight to realize this. I had always suspected it, ever since I first entered Parliament, and the first few days of our collaboration at the new Ministry of Fine Arts confirmed me in my shrewd estimate. On the second day of our term in office, he called me into his room. "Young feller," he said, using that rather unpleasant familiarity which elderly men of fifty-five think they are entitled to use towards young men of thirty-five, irrespective of the comparative talents and achievements of the two— "Young feller, we've got to make a success of this."

I was a little surprised at this, as it had never occurred to me to think that I was going to make anything but a success of it. But the old buster completely disarmed me when he went on, "Don't misunderstand me. You are all right. You're young, and you'll be in the Cabinet before you're fifty. It's different for me. This is the first real job I've had in thirty years." There were tears of emotion in the old chap's eyes, and he pulled his white moustache nervously.

"I've been a pretty good party man," he went on gruffly, "and it was a bit galling to be fobbed off over and over again. I've been Charity Commissioner, Vice-Chamberlain of the Household, and twice a Lord-in-Waiting. If they hadn't abolished them," he added bitterly, "I swear I would have been Whipper-in to the Royal Buck-hounds. The highest I've ever got was a measly Parliamentary Secretaryship to the Ministry of Health." Then his face brightened. "But I've got a real job at last, Fox-Ingleby, and if I make a success of it there's no reason why I shouldn't get the Board of Trade or the Colonies."

"Or the Admiralty, sir," I put in tactfully, and I was delighted to see the glow of complacency which my innocent perjury caused. A lot will be said in Heaven in defence of White Liars. The old fool could never get the Admiralty, or any of the dominant positions in the machine of Government, at a time when administrative talent—naturally it is not for me to say administrative genius—coupled with energy and youth, was knocking so imperatively at the door.

But I have always been strongly in favour of humouring the old, and although my tongue was in my cheek when I spoke those words, "Or the Admiralty," my heart was in its right place. I sincerely meant to please Pettinger. After all, it was at no cost to myself, and I succeeded.

It was a real pleasure to me to watch the poor old fool bridling at my three little words. No one, in my opinion, is worth his salt who does not strive his utmost to make up to the outworn and unsuccessful hulks, as it were, of life, a little of what they have missed upon the high seas of the world. So it was with myself and Pettinger.

"If I get a really big job," he said, "one of the Secretaryships of State, for instance, I shall die happy." He coughed violently to cover up this most un-English lapse into sentimentality, and waved his hand to indicate that the interview was over.

As I returned to my room, I wondered whether Pettinger deserved my admiration as a whole-hearted servant of his country more than my gentle, tolerant contempt for him as an old fogey. But predominant over my doubtful admiration and doubtful contempt was my determination to do everything in my power to make Sir Henry Pettinger's tenure of the new Ministry of Fine Arts a notable one. If it lay in my power—and if it lay in anyone's it lay in mine—to lift Sir Henry into one of the high offices for which his soul craved, then I would spare no toil to do it. Credit would come to the Ministry by my exertions, and I would see that it all went to the amiable Chief, who knew nothing whatsoever about the Arts. I, who had a humble smattering, would be happy to remain obscurely in the background if, by so doing, I could hoist Sir Henry Pettinger into his political paradise.

I suppose it was patriotically immoral of me. The welfare of the country and of the Empire ought to have come first. The man was really only fit for the job which he had tried to dismiss as a joke, the Kennel-keeper of the Buck-hounds. But somehow sentiment creeps in, even into the most realistic of minds, and when the tears glistened in Pettinger's blue eyes—which were watery enough at the best of times—I said to myself, "Dammit, he ought to have India, and I will work myself to the bone to help him to get it."

My task was nothing less than the moulding of the cultural sense of the nation, and it had two main heads. I had to guide taste into the right channels and I had to see that no one else guided it into the wrong. Thus it was just as important to discourage bad influence as to encourage good. To send a promising and impecunious young painter to an Art School with a Government grant was in itself a praiseworthy act; but it was useless from the national point of view if it was not accompanied by drastic measures to keep the most suggestive sorts of French literature from entering our ports. To help a young genius to Valhalla was one thing. But it was almost as important, from the national point of view, to see that our youth was not brought into contacts with those packets of French postcards which are labelled, *"Très rare, très curieux. Discrétion."*

I take a good deal of credit to myself—though, of course, Pettinger got the kudos at the time—for tightening up the administration of the Customs so that such authors as Joyce, whose name was either James or John—I forget which—Stein, Baudelaire, Louÿs, Anatole France, Proust, Freud, Jung, Rolland, and others, were intercepted at the ports by the special Pornographic section of the Constabulary which I created with men borrowed from the uniformed branch of the Metropolitan Police. These men, all of whom could read and write English fluently, performed admirable service in the detection of immoral literature.

Art Exhibitions also came within the scope of my department, and I closed at least a dozen objectionable ones which contained nudes and other suggestive subjects. It was always a matter of regret to me that I was unable to take strong action about Epstein's "Genesis". But the Marchioness of Risborough—a leader of taste and fashion, who was not only *persona gratissima* in exalted circles, but also the daughter of a millionaire steelmaker—had publicly declared her admiration of it, and so there was nothing for me to do except to declare mine. And now, looking back on it, I realize how right I was to choose Lady Risborough's opinion rather than the small advantages to be obtained from Epstein's gratitude. Small tradesmen who tried to sell miniature replicas of the "Genesis" were ruthlessly prosecuted, however, by my department on the charge of exhibiting, or causing to be exhibited, indecent figures.

My department also absorbed the Film Censorship and the Play Censorship. I took a broad view on both. Anything which reflected upon the social fabric of our times, upon the administration of our wonderful system of justice, upon the integrity of the Englishman in whatever circumstance he may find himself, and upon the virtue of our English women in whatever circumstances they may find themselves, was ruthlessly stamped out. And any propaganda which made it appear, even remotely, that Pacifism was desirable, was suppressed. Peace was of no use, after all, to those of us who had fought. We knew.

Oddly enough, it was easier to keep a firm, controlling, hand upon the Drama than upon the Cinema. I never could quite understand why this should be so, in spite of all the theories advanced by my underlings, none of whom had a glimmering of sense, except, of course, the Old Wykehamists, and they were dull.

But I came to the tentative conclusion, after a lot of thought, that the reason might be that the folk who ran the Drama were balancing on a precarious edge of finance, whereas the folk who ran the Cinema were inordinately rich.

The poor are always, and have been throughout the ages, more likely to offend against the canons of good taste than the rich. The lack of breeding, the spirit of revolt, callousness induced by slum-surroundings, insensitiveness to the true beauty, these combine to drive the poor all too often across the border which divides refinement from offence. The rich can be trusted not to err. And so it was that I found it easier to exercise my censorship of the Theatre than of the Cinema. Besides, a lot of the Cinema fellows were friends of mine.

In Architecture my policy was simple and straightforward in a British way. I laid down the cardinal British rule that sturdy individualism was the best, and that anyone could destroy what he liked (provided, of course, that it belonged to him). In other words, I encouraged the real-estate owners of the country to enjoy precisely the same freedom which I had allowed to myself at Lovely Mount. It was not for me to deny to my fellow-citizens what I insisted upon for myself. "So long as I occupy this position," I said in the House when the Estimates of my department came up, "I will not be a party to the proposition that there is one law for the rich and another for the poor, unless exceptional circumstances warrant the differentiation, and even then I should require to be convinced beyond a shadow of dubiety that the rich were sufficiently rich or the poor sufficiently poor to justify such an un-English discrimination." (I quote from Hansard.)

As a result of this liberal policy (I use the word "liberal" in its best conservative sense, and not in its dirty political sense), some notable architectural changes took place in my time.

Of course I did not get my own way all the time. Every reformer finds his obstructionists. But the only major set-backs which I suffered architecturally were my failures in the City of London and at Stonehenge. In both cases Meddlesome Matties were to blame. In conjunction with the Ecclesiastical Authorities a scheme had been drawn up by my department for enriching the life, both spiritual and aesthetic, of the new suburban communities which were springing up on the outskirts of London. It was, in effect, the earlier scheme of the Bishop of London, brought up to date, revivified, and informed with a new driving-force. The redundant churches in the City were to be pulled down, with all the reverence due to Wren's reputation and, of course, to the sacredness of the sites; the sites were to be reverently deconsecrated and sold to the banks and insurance companies, the financial stability of which is the cause of the eminence of London as the money centre of the world; and new churches were to be erected in suburbia on a standardized, and therefore inexpensive, model which had been designed specially for me by a young American architect from Denver, Colorado. He was a cousin of Winslow Starrett's and I pleased Winslow, the poor fish, by employing him. His name was Imer B. Pett. What a name!

But the whole thing fell to the ground (unlike, unfortunately, Wren's churches). For a grotesque outburst of what is called "Public Opinion" induced me, against my better judgment, to withdraw the scheme and leave suburbia to damnation for all eternity, or at any rate for the next few years. As a matter of fact, the whole deplorable business cost me two hundred pounds, for I had advised Winslow Starrett to form a small corporation which would acquire the copyright of the standardised church-model from his young cousin and sell it to my department, thus benefiting everyone and harming no one. Indeed I had made it perfectly clear to Winslow that unless this corporation was formed, with a generous allotment of the Ordinary shares to certain nominees of my own, there could be no question of our employing young Pett at all. My department, I explained, was a British one in every sense of the word and we could not buy from an American citizen but only from a British-controlled corporation or company. When the scheme was withdrawn, it was only fair that I should reimburse Winslow for a portion, at least, of his outlay. Winslow himself rather unreasonably thought that I should reimburse him with a percentage of his expenses nearer to one hundred than twenty-five, but that idea was quickly pooh-poohed. Winslow was left with the copyright of the model on his hands, for he had bought it on behalf of the new corporation from Pett. I often wonder what he did with it. But after all, the money stayed in his family. Winslow lost it, but Pett got it, and nothing can really be said to be lost if a cousin gets it.

The other failure which I suffered was in my attempt to co-ordinate the work of governmental departments and to join with the Air Ministry in popularizing Stonehenge with such things as tea-rooms, canteens, milk-bars, chocolate-kiosks, soda-fountains, and parking-places for motor-cars, in the immediate vicinity of the interesting Druidical remains.

This scheme also was defeated by the reactionary elements, headed by *The Times* newspaper and supported by every crank in the country. Fortunately the financial side of this failure was insignificant. My friend Toby Betchworth, who had somehow got wind of the proposal, had not actually bought the land round Stonehenge. He had only secured a two months' option, which had cost him a matter of three hundred pounds or so. Toby could well afford the trifling loss, and I laughed off his suggestion that we might split it. As I humorously pointed out, over a dry martini at White's, there was nothing on paper.

But against these two defeats could be set my victories along every new by-pass of those years. The activities of the Council for the Preservation of Rural England in the matter of Lovely Mount had by no means faded into oblivion in my mind. While it is certainly true of me that I have never forgotten a friend or a kind action, it is perhaps also true that seldom have I forgotten, even after many years, an enemy. It is the old fighting spirit of the Normans in me, I suppose. So it was with especial satisfaction that I defended the rights of property-owners alongside the new by-passes to build whatever they liked and to change whatever they liked. It is the literal truth that it is entirely owing to me that there is no hateful Continental regimentation of building on such great roads as the Kingston By-pass and the Great West Road.

This, then, was the background of my life during 1925 and 1926. It was a busy, vivid life, full of cares and responsibilities, but full also of the intense joy which comes of the consciousness of a big job well done.

My domestic troubles were a sorry contrast, and it has always been an enigma to me how anyone could have been so heartless, or thoughtless, or perhaps both, as to subject a public servant, in the heat and toil of the midday sun of his public service, to such mental torment as I was subjected to in those years.

CHAPTER XXII

It was in the autumn of 1925 that the firm of private detectives which I had been employing for several months, reported to me at last that Diana had gone off the rails and had betrayed my honour. She had visited a small hotel in Lincoln with Charlie Skellington-Green and had lived with him there for a week-end as man and wife.

To say that I was appalled would be to put it very mildly. That a potential liaison between the two had been, as you might say, simmering for a good long time was obvious to anyone of my perceptions. Hence the employment of the firm of private detectives. But somehow when the blow fell, it seemed almost staggering in its unexpectedness. My wife unfaithful to me! My wife preferring another man's arms to mine! Stabbing me in the back when I was up to my eyes in the work of the nation! And, almost the unkindest stroke, choosing Lincoln of all places. For not only had a Socialist won the seat at a recent by-election in which I had taken a prominent part in the campaign on behalf of our fellow, but also I had been departmentally engaged in an attempt to preserve one or two of the artistic and architectural glories of that ancient city. It was I, for example, who frustrated the iniquitous scheme to sell the Rose Window in the Cathedral to the new Methodist Church in Oklahoma City in order to provide funds for the restoration of the Cathedral itself. The scheme was in train, and might well have slipped through without the general public's knowledge. Fortunately I was on the watch. The price of liberty is, as we all know, eternal vigilance. But the price of the Rose Window was utterly absurd. Unless Oklahoma City is prepared, I said firmly, to treble its offer, and to put it through the reputable New York firm of Starrett and Starrett, Inc., the Rose Window remains in Lincoln. I will rush a Bill through the two Houses, I said, to prohibit the export of the window. Not while I am Under-Secretary, I said, will vandalism rear its ugly head in East Anglia.

Of course I so arranged matters that Sir Henry Pettinger got the credit for saving the window. For myself, it was nothing. But any little public kudos that he could acquire was another help towards Health or the Admiralty or India. Besides, if the suggested trebling of the offer, which Oklahoma refused to consider, and the small matter of the brokerage to Starrett and Starrett, Inc., had become public, it occurred to me that it was just as well that Pettinger should make the necessary explanations in the House. Where the credit lies, let the explanations lie also, as some poet or other has written. I have always been a devout admirer of Shakespeare, and I agree so profoundly when he says, through the mouth of Mark Antony:

> And though we lay these honours on this man,
> To ease ourselves of divers slanderous loads,
> He shall but bear them as the ass bears gold,
> To groan and sweat under the business,
> Either led or driven, as we point the way.

Naturally I do not mean to imply that Pettinger really was an ass, although of course he was, but I could not help feeling that it was undoubtedly his business, as Minister, to bear any divers slanderous loads that might be going about. But the necessity did not arise, and no one, not even Pettinger, ever knew of my attempt to save the centuries-old fabric of Lincoln Cathedral. I am perfectly well aware that if the hill-billies, or Ozarkians, or whatever the people who inhabit Oklahoma City are called, had accepted the far-seeing offer which I made them, there would have been no need for the Dean and Chapter of Lincoln to weary their declining years with appeals for funds to restore their heritage of splendour. All could have been done at the cost of a few square yards of glass. But my scheme broke down and, in consequence, their Cathedral nearly broke down too.

There was a curious sequel to the episode. The Society for the Preservation of Ancient Buildings, in gratitude for my firm stand in the matter of the window, elected me an honorary vice-president. In spite of my detestation of this meddlesome society after the Lovely Mount episode, I accepted the vice-presidency. It was a wise move, for I did not know for certain at that time that the whole story of my effort to save Lincoln Cathedral was not going to become public. If it does become public, I argued at the time, my action is certain to be misunderstood, and it will be a fine defence against any outbreak of ecclesiastical petulance if I can point to the official benison clapped upon me by the S.P.A.B. As it turned out, of course, nothing happened, and I might just as well have refused the vice-presidency.

To return: it was this very city, where I had fought so doughtily for the Party, and where I had campaigned so far-sightedly for the preservation of the historical monuments, that Diana and Charlie Green selected, out of all others in the land, to betray me in.

It is not my intention to set down in black and white, for all the fool world which runs to read, what I thought about Diana's conduct. There are certain reticences of soul which cannot be untied. There are inmost sacred groves of the heart in which no alien foot, however gentle, must be allowed to tread. Besides, no man who is a man will permit a single sentence or phrase to be spoken in derogation of his wife in any circumstances whatever. Still less will he, by word, written or uttered, or by thought, or by deed, provide the material from which any derogation of his wife could be constructed by strangers.

So I will suppress all my feelings of passionate and just resentment and will simply record the fact that Diana's behaviour with Charlie Green made Delilah seem by comparison like a cross between Martha, sister of Mary, and Florence Nightingale, O.M. It was not for nothing that Dante put four men, all traitors, and no women, into his lowest Inferno. If he had started putting women in, the place would have been so cluttered up that all sense of perspective would have been lost, and the place would have been just like any Presentation at Court. So let us leave Diana unscathed. She shared my bed and board for five years, and there is a soft, tender spot in every man's heart for a woman who has done that. Whatever she may turn out to be, traitress, or harlot, or common bore, or, as in Diana's case, all three, he cannot find it in his heart to throw the first stone. There is a great deal to be said, on occasion, for Scriptural precept.

I will say no more about her.

But when I think of Charlie Skellington–Green, it is a totally different matter. My blood boils, and it is with difficulty that I can restrain my pen. A fine thing it would be if a Minister of the Crown, the Minister of Fine Arts, with control of the Censorship of Literature, had to indict himself for the use of blasphemous language and slanderous invective on the initiative of his own department. But when I say Minister of the Crown, and Minister of Fine Arts, I am anticipating. I will be moderate. Let me state my case as temperately as is humanly possible.

Charlie was my friend, "faithful and just to me." Those are ironical words of Mark Antony's. I wish to God Charlie had been faithful and just to me.

He was my colleague in the Government. I had spoken on his platforms. I had wept at his defeats and rejoiced in his successes. And when he was defeated I had brought him to my home and made him a welcome guest, and begged my beautiful Diana to solace the youth in his distress with her gentle sympathy. But it was only metaphorically that I begged her to let his head lie upon her breast. It was only in the spirit of poesy that I quoted Browning's stuff about "the breast's superb abundance where a man might base his head." But he, and she—damn them both!—took my advice literally in a wretched tavern in my beautiful Lincoln.

I had put him up for my clubs. I had guaranteed his overdraft. Not only that, but I had completely hidden my chagrin when he unexpectedly paid it off, out of a legacy from some childish old family retainer, who had fitted him into his lace-collar and revolting buckled-shoes when he was a mewling and puking infant of six. I wish to Heaven he had mewled and puked himself into another and better world before he was seven. Through me he had climbed into circles of society unattainable otherwise. It was owing to a timely word from me that he gave up his chase of the dazzlingly alluring girl in the Burlington Arcade—High-heeled Hilda, she was known as—who certainly would have given him an exciting time and, according to my information, might have given him something else as well. It was on my advice that he put a packet on Woolavington's Captain Cuttle in the 1922 Derby at eighteen to one, before the betting shortened to tens.

I was, in fact, Charlie Skellington-Green's guardian angel.

He repaid my benefactions by taking my wife to Lincoln.

Well, it takes all sorts to make a world, unfortunately, and those of us who are turned into mugs, and worse, by our very simplicity, must just suffer. But Charlie Green was a bad judge of character. Or perhaps I should say a poor choice of cuckold. He thought that I, with all my tolerant philosophy and good-nature, would not object to being made into the universal, central figure of the traditional Parisian farce. He did not quite understand the sort of man I am, or the sort of

215

man that often underlies the apparently vague dreamer. And probably he reckoned on the known fact that I had heavy duties at that particular moment and that the range of my public cares was very wide. It was in that very week, for instance, that I was making the decision to stock the London Parks with sweet-william during the following spring, to be succeeded by potted begonias and calceolarias; that I was forbidding the cultivation of window-boxes in coast-guard stations because it took the attention of the personnel off their coast-wise watch; that I was suppressing a film which showed that painful and unmentionable diseases could be cured if taken in time; that I was arranging for an all-British exhibit of cricket-bats, cricket-pads, gloves, score-boards, popping-crease-markers, stumps, bails, and balls, in the forthcoming Exposition de Tourisme, Viticulture, et Énergie Hydraulique at Grenoble; and that I was painting Carlton House Terrace.

But if Master Charles thought that public responsibility and private dreams would immoblize me, he was sadly out.

I sprang to arms with all my accustomed decisiveness.

The report of the detectives reached me on a Monday in Le Touquet, where I was playing a little quiet golf with Violetta, and by six o'clock in the evening I had reached Belgravia via the Croydon air-port. Two telegrams, phrased in a guarded but emphatic manner, had ensured the presence of the two betrayers and, after I had poured myself out a glass of Amontillado, I began:

"I am not offering you a drink, Green, because there is no reason why you should drink in my house ever again. As for you, Diana, I am not offering you a drink, because I do not choose to."

This opening struck the right note of implacable sternness, and in set, measured tones, I told the guilty pair what I thought of them.

"We love each other," said Diana at the end, with

maddening tranquillity.

"That I know to be impossible," I replied with some warmth. "After being married to me for five years, you could not look at anyone else. But it is just as well that you should feel some sort of affection for him, even a transient affection. It will make your divorce a little easier for you."

"Are you going to divorce her?" asked Charlie.

" I am."

"Won't that make you out to be rather a swine?"

"Or you perhaps, even more?" I enquired blandly.

"That doesn't matter," he replied. "I was thinking of Diana."

"It is a time-honoured cliché, my dear Charles," I observed, "to say that you ought to have started thinking of her a little earlier, but nevertheless it is a very true one."

"Last year I spared you," said Diana, "when I had you in the hollow of my hand."

"That was entirely different," I pointed out. " It is always different for a man when his career is at stake."

"What about my career?" asked Charles, and again it had to be explained to him that he might well have thought of that before.

Diana asked if it was not unfair to ruin Charles when she had refrained from ruining me.

"My good girl," I replied a little impatiently. It was enough to make a Saint impatient. Nothing was to be gained by dragging up the past in this futile way; realism demands that only the present and the future should be discussed in a crisis—"My good girl, can't you distinguish between a wife's threat to ruin her husband and a husband's threat to ruin the man who has dishonoured his matrimonial couch? You have never been intellectually very bright, but surely even you can see that."

"I can only see that I was generous to you, and that you are not being generous to me," she murmured.

"Fiddle-de-dee!" I exclaimed with justifiable rudeness at this sophistry. "What do you expect me to do? Allow you to go sleeping all over England with Charlie, and make me the laughing-stock of the country? Thank you very much indeed, but you're not going to have me for a mug quite so simply. I may be green, but I'm not so green as all that. With apologies, my dear Charles," I added sardonically, "for the metaphorical use of your name."

He paid no attention to my witticism but said thoughtfully, "If Diana cross-petitioned and cited Violetta, nobody could get a divorce and both our political careers would be dished."

"You'll have a job to prove that I've slept with Violetta during the last month or so, my boy," I retorted triumphantly, "and that is all that matters, provided that I don't go near her while the case is going on."

"What about Le Touquet this last week-end?" he murmured, studying his finger-nails.

At that I confess I lost my temper. "So you've been spying on me, you dirty swine!" I shouted. "You're not content with seducing the wife of a friend and a colleague and a benefactor, but you must add filthy snooping as well," and I went on in that vein for a moment or two, winding up with the victorious paean, "and we were careful to stay at different hotels, you howling sweep, and not in the same bed as you did"—to refresh my memory I glanced at my detectives' report, which I had been brandishing in their faces— "in Room No.46 in the Black Bull in Lincoln, the third room on the left-hand side from the top of the stairs on the second floor. Black shoes, gent.'s, and green suède, Delman's, lady's. Double bed."

There was no real answer to that, and Diana turned on an emotional tap.

"What about Anne?"

"That will be for the judge to decide," I answered stiffly. I was not going to be diddled by sob-stuff. "But I should hardly think he is likely to take the child away from the innocent father and award it to the guilty wife."

"Dammit, man," cried Green, "you aren't going to take a kid away from its mother?"

"I should have thought the responsibility lay rather with you," I replied, and with that I went off to the Carlton Club, where my solicitor was certain to be drinking his evening glass of sherry.

Preparations for the service of the writ having been put in train, the next thing was to explain the situation to Violetta, and she arrived on the following day by the midday aeroplane. To my astonishment and, on reflection, to my gratification, she was furiously angry.

"Do you think I'm going to lead a pure, chaste, maidenly existence?" she exclaimed in that melodiously stilted brand of English which is employed so often by Americans, which comes from reading short stories in American magazines by illiterate authoresses, and which is invariably ascribed by Americans themselves to a sort of linguistic hangover from the golden age of Elizabethan prose. Wrongly ascribed. "Am I to pass the long night hours alone in my virginal dimity," she went on in a high-pitched Massachusetts shrill, "for nine whole months while your old English law creaks along? Not me." I am not at all sure that she did not say " Not this baby," but happily I am unable to recall all her painful eccentricities of speech. In essence, she flatly refused to agree to any such arrangement, and left me to choose between abandoning my divorce and abandoning her.

She was a foolish woman—most women are foolish, I have found in my long experience of the world and its follies—and she did not understand that there is a difference between those who can be blackmailed and those who cannot. My opportunity to divorce Diana had been long in coming, and it might be long in coming again, whereas Violetta, adorable though she was, could not be described as indispensable to my happiness, either mental or physical.

As a matter of fact, I had been getting a little bored with Violetta for some time. She was within a measurable distance of becoming as exacting as if I had been not only an American business-man with a face like a suet-pudding, but her husband at that. She had been several times on the very brink of ordering me about, and once, in Deauville, she had kicked up an undignified row in a street because I refused to carry a large brown paper parcel for her. She had also twice referred in terms of regretful affection to the tedious Winslow, and a woman who mentions her husband to her lover in any other terms than those of jocular derision is asking for trouble. The end, in fact, was approaching in any case, and when she gave me the choice between divorce and herself, I unhesitatingly made the right choice.

I do not use the word "right" from a selfish point of view. Please do not make any mistake about that. My sole motive was to save my innocent little daughter, Anne, from a household in which the Charlie Greens of this world are at liberty to carry on their promiscuous amours with the mother and lady of the house. It was unthinkable that I should let my love for Violetta selfishly ruin poor little Anne's life. A man who was capable of that would be capable of anything.

There is no question whatever that I, who have always prided myself on my modernity and up-to dateness, am laying myself open to the charge of being old-fashioned almost to the point of Victorianism when I discuss my attitude to children. But there—the risk must be taken, and there are those of us who can stand, unruffled, a good deal of criticism. Briefly, my attitude has always been that the child must come first. The parents do not count, not even the father. It is true that the father has to bear the burden of what his wife thrusts upon him—for, as I have already jotted down in my explanation of the Life Force and its effect upon short skirts and low-cut gowns, it is always the woman who insists on race-perpetuation by herself at the expense of a man, in theory any man but preferably and usually her husband. But we can be magnanimous enough to forget that we are the butts of a woman-made world. Fools we may be, but an understanding Providence has made us generous fools. So children always come first with us. The mothers kohl and paint and dance their macabre sarabands,

> Like strange mechanical grotesques,
> Making fantastic arabesques,

as that Irish bounder Wilde said, but it is the fathers who are everlastingly on guard at the nursery gate at the top of the stairs.

So it was with me and Anne.

It is true that I might appear, superficially, to have paid little attention to her. I had a vast range of other activities. There was my pre-occupation with national affairs, for example, and the care of my dependants on my estate at Grantly, and the various charitable balls at Dorchester House or Grosvenor House to which I lent my name and patronage, and my week-end visits, in search of earned recuperation and rest, to the seaside towns in the departments of Pas de Calais, Somme, Seine Inférieure, Eure, and Calvados.

But in spite of my wide responsibilities, I often found time to visit little Anne's nursery and to put the two nurses through a catechism about their duties and their qualifications. The child herself was, of course, the same as all other children of that age—entrancing for five, or even seven minutes, and then rather tiresome. But I never grudged the time spent in these visits to the nursery—for, when you come to think of it, the moulding of that sweet, fresh mind rested entirely with me—and it was always with a feeling of good work well done that I used to hand the brat back to her nurses at the end of my visit.

You will readily understand that, with this paternal instinct ablaze in my breast, I was not going to allow my little Anne, the apple of my eye, to be turned over to the tender mercies of Diana and her paramour.

CHAPTER XXIII

Violetta, not to put too fine a point upon it, kicked up the very devil. There is something strangely un-subtle in an American woman's behaviour in an emotional crisis. But, on reflection, I think I am wronging American women. Fundamentally they are no different to those of other hemispheres. They are only a trifle, perhaps, cruder. All women scream in an emotional crisis. The American note, or pitch, or key—I have never had the time to become a musician, so the technical jargon escapes me—is shriller than others. That is my experience. Violetta was, unquestionably, the shrillest thing that had ever come my way. She positively squealed with rage. It was very undignified. And, what made it even more awkward than the lack of dignity, she became almost unintelligible.

The feminine American voice occasionally sounds almost musical. When the feminine American owner of the voice is lying happily and snugly in one's arms, for instance, the voice can very nearly be compared to the song which the Sirens sang. Odysseus would have admired it almost as intensely as he admired the voices of those dangerous ladies, if he could have seen the owner of it in the circumstances in which I had so often seen my Violetta. So beneficial an influence does a New England body exercise over a New England twang.

But when the feminine American voice loses its charm, when it is piped up in chattering anger, when it is no longer murmuring sweet Pennsylvanian blandishments to a lover from a half-muffled rose-petal mouth, then it sounds like a high-powered circular saw at work upon a piece of corrugated iron.

So it was with my sweet Violetta.

Within thirty seconds of my telling her that I had decided, after careful consideration, to go ahead with my divorce and that she could do what she liked about it, she sprang out of bed, pulled up her garters, as all women do when they spring out of bed—it is a reflex action—and flew into a rage.

"You howling swine," she screamed. When I say "screamed," I mean that she made the loudest noise which a woman dares to make when she is wearing stockings, garters, and one ear-ring, the other having fallen off at an earlier stage.

I rearranged the pillows and lay back, sleekly, and looked at her. "Sweet one," I said, in that purring tone which never fails either to infuriate or enchant a woman, according to her mood and according to the way in which the words are spoken, "as you stand there, your body would be the loveliest thing that God ever made, if it was not that God has also made the London climate."

"What exactly do you mean?" Violetta asked, tapping the ground with her right heel in the traditional way in which women try to convey the impression that they are uncontrollably angry.

I jumped out of bed, picked up her dainty black shoes, with their enormously high heels, knelt down in front of her, put the shoes on her small feet, kissed both her insteps, and then looked up at her.

"What's the idea?" she said coldly.

"Only to help you to tap the ground harder," I said with a cheerful laugh.

She tried very hard to keep her temper. I will say that for her.

"What did you mean," she went on, with a superb affectation of indifference, "when you said that I would be lovely except for the climate?"

"There's a large black smut on your divine left breast," I replied.

That was the end of a wonderful romance. Those words finished it. And yet, and yet, how unfair it was. Why, in the name of reason, should Violetta have chosen that simple sentence as the excuse for throwing me aside like an old glove? What justification had she for such relentless cruelty?

Consider my position. There she was, standing in front of me in all her dazzling whiteness. There it was, the flawless body which I had adored for so long. But there was a black smut from our detestable London climate upon that exquisite breast. A boor, a clown, an animal, a clod to whom beauty meant nothing, would have said, "Oh well, it doesn't matter," or "Anyway, what is the difference between black and white?"

I could not say anything like that. I am, whatever else can be said against me, an amateur of beauty.

The tiniest flaw in a work of Art or Nature is as distressing to me as a vulgarism.

What was I to do? Was I to say, "Beloved, you are the loveliest thing in the world?" Or was I to say, "Violetta, there's a black smut on your left breast?"

I am an honest man, and I spoke the truth.

The result was cylonic. Violetta exploded into a frantic rage. She snatched off the high-heeled shoes, which had been so chivalrously clamped on to her feet a moment before, and flung them at my head with the usual result of feminine throwing. I kept quite still, from long experience, while the shoes crashed out of the window into the street below, and she followed up the shoes with a few hair-brushes, clothes-brushes, and bottles of scent. The street below, Park Lane, must have looked like the Caledonian Market for a few minutes. I remember to this day the crash of an ormolu clock as it struck the pavement, while the tinkle of glass was like the sound of April rain in a birch-wood. At the end of the first phase, Act One as it were, Violetta stood in front of me, panting, magnificent, many-curved.

"Well," she said venomously.

"Beautiful," I replied; "you have gone a long, expensive, and roundabout way about it, but at least you have succeeded, with all your voluptuous physical exertions, in shaking off the black smut."

That was meant to soothe her, but it did not. She stopped throwing things and turned to invective. But I was tired. I had reason to be. An imperious gesture brought her to a halt.

"Violetta," I said, with a sort of masterful tact, "the behaviour of a fishwife is not excused even by a pair of legs as beautiful as yours, nor can I allow the language of the Lower East Side of your filthy New York City to be carried off by the undeniable fact that your body, when unblemished by smudges, is perfect in shape, texture, and colour."

She stormed more than ever like a harridan at this, and finally I had to leave her flat without saying good-bye.

It was a painful ending to what had been a lovely episode. There had been a fragrance about our relationship which one rarely finds in this dark world. Violetta would have been the ideal wife for me, once she had got rid of that stupid American notion of thinking for herself instead of behaving like the normal woman of all time and accepting the thoughts of her husband. She had a wit almost to match my own, charm to grace my table, voluptuousness to adorn my bed, vivacity buoyant enough not to drain my stores of vitality, and an adoration of me. But the temper which she displayed over this matter of my divorce, the language which she used, the commonness which she involuntarily exhibited, made me understand that I was right in my first instinct. Violetta was a mistress, not a wife. So I parted from her without very much of a pang, except perhaps an occasional sigh of regret for the delectable contours of her person.

It took precisely twenty-four hours for the truth of that old gag about Hell and a Woman Scorned to be painfully brought home to me. One has always known in theory that the Woman Scorned is a pretty fierce object, and that poets and playwrights have made great use of the theory. But in practice one has usually found that however much one scorns a woman—that is to say, refuses to continue being her lover after a fortnight or so, and pensions her off with a bangle or a brooch or whatever chances to be the fashionable gift of the moment wherewith to discard a boring mistress—it makes no real difference to her love. She goes on adoring just the same. Now that I come to think of it, perhaps that is the real meaning of the word Hell in that proverb. To be adored by a discarded mistress is pure torture. One takes them out to dinner twice a year and each time they contrive to burst into tears in the Ivy Restaurant when it is crowded with friends and gossip-writers and, worst of all, women who are madly anxious to be in the position that the discarded mistress once was in. One sends the poor discarded sweets a Christmas present of a book-token or a *foie-gras* pie, and they ring up every morning for a fortnight to thank you. In the end, one finds them on one's doorstep, when they are trying to pay a last desperate call, or play a last desperate card, whichever you like to call it, and one slaps them on their shell-pink ear and they adore one more than ever.

And that certainly is hellish, because it makes one look ridiculous. Poets and playwrights are very glib and spry with their aphorisms, laying down the law about this and that most confidently, but they never explain the really important things which worry us poor illiterates.

Why is it that a man who is notoriously worshipped by a woman looks, feels, and is, an ass, whereas a woman who is notoriously worshipped by a man moves through the world like an Empress? If a man is scorned, it must be, I imagine— indeed, I have often been told—very unpleasant indeed for him; but the woman who has done the scorning would be indignant if he did not still weigh in with his flowers and his sighs, and if he did not parade his broken heart before that part of the world which matters. But when it is the other way about, the man simply becomes a figure of fun.

So when there is any scorn being distributed by either party, it is the man who gets the worst of it always. The best thing is, I suppose, to fall in love with someone who falls in love with you. But there is much food for thought in the words of Alexander the Great when he captured Stateira, the wife of Darius of Persia. Stateira was by repute the most beautiful woman in all the Kingdom of Persia—and that went from the Mediterranean Sea to the valley of the Indus and south to Memphis and north-east to Samarcand—and when the jubilant captains announced their prize, obviously thinking that they would get at least a fortnight's holiday when Alexander saw the lovely creature, they were sadly disappointed when Alexander refused even to see her, speaking the memorable words, "Women are a torment to the eyes and it is best to avoid temptation."

How right he was. And how easy it is to make such slick remarks. And how hellishly difficult it is to act up to the spirit of them. And how ludicrous it is to want to try to act up to the spirit of them.

To return. Violetta was the exceptional woman who proved to me that once in a while poets can stumble upon a part-truth. She certainly was a Fury, and it was difficult not to admire her American efficiency in the technique of hatred.

It went for nothing with her that we had been exquisitely happy together for more than two years; that we had slept together in almost every beauty-spot in the South of England (as the sweet Violetta was an American citizeness, I had naturally pandered to the American Niagara-Grand-Canyon complex, and tried my best only to sleep with her in famous English beauty-spots); it went for nothing with her that not once but a score of times I had taken risks for her sake which might easily have ruined my wonderful, almost meteoric, political career; that I had been—this can be said without the slightest suspicion of boasting—a better lover than she would ever have found upon the North-American Continent; and that I had truly and sincerely loved her.

All that went for nothing.

Within twenty-four hours of leaving Violetta, I received a cable from Winslow warning me that he was going to divorce her and cite me as co-respondent.

Think of the swiftness with which she had acted. Think of the decisiveness of mind she must have possessed all the time. I had thought of her as a lovely and voluptuous pussy-cat, with a contralto purr, and a fondness for being stroked, and a smooth, responsive body. It had somehow never occurred to me that she might also have the feline claws and the feline temperament; that she might lie on her back, glossily, paws in air, playing gently and liking the world, while all was going well for her; but that she would become a wild-cat, a tearing, raging, terrifying lynx, when things went badly for her.

In the day and night which had elapsed since she had behaved so outrageously and had used such Americano-Billingsgate language to me in her flat in Park Lane (the rent of which, incidentally, I had been partly paying for through the commissions which Winslow had been raking in from my business in Wall Street), Violetta had grabbed (a word which perfectly describes her more temperamental and coarser gestures) the transatlantic telephone to Winslow and had ordered him to file a suit instantly, naming me as co-respondent.

I learnt afterwards that at first he had strongly objected. Poor fool! Strong objections from an American husband to a course of action proposed, which is the same thing as ordered, imperatively, by an American wife, are like a straw barricade against a north-east gale.

It is true that her telephone-call cost her forty-two pounds, at a pound a minute. But that was not due to Winslow's Sales-Resistance, as I believe the expression is. Violetta broke down the poor old boy's spirit in less than seven minutes, and the other thirty-five pounds was the price which the ordinary American man or woman has to pay for his, or her, incapacity to let well alone. After they have stated a case, about half as clearly and about one-quarter as concisely as any Englishman would have stated it, the Americans have to state it again in a different way, and then, just to make sure, in a third way, each becoming more prolix than the last.

Thus Violetta's original seven minutes expanded into forty-two, with a corresponding expansion of the telephone bill.

But the result was the same for me as if she had confined herself to the economic seven. Winslow telegraphed his intention to cite me as co-respondent.

CHAPTER XXIV

It will be obvious that I was in a very awkward corner. Indeed it is no exaggeration to say that I was faced with the ruin of everything I had laboriously built up and—what was infinitely worse—with the simultaneous shattering of every ideal which I had preserved unsullied in my humble passage through life.

It was bad enough that my political career should be blasted just at the moment when I was winning my spurs in the new Ministry; bad enough that the country should lose all the artistic improvements which I was planning to introduce into its everyday life, and should lose them at the hands of Americans, too; bad enough that the country should lose the services of one of the few survivors of the war generation who had the talents, and the public spirit, to continue to serve the common weal after the end of the war.

But all that could have been borne. No one—yes, I repeat it—no one is indispensable.

The rending of my ideals was a totally different matter. That was irreparable.

It was a bitter thought to me that Winslow Starrett, my friend, my old familiar friend, whom I had trusted so implicitly with a very large part of my fortune, should have turned and bitten the hand, so to speak, which fed him. It was a bitter thought to me that Violetta, whom I had adored so faithfully and so long, should have become a vulgarian Jezebel at the prospect of a few months of enforced chastity. Where are your pedestals now, Edward Fox-Ingleby? I mused sadly. Where are your goddesses? What use has a lifetime of chivalry been to you, a lifetime of reverence and service? All you get as a result, I said with a sneer at my ludicrous and pathetic quixotry, is treachery and disillusion. Worship them as you may, I said, you will find them merciless in the end.

And they will not even be merciful to their own sex. Violetta was not merely trampling me, who had loved her, into the mire. She was ruining Diana's chance of a divorce as well. For if I was co-respondent in one suit and plaintiff in the other, the King's Proctor would have the laugh of his life, and it was not to be supposed that I would humiliate myself to the depths of being the guilty co-respondent in the one and the guilty respondent in the other. If I had sinned, through an overwhelming, and therefore perhaps pardonable, love, so had Charlie Skellington-Green sinned, through his beastly animal desires; and if I was to suffer, so was he going to suffer. Thus if Starrett brought his suit and cited me, Diana and I would be tied together for life, and at least Charlie Green would be stung.

Nor was this all. Violetta was striking at me, at Diana, and at the miserable Charlie. But—and this was completely unforgivable—she was striking also at my poor, sweet, innocent, little Anne.

Obviously, whatever happened, I could never go back to Diana. And if, by some monstrous blend of injustice and ill-fortune, a judge could be found who would overlook the infamy of the Black Bull at Lincoln, Diana might ultimately manage to divorce me and secure custody of Anne.

Think of the life to which Violetta would then be exposing my precious little one: a life under the same roof as Charlie Green, the seducer of his friend's wife. Paramour Green, I have no doubt our mutual friends would soon have been calling him, just as I have no doubt that those same dear mutual friends would have been calling me Fox-Cuckoldby, or even worse.

No. It was not to be borne.

Heredity is a queer thing. My father—rest his strange, liberal soul—was admired for several qualities but never, so far as I ever ascertained, for quickness of mind. My grandfather's slowness was as proverbial in Midhamptonshire as his sureness. Yet I have only been proud of one real talent in my make-up, besides the talent for making and keeping men friends (naturally I take the pleasing of the fair sex as an art and not as a talent), and that is promptness to act in a crisis. Napoleon, my hero, said that in an emergency it was better to do the wrong thing vigorously than the right thing vacillatingly, and on the whole I am inclined to agree with him, although the first of the two alternatives has never actually come within the semicircle of my horizon.

I had to act, and act with devastating swiftness and effect.

I did. I cabled to Winslow begging him in the name of our old friendship not to do anything drastic and irrevocable for a week, and then, without a word to a soul, I caught the *Mauretania* and sailed for America.

CHAPTER XXV

I kept myself very much to myself upon the liner. There are times upon transoceanic travel when one is prepared to join in the simple festivities of ship-board with the most personable of the young women among the passengers, or even in the less simple festivities if one or two happen to be more personable than usual.

But on this occasion I was preoccupied with serious thoughts, and I had even arranged to have my name kept off the passenger list.

My political future was in the balance for one thing; for another, my chance of divorcing Diana and obtaining custody of Anne was on the brink of falling down; for yet another I was facing the possible ignominy of being worsted by Charlie Green; and, as if all that was not enough for any man to bear, there was the critical financial aspect of the whole business.

For I had entrusted more than a half of my entire fortune to Winslow Starrett to be invested in American stocks. He had his hands upon nearly two hundred thousand pounds of mine at that very moment, and it made me break out in perspiration, even when I was standing in the cool breezes of the boat-deck, to think what might happen if it occurred to him to sacrifice his professional integrity to a desire for revenge. He might play the very devil with my money out of sheer malignant spite.

The only bright gleam upon a cloud-menaced sky was that Americans are, in the main, slow thinkers, and that Winslow was conspicuously slow even among his compatriots. The dastardly scheme might not have occurred to him in the five days which must elapse before I could reach New York. There was also a second gleam, fainter but still just discernible, that he might be sufficiently honourable not to commit such a black breach of trust. I put a good deal less trust in the latter chance than in the former, because it has been my sad experience in life that most men miss opportunities of playing a scurvy trick only through stupidity and through failure to grasp the opportunity, rather than through a sense of honour.

On the third day out I reached the conclusion that my only hope of getting a breathing-space lay in Winslow's slowness of intellect, and that in the meantime there was nothing which I could do about it. So I came gracefully out of the romantic aloofness which had so intrigued the feminine portion of the passengers, and allowed one or two of them to entertain me in a manner which was, I fancy, highly satisfactory to all concerned.

But in spite of these small diversions no traveller to America ever saw the Manhattan Sky-Line with greater thankfulness than I did. As a rule it has always seemed to me to be a tedious affair, as a whole series of Christmas cakes must appear to one who dislikes Christmas cakes anyway, but on that April morning in 1926 it was the battlement of the Promised Land.

Within half an hour of passing through the Customs, I was closeted with the senior partner of a brilliant firm of lawyers whose acquaintance I had made in London in the previous year.

There was not much time for preliminary talk and explanation, however, for at any moment the story might "break" in the New York evening papers that no less distinguished a personage than the British Under-Secretary for Fine Arts had arrived, practically incognito, in the

Mauretania that afternoon, and once Winslow was warned of my arrival he might be galvanized—if such a term can be used of an American business man—into some sort of disastrous activity.

Fortunately my lawyer friend, Hewitt C. Bole, had been a Rhodes Scholar in his day and had learnt something of British methods during his residence at Oxford and his subsequent frequent visits to London, and I was able to give him a rough outline of my situation three times in under the hour. When, at the end of the third telling, Hewitt C. Bole had grasped the main essentials, he seized his hat, summoned his assistant, two experts in accountancy, and a stenographer, and we sallied out like knights of King Arthur's Table to beard the monster in his Down-town lair.

When we reached Winslow Starrett's office in Nassau Street, Bole alone sent in his card. The surprise was to be complete.

And it certainly was. Poor Winslow was completely taken aback for a moment and he goggled at me in a really comical way. Then his puffy, unhealthy face flushed. That is to say, a faint tinge of pink, which was as near a flush as such an anaemic creature could ever achieve, crept into those pallid stretches of cheek.

"You scoundrel," he spluttered, "you cheating, dishonourable, double-crossing, wife-stealing scoundrel."

Whatever may be said about the speed at which the American mind moves, there can be no question about the smoothness of their organization. Hewitt Bole had said no word nor made the slightest gesture, but the stenographer had already produced a note-book from nowhere and was unobtrusively jotting down poor Winslow's actionable remarks.

"You low, dirty skunk," he went on, and then he suddenly saw the stenographer, stopped, and sat down.

"Quite so, Mr. Starrett," said my lawyer in what he

imagined to be his best Oxford manner—as indeed it probably was— "but in the meanwhile we have come on other matters. My friend, Mr. Fox-Ingleby, would like a statement, if you please, of the position of his account with you."

"Why, certainly," replied Winslow, probably relieved at being able to return from the unfamiliar world of personal problems into a world with which he was so infinitely more familiar.

"You mean," he went on, "that Mr. Fox-Ingleby would like to know how his account stands? That is what you require, Mr. Bole?"

"That is so, Mr. Starrett," replied the lawyer. "My client wishes a financial statement from you."

"I take your meaning, Mr. Bole. Your client wishes a financial statement from us."

"That is so, Mr. Starrett."

"In that case, Mr. Bole, I shall be happy—" Winslow broke off coughed, glanced sullenly at me, and went on, " I shall, of course, be prepared to let him have one."

"At once, please, Mr. Starrett."

"You mean now, Mr. Bole?"

"If you please."

"Nothing could be easier." Winslow rang a bell, and within ten minutes, with a pile of books before him, he had opened a lecture on my financial commitments in the New York stock-market.

There is no need to go into boring details. Roughly speaking, Winslow had divided my money into two halves. One half he had invested in Industrials which were steadily on the rise, such as United States Steel, Duponts, General Motors, and so on, and this half was to remain invested for capital appreciation. With the other part of the money he was, frankly, speculating on my behalf. He was, in fact, acting in general accordance with the broad instructions which I had given him in London.

Altogether, he had made profits for me, in the short time during which he had been operating, of about one hundred thousand pounds in the solid, unspeculative side of his activities and of about fifty thousand on the speculative side. It appeared that Winslow was more successful at slow caution, than at dashing raids upon the markets.

I sat back in my chair with a sigh of relief. Not only had the old fool failed to see his wonderful chance of double-crossing me, but he had actually made a large sum of money for me. Both aspects of the situation had their comic angle, as you will admit, but I was sufficiently master of myself neither to cheer nor to smile.

When the exposition was over, Mr. Hewitt C. Bole puffed out his chest and was obviously about to deliver himself of some weighty pronouncement. But there was no time to wait for that sort of thing. Going straight to the point, I chipped in, "And at present all these stocks are held in your name, Winslow?"

"They are—Fox-Ingleby," he used my surname pointedly, "they are, provisionally."

The lawyer managed to intervene at this point. He had been gazing alertly, in Oxonian fashion, at the list of securities in which the second part of the money had been invested on margin—the speculative list, that is to say—and he said, "Pardon me, Mr. Starrett, but I think that some of these concerns, notably Cereals Inc., Mammoth Coloso-phone Films, and Public Utilities of Nevada, in which you have bought margins on a large scale on behalf on my client, are of a very high degree of uncertainty."

"There are three observations which I should like to make upon that observation, sir," replied Winslow, turning the full light of his typically honest American eyes upon the lawyer. He was so taken up with his professional duties towards me that he had entirely forgotten Violetta. At that moment he looked exactly what he was, the embodiment of a certain sort of slow American integrity.

"And my three observations, sir, are these. In the first place, this gentleman is also a client of mine. In the second, it is an axiom of this life that in no sphere of this life can there be speculation without uncertainty. And in the third—and this will show you the confidence which I have in my own professional judgment—in each of those three stocks which you mention—Cereals, Mammoth Films, and Nevada Utilities —I have invested a considerable part of my own private fortune on precisely the same terms as I have invested your money, Edward."

I was enchanted. He had completely forgotten Violetta, for the moment. Things were moving with exquisite smoothness. Card after card was appearing in my hand. Winslow had forgotten Violetta.

I would soon be in a position to jog his memory.

Papers were quickly produced which convinced the shrewd Bole and his sharp-nosed colleagues that Winslow had actually bought on his own behalf about fifty thousand pounds' worth of margins in those three stocks.

"You must be a very rich man, Mr. Starrett," said Mr. Bole respectfully, " to risk such a large sum in three such concerns."

"Oh, we are all gamblers nowadays," replied the poor creature. "But everything is soaring, and it really isn't a gamble at all."

"All the same, I'm not happy about it," said Mr. Bole, but I interrupted.

"Then I tell you what we'll do," I said briskly. "You've done magnificently, Winslow, old fellow, quite magnificently. Now just transfer all the solid stuff to me right away, and all the margins except those three. Hang on to those and carry on your stout work."

"I had thought that I didn't want to handle your business any more,' said Starrett vaguely and uncertainly. He obviously was only making a gesture to the conventional moralities. It stood out a mile that the prospect of losing his commissions on such a large volume of business was torture to him. And after all he had never really loved her.

I laughed gaily and slapped him on the shoulder.

"We can talk about that later," I said. " I'm over here for at least a week. Anyhow, carry on for a day or two, and then we can discuss it again. Dammit, you can't drop a client in mid-stream."

He brightened a lot at that. "Very true," he said. "Yes, very true."

"Good," I cried, giving him another cheerful slap. "Well, I must be off. Mr. Bole and his friends will stay to fix up the transfers."

If ever a man felt that he had a duty to his country, I was that man as I walked Up-town from Winslow's office to the Savoy Plaza Hotel and read in the evening papers that the General Strike had broken out in Britain. For it was May the 1st, 1926. The Government, the nation, nay, the Empire, needed young men with cool heads, and firm minds, and experience of hard knocks, to pull them through this terrible crisis. And Winslow, the fat-faced, flabby, half-witted nincompoop, was actually proposing to deprive them of my services at this very moment. With one Minister clamouring for defence for his pet power-stations, and another for defence for his pet milk-supplies, and a third for his pet pumping-appliances in the coal-mines, what chance would my lovely Ancient Buildings have, or my Open Green Spaces, my Vandycks and my Turners and my Hubert Herkomers, my model villages and my coastguard stations? Who would clamour for their defence if the miserable Winslow forced me to resign from the Government? Not Sir Henry Pettinger. "Pet Pettinger," I angrily christened him as I crossed Twenty-second on my way up Fifth Avenue. Was he the man to stand in the gate and fight for the beauties of England? No, no, no. A thousand times no. Yet the fate of those beauties might even at that moment be lying in the hands of a scrubby little New York stockbroker. Salisbury Cathedral, and the Roman Baths at Bath, and The White City, and Bodiam, and the rest, might be destroyed, with all their history, by a thunderbolt wielded by a worm from an office in Nassau Street, Manhattan, New York City.

It was not to be borne.

That evening Mr. Bole visited me in my hotel, and, when the coffee and brandy had been brought up to my suite, we put our heads together.

The next day was famous in the annals of Wall Street for a sudden bear attack upon Cereals Inc., Mammoths, and Nevada Utilities.

I rang up Winslow's people every quarter of an hour or so, anxiously enquiring about the fate of our margins, and at about eleven o'clock Winslow came on the line himself. He sounded a little anxious. Things were holding up, he said, but renewed pressure might be serious. I gave him a few words of encouraging advice, and reported our conversation to Bole.

At half-past eleven a fresh wave of selling swept the markets and Winslow came on the line again. This time he was in a state of feverish panic. The margins were on the point of being engulfed; would I put up more money to save them and stem the tide?

"Dollar for dollar with you, my lad, up to a hundred thousand dollars apiece," I said.

"You're a good man, Edward," he replied huskily, and rushed back to the floor of the House.

But it was of no avail. As Bole had said on the night before, those three stocks were suspect already, and the persistent attack on them for an hour and a half confirmed the suspicions of all wise men. Everyone clamoured to unload, and by one o'clock every cent of our money was lying at the bottom of the sea. There was a strong rally in all three later in the day, but that, of course, was too late for us.

When it was all over, at about four o'clock in the afternoon, I lay back in a big chair and ordered a bottle of champagne. Phew! I needed it. All day I had been playing for big stakes, and that is an agonizing business even for the toughest of professional gamblers. But for a sensitive and inexperienced man, it is nothing short of hell. However, it was over at last, and I put through a call to Winslow's office and asked him to come round to see me.

He was paler even than usual when he arrived, and he looked like a man who is completely done, with his tousled hair, rumpled clothes, and stains of dried perspiration on his face. I had ordered a second bottle of champagne and I gave him a glass.

"Good God," he cried, after he had gulped it down and I had refilled it. "What a disaster! What a calamity! I have lost three hundred thousand dollars. I am ruined, utterly ruined."

It was typical of the man—a stockbroker, mind you—to think of his own losses before those of his client who had trusted him. I was shocked.

"And what about me?" I asked coldly.

"Yes, you too," he added in a perfunctory way. "But who would have dreamt of such diabolical bad luck?" he wailed on. "I had certain information that within the next few days big interests, very big interests indeed, were going to deal exclusively in those very shares—still are going to, for all I know—but it won't help us now. It won't help us now. Oh, my God!" and the great baby actually burst into tears.

"Pull yourself together, Winslow," I said sternly, "and listen to me. Are you pretty well cleaned out?"

He nodded bleakly between half-stifled sobs.

"Very well. I will give you a present of fifty thousand

pounds—two hundred and fifty thousand dollars—to start you off again."

He jumped to his feet and stared at me incredulously.

"You mean it?" he gulped.

"You ought to know by this time, Starrett," I said icily, "that an Englishman's word is his bond."

He mumbled an apology, and I went on. "There would be, of course, one or two trifling conditions. You must drop all idea, for instance, of citing me as Violetta's co-respondent."

"Sell my wife to you for fifty thousand pounds!" he exclaimed, that odd look of integrity coming into his eyes again. "Never. I would sooner beg in the streets than commit such an infamy."

The spirit of Bunker Hill and Lexington glowed in him.

"You may have to in any case, old boy," I remarked, lighting a cigar.

"I still have a few thousand dollars left," he cried defiantly.

I took a few long pulls at the cigar to get it going and then said casually, "You said you lost three hundred thousand dollars. I thought you only stood to lose two."

"There was my original two, and the extra hundred thousand that you and I agreed to put up each."

I shook my head sadly and smiled.

"Oh no," I murmured. "Oh dear no."

"But you said on the telephone—" he gasped.

"On the telephone?"—this with my head cocked at a quizzical angle.

There was a long, long pause. You could almost hear the long-unoiled creaking and groaning of that ponderous mind.

At last he sat down in his chair and said, "Very well. I quit. The pot is yours. What do you want me to do?"

"Have another drink," I said, "and listen."

I felt exactly as Wellington must have felt at that decisive moment at Waterloo when he did not say "Up Guards and at 'em," but something else which at the moment I forget.

"This is what you are to do," I said. "You are to cable to your London solicitors instructing them to drop any proceedings they may have begun against me."

"They have not yet begun," Winslow muttered.

"Good. Then you will cable to them at once instructing them to begin immediate proceedings against Violetta, citing Sir Henry Pettinger, baronet, of 180A Hill Street, Mayfair, W. 1, as co-respondent."

"But I've never even heard of him!" exclaimed Winslow. "Is he another of you?"

"You are hardly in a position to be offensive, my dear fellow," I began blandly, and then I suddenly saw the implication of his remark, and the blood rushed to my temples.

"How dare you suggest that I shared Violetta with anyone else?" I exclaimed furiously. "And how dare you insinuate that I'm the sort of man that a woman wants another man when she's got me?" I was so angry that my grammar went all to bits. The sense, however, was pretty clear.

I continued more calmly, "Besides, are you not slandering your wife's reputation in attributing promiscuity to her? Is this your vaunted American chivalry? No, no, Winslow, I won't have it. Don't say that sort of thing again. Now, we'll start again. You'd better write Pettinger's name down. There are paper and pens on my desk. Write from my dictation: 'On the grounds of their misconduct at the Grapes Hotel in Tewkesbury, Gloucestershire'"—I consulted my diary— "'on the nights of the twenty-second and twenty-third of January 1926.' Furthermore, you will instruct them to claim twenty thousand pounds damages—" Winslow looked up eagerly from his unaccustomed labour of receiving rather than giving dictation.

"It's no good putting on a dog-expecting-bone vaudeville act like that, Winslow," I said, perhaps a little brutally. But it had been a trying day, and anyone's nerves might be forgiven for being a little on edge. "You're going to claim twenty-thousand pounds, but you aren't going to get them, because the case will be dropped long before it reaches the Courts."

Winslow passed his podgy hand across his brow. "I don't understand," he said drearily.

"No," I replied, "perhaps not. But the point is that I do. Have you got all that written down? Then read it over."

After the half-dozen spelling mistakes which Winslow had made had been corrected, the matter was finished.

And that is the story of how victory was snatched at the last moment by a combination of audacity, opportunism, and brains, fired and inspired by a passionate determination to help my country in her calamitous need.

Nothing remains but to sketch, in a few words, the aftermath of battle. On the following morning, having sent one of Mr. Hewitt C. Bole's clerks with Winslow to the cable-office to make certain that the cable was actually sent, I sat down with Mr. Bole himself and his accountants to examine the profit-and-loss account of the carnage, so to speak, of the Armageddon of the markets.

My fifty thousand pounds' worth of margins was, of course, a dead loss. On top of that I had thrown, altogether, nearly two hundred thousand—almost a million dollars—into the great attack upon my own shares, and I was a little staggered to find out, for the first time, how nearly the whole of that had been lost as well. It was touch-and-go at about twelve-thirty, said Bole. But when the other fellows came tumbling in on our side at one o'clock, then, of course, we were in clover.

I must say Bole managed the whole thing with amazing cleverness. His timing was perfect, and he started buying in again at exactly the right moment. The result of it all was, by the end of the day, we found ourselves in the delightful position of having contracted in the morning to sell a certain number of shares for approximately three-quarters of a million dollars, and of having, in the afternoon, bought the requisite number of shares for two hundred thousand dollars.

In short, we hauled in about five hundred and fifty thousand dollars, which left me, after deducting the loss of my margins, a clear net profit of about ninety thousand pounds sterling.

Of this sum, it need hardly be said that fifty thousand went straight to Winslow in accordance with my promise to him over the telephone. It had never been my intention for one instant to repudiate my bond in this matter, even though it represented an unprovable contract, and if Winslow liked to assume that I was a blackguard and to adjust his behaviour accordingly, that was his affair.

I returned home, then, with a swag of forty thousand pounds plus the original capital entrusted to Winslow, like Genghiz Khan or Tamerlane returning from one of their raids. All was saved, Fortune, Career, Honour, and Britain's Fine Arts. The possibility of a divorce case against me, either as respondent or as co-respondent, had been extinguished. Charlie Skellington-Green could safely be ruined. I should be free of Diana. Anne would belong to me. My Honour was untarnished. As for poor old Pettinger, he strenuously denied the allegations against him, and in the end, after a great deal of most unsavoury publicity, the divorce suit came to nothing, exactly as I had prophesied to Winslow. After all, you can't expect to go about citing any Tom, Dick, or Harry as co-respondent when you want to divorce your wife. There is still a certain amount of justice in this old country of ours (though what goes on under the Poor Persons' Divorce Procedure I do not profess to know nor do I care), and it is still necessary, thank Heaven, to bring evidence before the Court if a charge is to be substantiated. Winslow had not a scrap of evidence in support of his charge, and the whole thing fell to the ground. But the fact that Pettinger and

Violetta had actually spent that week-end at Tewkesbury, in the same hotel, aroused the very sound British instinct that where there is smoke there must also be fire. It never came out, of course, that Pettinger and I had been on an official visit to Tewkesbury in connection with the repairs to that dream-like Norman tower of the Abbey, and that I had taken Violetta along with me. By some queer prompting of intuition—call it what you like—I had dimly foreseen that that visit might ultimately be of use to me, and I had spent a quiet and skilful five minutes with the hotel register before we left. It is hardly necessary to add that Pettinger was completely innocent, but the register certainly looked bad, and the register and the rumours combined were too much for the poor old chap, and he was forced to resign the Ministry of Fine Arts. He retired to North Wales, and now broods over bee-hives, I believe, and over his dead ambitions.

I got the Ministry.

CHAPTER XXVI

And so I triumphed, as true merit is always bound to triumph in the end. You will never find me among the defeatists who think that merit goes unrewarded in this world. Pessimism has never claimed me as an addict. There is something magnificent, I have always been certain in my innermost being, in the invincible integrity of the human soul, and those of us who have clung fast to that integrity are entitled, surely, to our share of the ultimate magnificence. Those of us who have fought for what we have believed to be right, to be true, to be in accord with the dictates of a Supreme Being, may at least claim a small amount of consideration when we face Rhadamanthus at the Golden Gate of Heaven.

What I am trying to say is this: I triumphed in the worldly things of life, as I expected to. But even if I had been a worldly failure, there would still have been the strong consciousness of duty done, and of righteousness strictly pursued, which would have more, far more, than compensated me for material defeat. That I was a worldly success was, actually, a great satisfaction to me. But of infinitely greater importance to me was my steady refusal to sell my soul.

My principles guided me, and those of you who have read this small book will be able to judge whether my principles were good or not.

Just consider, for a brief moment, what I had done in those thirty-eight years of my life.

I set a standard of conduct in the pre-war life of this unhappy land. It was by me and my friends—their names escape me as I write, but you will find them if you turn back the pages of this book—that the last flicker of the *flâneurs* and *boulevardiers* was lit. We were the nineteenth-century Parisians of the London of the early twentieth.

We made Mayfair. We extinguished the dismal Belgravia. The blooming of Curzon Street and the ostracism of Eaton Square were both due to us. And so was the financing of Maida Vale. Sweet Maida Vale! I kiss my hand to you and your bijou residences and your bijou girls. Alas, the snows of yester-year! Melted, melted, as our hearts and our bank-balances were! Some fool poet, some hack-genius, the sort of man who writes for the evening papers, might well follow in the footsteps of the frog Villon, and write a poem with the refrain, "Where are the girls of Maida Vale?"

We are all gone now, we who made the London of our day. Some are old, and some are fools, and some are both, and most are dead. But do not forget us, you who come after. Sneer at our greying hairs, at our spreading waistcoats, but do not forget that we were the last of the orchid-laden gallants of the stage-door. What is the stage-door now but a desert in which nothing flowers except pansies, and in which no fairy-stories live, but only fairies. In our day no girl who came out of a stage-door was safe for miles round unless one of us was defending her against the rest of us.

And it was I who led that mode of life, and set that standard of glorious, Gascon, swaggering, gay nonsense.

Then do not forget that I and my friends helped to win the war.

That I helped to save Ireland.

That I helped to reconstruct the world after the war.

That I helped to make Britain a better place to live in, by devoting my services to the Government of Britain in Parliament.

That as Minister of Fine Arts I laid down a broad basis for a new national culture, just as Pericles or Ruskin did in their days.

And above all, do not forget that I devoted these years, nearly forty, of my life, to the attempt to make the world a better place for women to live in. If you have read these memoirs aright, you will have understood that my whole existence has been governed by a passionate desire to help women in their too-often difficult path through life.

That has been, beneath a casual, perhaps flippant, exterior, my deep purpose. And it will be a disappointment to me if you do not agree that I have succeeded to such small extent as my powers permit.

Diana, Violetta, my daughter Anne, and all the odds and ends who have from time to time flitted in and out of the shadowy room of my existence, not one of them can have left my life without a greater richness of mind and experience than that with which they entered it. For myself, I may have lost. Probably I did. But they, bless their sweet little hearts, can have done nothing but gained.

But whether you understand this essential motive which underlies my every action, or whether you do not, I am prepared to rest content upon the verdict of posterity. I am and always have been and always will be a champion and a servant of womankind.

Let us leave it at that.

And so I bring my memoirs to a close. There is nothing more to say.

In May 1926 I had defeated all my enemies. I was a Minister of the Crown. I was rich and young and a bachelor again. I was untarnished by public scandal. I was respected and honoured by all. And I was at peace with myself.

APPENDIX

One last word. Some of you may be wondering how, with all my multifarious activities and deep responsibilities, I found the time to study the technique of writing, to write this book, to arrange all the complicated details of drawing up contracts with publishers, and to see the proofs through the press.

This is what I did. I employed two assistants. One was a supremely efficient stenographer, to whom I dictated in my spare time at my house. She was admirable in every way. The other was a revolting youth, covered with spots, who ran round the town verifying references and digging out facts. He was a writer himself in a humble way—a bit of a poet and novelist, I believe—and when I was too busy with other matters I allowed him to tinker with my typescript and alter such sentences as might have slipped out of grammatical harness. In fact I allowed him to do quite a lot of the hack work. He was very poor and unsuccessful at the time—though I rather think he is quite a well-known dramatist now—and I paid him a few extra shillings for the work, although I might well have knocked something off his weekly wage for the extra experience which I was giving him.

As for placing the book with a publisher, I employed an agent, who did all the work, secured the publishers both here and in America, drew up the contracts, and advised me most skilfully throughout in the matter of getting the book through the press.

It was my agent, indeed, who insisted upon the insertion

of an important clause in both the English and American contracts. In my immense preoccupations, the small details of a business to which I was unaccustomed had escaped me, although, of course, if I had had the few necessary minutes, they could easily have been mastered. In the circumstances, it was fortunate that I had an agent to look after my affairs, and I did not for one moment grudge the ten per cent commission which I had contracted to pay him on all my gross receipts.

Briefly, the clauses which the agent insisted on forcing upon the publishers were in connection with the fluctuating exchanges. The pound at that time was standing at $3.55 in New York and about the same in Canada. If, during the sale of this book, the pound rose to, say, $4.50 in both countries, I would obviously be a serious loser on both contracts—the Canadian rights having been retained with the English rights.

The agent, an admirable fellow, therefore arranged that if, within six months of the publication of the book, the pound went beyond $4.50 in either country, new contracts should be drawn up.

It was a wise precaution and everything turned out for the best. Within two months of the signature of the contract, the pound began to rise. On the date of publication, it stood at $4.25½, and six weeks later it passed the crucial mark. New contracts were obligatory.

By this time I was pretty well *au fait* with the technique of drawing up contracts with publishers—besides, I had the agent's original contracts before me, drawn up by an expert hand, to copy from—and I therefore told the agent that his services were no longer necessary. I would draw up the new contracts myself. Naturally I thanked him for all that he had done, and offered him, without prejudice or admission of liability, a ten-pound note in full discharge of any implied debt from me to him. He refused it, with some remarks that a lesser man might have taken to be actionable, and I put the note back in my pocket. Later in the day I gave it to my admirable stenographer, for all the extra, and most able, work she had put in.

So far as I remember, I also gave a present to the spotty little devil who had dug out facts for me from the Libraries and Museums. Ten shillings, if my memory serves me.